The Cross by Day,
the Mezuzzah by Night

The Cross by Day, the Mezuzzah by Night

Deborah Spector Siegel

The Jewish Publication Society
Philadelphia
1999 • 5759

The Jewish Publication Society
2100 Arch Street, 2nd Floor
Philadelphia, PA 19103–1399

The Library of Congress has cataloged the cloth edition of this title as:

Siegel, Deborah Spector
    The cross by day, the mezuzzah by night / Deborah Spector Siegel.
    -- 1st ed.
        p.   cm.
    Summary: Because she is a Marrano, thirteen-year-old Isabel
suffers the harrowing experience of expulsion from Spain during the
reign of King Ferdinand and Queen Isabella.
        ISBN 0-8276-0597-8—cloth
        ISBN 0-8276-0737-7—paper
        1. Jews--History--70-1789 Juvenile fiction.   2. Spain--History-
-Ferdinand and Isabella, 1479-1516 Juvenile fiction.   3. Inquisition
Juvenile fiction.   [1. Jews--History--70-1789 Fiction.   2. Spain-
-History--Ferdinand and Isabella, 1479-1516 Fiction.   3. Inquisition
Fiction.   4. Jewish Christians Fiction.]   I. Title.
PZ7.S5745Cr   1999   99-20683
                                                          CIP

06 07 08 09   7 6 5 4

To the Jews of Spain,
 who found themselves without doorposts
 to hang their mezuzzahs,

to the Marranos
 who were forced to keep their mezuzzahs hidden, and

to the wonderful family
 who dwells behind my own golden mezuzzah:
 Howard, Joshua, and Noah

... We have decided
to order all Jews, men and women,
to leave our kingdoms
and to never come back. ...

All must leave our territories
on the first day of July,
fourteen Hundred Ninety-Two
and never return,
under penalty of death. ...

〜〜〜

FROM THE EDICT OF EXPULSION,
31 MARCH 1492,
QUEEN ISABEL, KING FERDINAND OF SPAIN

Contents

I Reveal My True Identity

or thirteen years my name was Isabel. I was Isabel Caruso de Carvallo, of Seville, Spain, baptized in the year of my birth, 1479. Like so many other infant girls, I was named in honor of our great "Catholic Queen," Isabel of Spain. It was a proper Christian name for the daughter of good Spanish Catholics, Paulo and Maria Caruso de Carvallo. For above all things, in that cruel realm, one *must* be a good Catholic.

They called me Isabel. But that was not my true name. I carried another secret name given to me also in that year of my birth: Ruth. Ruth de Cojano, descendant of the tribes of Abraham, Isaac, and Jacob; of Sara, Rebecca, and Leah, a daughter of the house of Israel. I am a *Marrano*, a "secret Jewess," though this astonishing fact was not revealed to me until four years ago, on the very day I turned thirteen, the age of Jewish adulthood. Only then was I told the shocking truth of things.

Ruth—that beautiful name of the biblical heroine who adopted the Jewish faith for her own—was a name I was never allowed to hear roll lovingly from the tongue of family and friends. For you see, an Old Testament name in Seville was like the kiss of death. It was one of the "telltale signs" of the secret Jews.

Though we Caruso de Carvallos had been practicing Christians for a hundred years, devoted to the Church and giving many tithes, our Church records were boldly marked to show that my great grandparents, Avram and Ruth de Cojano, had once been Jews converted to Christianity by force. The Church and the whole of society labeled us *Cristos-Nuevos*, meaning "New Christians." Only "Old Christians" in Spain may hold the coveted documents of *limpieza de sangre*, "purity of Christian blood." Such documents prove that a family is not tainted by the blood of Jews.

Until the year of my thirteenth birthday, I lived nearly the whole of my childhood blissfully unaware that we were not what we seemed—good and proper Catholics. Still, I had sensed from time to time that our family was different somehow. Unusual prayers were uttered in our home. Papá and Mamá would worship at odd times and in different ways than the Church demanded. On many a Friday night, long after the servants had retired, Mamá and Papá would creep down to our cold, musty wine cellar to light candles and pray yet again. I thought them simply to be memorial candles for the many Catholic dead. And the late hour to be one of Mamá's ideas. She always did have a fondness for enlivening things, inventing new and intriguing celebrations and entertainments. Like her Christmas Eve celebration held outdoors in the courtyard, so that our guests could search for the star of Bethlehem. Our home was often filled with prominent guests and court officials. It was one of the things people loved about her—that delighted Papá and me too—her capacity for bringing mystery and excitement to ordinary events.

How often on those Friday nights did I follow my parents, slipping downstairs to stare into the dancing candlelight beside them. Only rarely did they object to my presence. They were relaxed and unworried, secure as most Marrano families were, that their high rank in Spanish society was secure, that their small transgressions in Jewish prayer were private matters of the heart, not public crimes of shame and heresy.

But that year before I turned thirteen, the Friday night candle-lighting ceremonies grew increasingly less pleasant and more hurried. Papá began to bolt the door after us. And my parents grew nervous and wary, as if my presence at the cellar meetings made them uncomfortable. Finally, one Friday in May, Papá commanded me sternly, "Do not mention or mark this occasion with the servants, not ever!"

"But why, Papá?" I asked, surprised at his vehemence.

"It would shame or embarrass them that we said so many more prayers than they," he answered more softly, kissing me on the head.

I thought little more of the matter. As a high official, Papá had often advised me to silence and secrecy in various matters of court discretion.

Little did I know that those Friday night candles were lit to bring on the Jewish Sabbath, the holy day of rest—an act of highest heresy for Christians, punishable by death!

That year there were other odd things that I could not ignore in my parents' behavior. There was the time my baby brother, Manuel, was baptized in the Catholic faith, a week after his birth. Mamá held him as the priest poured the baptismal waters upon his tiny forehead. Yet I saw my father, upon returning home from church, quickly wipe the holy water from his head and descend with the baby to our wine cellar with a bearded man in strange dark clothes. When I went to follow them down, Mamá pulled me back saying, "No, Isabel. You may not go this time. This is men's business." And I heard Papá latch and lock the door behind him as he did at our Friday night family meetings.

"But why do they take the baby with them?" I asked in astonishment, for Mamá hardly ever let the baby out of her sight.

"They talk of his future," she said curtly, in a way that told me the discussion was closed for further questioning.

Now, of course, I know that the strange bearded man was the Marrano rabbi who was secretly brought to perform the sacred ceremony of circumcision, the ancient male covenant of the Jews.

For as far back as I can remember our small moments of Jewish life have been enacted this way, secretly, in the dark cellar of our house. Before my very eyes, yet unknowingly to me.

Until the day I turned thirteen, Papá and Mamá never actually told me that my family are what the Catholics scornfully call Marranos. It is the Spanish term for "swine," the animal of uncleanness which Jews are forbidden to eat. It is the word that has come to mean "secret Jews," those who have not entirely forsaken the ancient laws of Torah, who risk their lives to taste a bite of concealed matzah once a year, or to hear the words of the Passover seder or to express their love for the one God of all Creation, Adonai. For such small tendings of their souls, Marranos may be tortured, then burned alive at the stake.

Sí, that is what I have said: burned alive!

How I cried when I learned that we were such detestable Marranos, that we would be forced to leave Seville, the glorious city of my birth; and Spain, the ancient kingdom of my ancestors. That there would be no farewell fiestas, no loving words, no parting gifts, no final tearful embrace with Teresa, my best friend, my dearest friend in all the world. That our leave-taking of our beloved homeland would be a terrible, swift escape from the fiery arms of the Inquisition.

Papá, who had risen to the high office of royal tax collector over all Seville, began to feel watchful eyes upon him as he made his rounds about the city. Priestly spies, he told us, were everywhere. Once, returning home after dark, he came upon two men in friar's cloth peeking through our window. They scurried hastily away as my father approached, not wanting to cause alarm. They prefer to carry on their dirty work in secrecy.

Mamá and Papá began to fear that it was only a matter of time before the spies might try to secretly bribe our servants for proof of our "impure Jewish acts." For a New Christian to incite suspicion of any kind—to wash the hands frequently as a Jew, to refuse to eat pork as a Jew, to fail to kindle a fire on Saturday, the Jewish Sabbath, like a Jew— is to risk the inescapable processes of torture and death.

When I learned the truth, it was midway through the year 1492. A year of glory and fame, so many said, for Spain. Alas, for the Jews and all their descendants it was a year of infamy. It was, in fact, a year of infamy for *all* people not lucky enough to be born Old Christians. A ten-year war had just been won against the Moors of Islamic faith who had resided for centuries near Seville in the kingdom of Granada. All the Moors—even folk we had known—were put to the sword or sold into slavery! And then two great edicts came forth from our sovereigns, King Ferdinand of Aragón and Queen Isabel of Castille.

One royal edict was thrilling, for it granted the means for renowned explorer, Cristobal Colón, to find the passage to India and all of its riches and worldly knowledge for the progress and glory of Spain.

But the other edict was backward and cruel: the king and queen ordered the expulsion of all the known Jewish people from Spain—tens of thousands of human beings chased away, like rats to be gotten rid of at the hands of royal exterminators.

Think of it: our queen and king decided to brutally expel the Jews, ancient people who lived productively, in harmony, upon the land for more than fifteen hundred years, centuries before Spain knew its first Christians.

Not that the Jewish people have been treated with much kindness in Christian Spain in recent times. For more than a hundred years the monarchy had decreed that Jews live in walled-up crumbling neighborhoods called *Juderías* and forced to wear humiliating pointed "Jew's hats" upon their heads and yellow circles upon their lapels when they ventured forth to earn their livelihood. Many towns—even my own Seville—no longer allow Jews or Juderías within its borders. In cities where the Juderías are allowed, Jew-haters and fanatics have been given free reign to inspire dangerous mobs to attack and murder people within their very synagogues and homes behind the Judería walls.

But the worst was yet to come. On March 31, 1492—three months before I turned thirteen—the king and queen decreed that all Jews must leave and never come back under penalty of death. Even the king and queen's honored Jewish finance ministers, Don Abraham Senior and Don Isaac Abrabanel, were ordered to leave. The Jewish people were given only three months to flee all the kingdoms of Spain. There was much chaos and agony as they scrambled to sell their homes and belongings, to choose a foreign land for their destiny, to secure the means of travel, to say good-bye forever to the only homeland they and their ancestors had known since the time of King David.

Then, whether very young or very old, whether sick or in the throes of childbirth, the Jewish people were forced to leave their towns and walk to the nearest ship's harbor—whether it be a few day's walk or a harrowing journey of many weeks. Huge numbers of distressed Jews clogged the roads from north to south and from east to west. Rabbis were known to move among them with words and prayers of encouragement as they walked in long, miserable streams past the gates of all the Spanish cities where they were not allowed to enter for brief rest or refreshment.

Thus, the unmistakable crying and weeping of the passing unwanted Jews was heard daily outside the walls of our great city of Seville.

With my own eyes I saw them, not yet knowing they were my people, as they trudged in stricken groups moving south along the roadways toward the Port of Cadiz where ships would take them away.

Oh, how I felt the generous pity of one who feels safe from harm's way, not yet realizing that the fates of Jews and Marranos and New Christians alike are all interwoven as one, like the threads of a great tapestry.

I had lived a sheltered life, fussed over by Mamá and the servants, spoiled by Papá, fed fine foods, and dressed in silk and brocade. Perhaps that is why, when I began to see the brutalities of life around me, the vision of the fleeing Jews came as a very great shock to me. Papá and I had been returning home together to Seville in a hired carriage when I saw them along the road. It was early April, just a day or two after the March Edict of Expulsion. Yet it was nearly three months before my thirteenth birthday. Three months before I would learn that there were immense and dangerous secrets in our family. That we ourselves, were Jews—secret Jews.

Two

I Witness the Expulsion of a People

Our carriage lurched and bounced along the bumpy shoulder of road that led to the town of Seville. We had come upon a large stream of people blocking our way, forcing our carriage to the side. I pulled back the curtain and stared out in great curiosity.

"Papá, who are all those people? Where do they come from? And look, that woman carrying a baby is crying. Do you suppose the baby is sick?"

The compartment of our coach was steamy and hot. My father had been leaning against the cushion, arms crossed, eyelids drooping downward in sleep. At the sound of my voice, he opened his eyes and leaned forward to look out the window. We had come from the countryside where Papá, as royal tax collector, had taken me on his rounds to nearby farms and villas. I often accompanied him for I loved to see the chickens squawk upon their eggs and the hills of silkworms spinning their sticky strands and the farm children milking the goats. Now on our return trip, as we neared the city gates, our driver had been forced to slow down, increasingly detained by the dozens of people walking along the main road and the armed soldiers on horses who moved in and out among them. They seemed to trudge in lines of human misery, their heads bowed, clutching children and possessions to their side. Somewhere in the distance, I heard the pleasant sounds of flute and mandolin making strangely merry music in the midst of the forlorn-looking people.

"Are they coming to live in Seville, Papá?"

Father turned away from the view and leaned back against the cushion. His face had taken on a grim expression.

"Seville, I daresay, expelled them long ago. It is the exodus, Isabel, the exodus of every Jewish man, woman, and child from Spain."

The tone of his voice was so serious and final that we both fell silent for a time as the horse lurched and pulled us through a deep, jagged hole. I could hear the driver sitting above us, outside the coach, curse the condition of the road.

"Why should they leave, Papá, why should they want to leave?" I asked, for I couldn't imagine wanting to leave my beautiful, native Spain.

He sighed deeply. "They leave . . ." he began, his voice breaking, "they leave . . . because they are unwanted, cast out." He said the words softly but suffused with anger.

"I don't understand, Papá. Who makes them go?"

"Isabel," he said wearily. "Do you never stop asking questions?" I shrunk from his tone, knowing how his irritation could sometimes turn to stormy rage. I had begun to notice how he often grew impatient with my questions, as if I asked forbidden things. The coach rattled on for a time and I looked out the other window where I could see only the trees of an olive grove. After a few moments, Papá turned back to me and his expression softened and instead of further scolding he said, "Isabel, in June you will celebrate your thirteenth birthday."

"Sí, Papá! June the fifteenth!" I replied happily, thinking he was going to discuss some celebration or feast plans which he and Mamá had in mind. Instead, he stared out the window and said something in the barest whisper of a voice that astonished me.

"The year of Jewish adulthood."

I frowned and looked questioningly at him. It was a strange observation from my father who was a lay deacon in our great cathedral, the Church of Santa Maria del Popolo. My eyes fell upon the glint of the silvery cross Papá always wore about his collar. A strange comment, I thought. But then I suppose his mind was upon this disturbing vision of the Jewish exodus.

"Where are they going, Papá?" I asked, risking irritation again. I leaned toward the other window again and saw this time an exhausted-looking old man drop his satchel of belongings. He fell to his knees to retrieve his belongings and began to cry as many pairs of feet inadvertently trampled the objects into the dust. I looked away, shocked and disturbed by the desperation of that poor old man.

"To the Port of Cadiz, where the ships await to put them to sea like so much human driftwood." This time Papá didn't wait for my next question but began to speak.

"Isabel, you will soon turn thirteen, the age of maturity. There are many things you will need to be told."

I did not like the tone of Papá's voice. It was ominous, as if bad news was forthcoming.

"For now, I want you to understand what is happening to those unfortunate people in the street, people whose descendants have lived in Spain generation after generation, even unto ancient times," he said, his voice cracking with emotion.

"Sí, Papá," I said proceeding to fan myself rapidly. The heat inside the coach was suffocating, increased somehow by the heat of Papá's emotions.

"Once I believed that our monarchs, King Ferdinand and Queen Isabel, for whom you are named, were among the continent's most enlightened rulers."

I fanned vigorously and nodded. Papá seemed to be talking not so much for my benefit but to release some turmoil within him.

"They have done so much for the progress of Spain. They made the cities safe from the murderers and thieves who overran them. They approved the voyage of the great mapmaker, Cristobal Colón.

"And as for the Jews, it is well known that the king himself is descended from Jewish conversos. At the high court itself, Jewish men have been trusted advisors and confidants of the king and queen. There is the queen's advisor, Don Abraham Senior, and the royal financier, Don Isaac Abravanel. In fact the king and queen owe even their marriage to Don Abraham Senior who raised a princely fortune so the impoverished Ferdinand could marry the wealthy Isabel! But now," he said and gestured toward the window, "they undermine their reputations for greatness and humanity. First they destroyed the Islamic Moors earlier this year. Now they expel the Jewish people."

"But why must these people, the Moors and the Jews, all be gotten rid of Papá?"

"I'm afraid the king and queen have listened to their fanatic church advisor, the hated monk, Tomás de Torquemada. We must hear his

19

words uttered daily from every church pulpit in the province of Castille *'One people, one nation, one religion.'* In the name of this cruel oneness only true Christians shall be allowed to reside within the borders of the land. It is just as it was for the Islamic people of Granada, Isabel," Papá said dejectedly.

I understood about the Moors. I could never forget the day the trumpeters and troubadours marched up and down the streets of Seville singing of the king and queen's great victory over the people of Granada after the ten-year war. The town criers said that no more would the tainted Muslim inhabit the holy Christian Kingdom of Spain and that the remaining Muslims left alive would be sold into Portuguese and African slavery. Great joyous cheering went up in the streets. Royal banquets and knightly jousts were held to celebrate the Spanish victors.

But my mother wept. In her youth she had toured the nearby province of Granada many times with her papá, a merchant who did business with the Arabs. She had found the Islamic Moors to be a gracious and learned people, and she wept to think of such a place of beauty besieged by catapults and the terrible cannons of fire, its flowing fountains, ancient Mosques and gilded minarets, destroyed. Gone in fire and smoke were the brilliant Islamic Moors who had brought so much art and science and prosperity to Spain. And now Papá was saying that the unarmed and defenseless Jews, more ancient to the land than even the Moors, were to be officially banished.

"Isabel," he said gesturing toward the coach window, "two days ago, the thirty-first of March, the king and queen ordered all the Jews of Spain to give up their homes, their livelihoods, everything they hold precious and dear. Where they go is of no importance to our Catholic monarchs, only that they get out of Spain no later than the thirty-first of July. In hunger and anguish now, you see them. They trudge the roads of our land from north to south, traveling in long human lines of fear and misery. Everywhere the people of Spain take pity on them and beg them to convert to Christianity to escape their fate. But the Jews are proud and noble, and most refuse even as they collapse along the roads."

"It is mean, Papá, so very mean! Why does our queen destroy those who live peacefully upon the land?" I asked in dismay. I had grown up adoring the queen, carrying her name proudly. At the time of my birth it was said that she held court in Seville each week. The beautiful red-haired queen allowed one and all, no matter how humble or uneducated, to gain audience with her. I myself dreamed of meeting her one day. "Why would she make war with the Moors and expel the Jews, Papá?"

"Simply because they are Jews and not Catholics," was my father's bitter reply. "But our monarchy is not merely cruel to its non-Christian peoples. It behaves with royal stupidity. A country cannot prosper and survive without the talent and genius of its many races. It is as if Spain cuts off its own limbs!"

My father had so worked himself into a temper, I dared not rile him with more questions. I felt a wave of relief as our coach left the road and turned into the majestic gates of my home town, Seville. The horse began its familiar clip-clop across the cobblestones. Soon we would be home. I tried not to think about the woman crying over her baby or the old man trying desperately to retrieve his trampled possessions.

As Papá and I disembarked in front of our dear, familiar house, I crossed myself and thought, Praise God we are good Christians and not the luckless Jews.

Three

I Am Consoled by
My Best Friend Teresa

I must tell about the hanging *sanbenitos*, the horrid garments of shame, and the fear that follows New Christians even into the sanctity of the Church, and of hateful old Doña Martinez. But most of all, I must tell about Teresa.

Teresa, beloved Teresa, my oldest of childhood friends! Her father, the Marques de Rodriguez, was of landed nobility who had lost much of his ancestral property to kings and taxes. Yet still. he was so rich that he spent his days in travel or in hunting parties at his villa in the country. Teresa's mother, the marquesa, could not tolerate the noise and rowdiness of his country life. So she had taken a fine house in Seville, down the street and around the corner from our own, where she and Teresa and the younger children were looked after by servants and slaves.

For many years the Marques de Rodriguez and my father treated one another with great civility. Yet I always sensed, beneath the polish of their courtly manners, they did not like each other very much. But this was the business of menfolk and mattered little to Teresa or me. From the moment our mothers brought us together at the age of six, they called us "the twins" because we had both been born in the same year and because we quickly became as inseparable as twin sisters.

Yet inseparable as we were, and both born to wealth and privilege, we both understood that she was more fortunate than I. There were two reasons. One was that she had her very own horse—*El Rápido*, "the swift one"—a beautiful Arabian stallion that she was allowed to ride whenever she went to her family's villa in the country. And the other was that her family owned the document coveted by all of Seville: the limpieza de sangre, "the purity of blood" certificate. It meant that her family had always been true Old Christian with not a trace of Jewish blood in them.

It was at the age of ten, at Teresa's house, when I learned for the first time how valuable a thing was this title Old Christian. Teresa and I had been sewing costumes for the Queen Isabel dolls we were making in the library with bits of fine leftover velvet and brocade. I chanced to look up and see on the wall a certificate entitled Limpieza de Sangre in a prominent gilt frame. When I asked Teresa about it, she said that the document proved that no Jewish blood lines ran through her old *hidalgo*, "aristocratic" family.

Several years earlier, her father, the marques of the once powerful de Rodriguez clan, had hired the best heraldic historian in Seville to trace the family tree back nearly five hundred years. The Church had been shown the historian's tree of the Rodriguez clan and, in return, bestowed the grand certificate upon the marques. It had been, Teresa said smiling, a cause for great celebration, giving her father an excuse for one of his wild parties in the country, away from her mother's scrutiny.

"I don't think we possess such a certificate," I had said to Teresa, frowning. "I think our family has been Christian for only a hundred years."

Teresa, busily sewing a black velvet cape for her doll, said, "Perhaps you don't have one. Most families in Seville do not. For us, it is what we consider a little icing on the cake. You know how Papá loves his old hidalgo ancestry." She held up the cape for me to see.

I nodded my approval at her handiwork. "But why doesn't most of Seville have this limpieza de sangre?" I persisted.

"Because they have the taint of Jewish blood in them, of course," she said. I looked up at her sharply, startled. She looked back at me in horror, realizing she had let slip something awful and insulting. "Oh Isabel! I am so sorry. I didn't mean it that way," she apologized. "A hundred years of being Christian, is a *very* long time," she tried to say consolingly.

As soon as I got home, I asked Mamá about it. She was folding clean bedclothes into the linen cupboard.

"Don't fret about it," Mamá had said, barely glancing at me. "Half of Seville traces its ancestry to the Jews of ancient times who fled to the kingdoms of Spain after the Roman destruction of their Temple. Many, like our families, the Carusos and the Carvallos, came a little later to Christianity, that is all," she explained with a note of irritation in her voice. "You know how the Church loves its baptized converts." I could tell Mamá was uncomfortable with the discussion and wished it to be over. But her words brought me no comfort.

"But Teresa says those without it are *tainted* with the blood of Jews!"

Mamá's face colored. She shook the pillow coverlet that she held, almost angrily. "It is only a little taint, Isabel. After a hundred years, hardly a taint at all. Stop making so much of it! And never speak of it in public. It is very rude and uncouth to talk of people's ancestries!"

So for the next few years, I put my concerns about the limpieza de sangre, to the back of my mind. What Mamá had said seemed largely true. For as I grew older, I heard relaxed and easy talk among my parents' friends and court acquaintances about the New Christians of Seville. They often said how Seville was known far and wide as a *converso* town—a town of converts to Christianity whose wealth and success in many areas of life sustained the Church. People often joked that without the New Christians, the churches of Seville would have to shut down.

Though I wondered if the "slight taint" of Jewish blood would ever leave my veins, it never mattered to Teresa. Hardly a day went by when she did not want to see me, or I, her. Since we had been very young children, Teresa and I went to the morning mass together, arm in arm, following behind our mothers. But in 1492, as we approached our thirteenth year, the age of betrothal in Seville, we were granted permission to attend the morning Ladymass, the special mass held for women and girls, by ourselves.

For weeks, the marquesa had not been going with us anyway, having taken to bed as she often did, with vague complaints, her servants watching over her anxiously. And then my own mamá stopped going too, when she gave birth in early spring to my baby brother, Manuel. He was my parents' third child, for there was also my grown brother Tomás, who had left home five years earlier to join the Dominican Friars. Mamá, alas, had lost several infants to fever and

25

premature birth. The new baby, so healthy and strong, was a miracle to us all. She taught me from his earliest days to bathe and swaddle him. Except for our oldest servant, Marta, whose eyesight was failing, Mamá did not, *dared not*, trust any other servants with his care because of his circumcision.

One bright clear morning, not long after my disturbing sojourn with Papá, in which I had seen the fleeing Jewish ones, I called a hurried good-bye to Mamá, for church bells had rung their call to morning prayer.

"Do not forget your Book of Hours, Isabel!" Mamá called from the bedchamber where she was nursing Manuel.

"No, Mamá," I called. "I have it."

"Nor your rosary purse! Nor alms for the poor!"

"Yes, Mamá," I said laughing. "You remind me everyday. And I never forget," I called back as Pascua, our servant girl, waited to open the door.

"And do not dawdle along the way to Teresa's in case ruffians should be about!" Mamá persisted.

Pascua looked impatient, rolling her eyes upward.

"I shall run quickly to Teresa's, Mamá, not stopping even to sniff at the baker's fresh almond cakes," I said and nodded to Pascua to open the door.

She swung it open, as Mamá called out yet again. "Don't get yourself into a sweat, lest you ruin your silk and perhaps become faint in church!"

This time it was I who rolled my eyes and Pascua allowed a giggle to escape. I shouted, "Good-bye, Mamá; don't worry!" in the open doorway, then hurried out before I could hear another of her nervous instructions. Pascua closed the door quickly to aid my departure. We were both used to Mamá's worrying and fretting over the many details of our lives.

Soon I was around the corner and standing in front of Teresa's grand house. As I raised my hand to the iron knocker, Teresa herself threw open the door, laughing. "How you dilly-dally, Isabel," she said teasingly, "I've been waiting for hours!"

She swept out and slammed the door, barely pulling her silk skirts through in time. She took my arm and we gaily walked the short distance to the great cathedral, arriving just before the heavy doors were pulled shut by the dour friar who never looked anyone in the face.

Once inside the church, Teresa whispered in my ear, "There she is, there she is!" It was old Doña Martinez whom everyone shunned like the plague. Doña Martinez was a bitter, tongue-wagging widow who found fault in everyone, especially those who did not live up to her standard of piety. It was said that even her grown children avoided her and had moved far away to the country. Ever since she discovered that Teresa and I had begun coming to mass without our mothers, she watched us suspiciously out of the corner of her eye almost continuously. If we whispered or lapsed into conversation even a moment, there was Doña Martinez shaking her finger and looking at us with contempt.

I complained of her to Mamá, but she said to be kind, that Doña Martinez was a lonely old woman who has only her dead husband's wealth for companionship. But Mamá did not realize how mean and spiteful she was, watching our every movement.

We tried to move as far away from her in the pews as possible. That day, we were lucky, having found space near the lattice-work windows far from the old woman, who was sitting across the aisle, glowering at a fidgety boy on her right.

Comfortably settled between the end of the pew and Teresa, I was able to lose myself in the many different feelings of the Mass, the melancholy of the chanting, the fiery words of the priestly sermon, the sensation of angelic transformation when we held the host upon our tongues. I lost myself in the feelings this day all the more because Doña Martinez was not looking over our shoulder. Teresa and I were able to whisper several times to one another without dread.

At the end of services, Teresa took a ducat to purchase a candle for her uncle who had died recently in Córdoba. I waited near the beautiful carved statue of Our Virgin Lady, a gloomy corner of the church lit up by her presence. I stared up into her kindly eyes which looked with rapture toward the sky. I tried to imagine the angels she was envisioning.

Suddenly, without warning, I was startled out of my pleasant reveries by a most unpleasant poke.

"Seeking absolution for the many sins of you and your family, I see."

I turned and found myself looking into the sour face of Doña Martínez.

"*Buenos días*, Doña Martínez," I said casting my eyes down resentfully. "I was just admiring the Blessed Virgin."

"You should do more than admire. You should beg for mercy, Señorita Carvallo. People like you need all the mercy they can get!" she hissed none too quietly.

I looked anxiously around for Teresa who was still across the hall on her knees near the candles.

"I don't understand what you mean, I am sure," I said in as uninterested a tone as I could muster.

"*You don't understand what I mean,*" Doña Martínez mocked me in a harsh sing song voice. "Well, my dear it would behoove you to find out! For don't you know what happens to people such as you?"

I did not look at her as I spoke but stared up into the Virgin's mild eyes, trying my best to ignore the old woman and to ask Our Lady for special patience. For I had the greatest urge to slap the smirking face of the old woman.

"They burn, señorita, they burn, along with all their wealth and fine possessions, in the baptismal fires of heretics and Marranos!" She spat the word "Marranos" out so forcefully I could feel the terrible spray of her spit upon my face. I stood there as deaf-seeming as possible staring up at the face of Our Lady, in fierce concentration.

"Do you not pay heed to the sanbenitos hanging here in the Hall of Impurity? Do you not think of the fate of the heretics and Marranos who wore them?" she insisted, her voice growing shrill and pinched.

I shivered at her words. In the entryway of our great church was a hallway devoted to displaying sanbenitos, the garments of shame worn by heretics who either did public penance or were burned at the stake. After the heretic was burned, his or her sanbenito was hung upon the walls in the church for public display. The sanbenitos were to serve as a reminder to all, of the terrible fate awaiting those who did not practice the purest and most sincere form of Christianity approved by the archbishop. The hanging of the sanbenito did not only punish the heretic, but brought disgrace and impoverishment upon the family of the heretic as well, for generations to come.

Since my earliest memories, the sanbenitos had frightened me. They looked like empty shrouds and ghosts hanging high on the church walls, so limply. Whenever I passed the Hall of Impurity, I shuddered and cast my eyes away.

"What is all this talk of heretics and Marranos in Blessed Mary's presence?" It was the strong, melodious voice of Teresa, who had come unnoticed behind us. I crossed myself in great relief.

Seeing Teresa de Rodriguez, Doña Martinez put on her most ingratiating smile. "Now here is a fine Old Christian girl if ever there was one," she croaked.

Teresa, unsmiling in return, repeated the question. "What was that, pray, Doña Martinez, that you were saying about your involvement with heretics?"

"I said nothing of the sort!" the old woman said with a look of horror. I could not help cracking the barest hint of a smile. That was a clever remark for Teresa. For she knew, as I, that even knowing a heretic could implicate someone with the Holy Office of the Inquisition, the official agency of torture and burning of accused ones. The Holy Office, run by friars and monks, was spoken of in terror in Seville and all of Spain.

"I was only speaking to Señorita Carvallo about the wages of sin and of what happens to certain Judaizers who taint our glorious faith!" said the old woman, who had put back on the smile. She nodded and began to back off when Teresa did not reply. Though she was small, hardly taller than we were, it did not diminish my fear of her.

"No such thing concerns *us*," said Teresa loudly to the back of the retreating woman. "We are *both* from the finest Catholic families of Seville," she finished. We watched in silence as the exasperating old woman had scooted off into the gloom of the passageway pulling her black lace mantilla closely around her head.

As we began our walk home, I squeezed Teresa's arm in gratitude. "You chased her away so cleverly," I said gratefully, then added, "At least Doña Martinez likes you, you fine Old Christian girl," I tried to joke.

"Pay her no mind," said Teresa scoffing. "She is like an old black spider in her black lace, spinning her webs."

Even though we stopped to buy sweet almond cakes on the way home and Teresa kissed me at her door and stroked my cheek, I was unconsoled. Never before had anyone spoken so openly, so brazenly of my Jewish ancestry. I wondered what gave her such courage to speak to me in that way. And I walked the rest of the way home feeling a cold icy dread from those "spinning webs" of Doña Martinez.

four

I Learn Our Family Secret

I told Mamá that very day about hateful Doña Martinez. But this time she did not scoff at the words of a bitter old woman as I had expected her to.

Her eyes filled with dread and she said, "Isabel, I don't want you to go to church alone again with Teresa. Not unless the marquesa or I are with you."

"But why, Mamá? We are old enough to go unchaperoned now. The church is so near to us. . . ."

"No, no," she shook her head vigorously. "You don't understand. You must be more careful. It is not only Doña Martinez that we must worry about. There are so many others as well." Mamá paced the floor wringing her hands nervously, as if groping for words. "You see, my darling," she said turning to face me, "tremendous changes have been decreed in the land. . . ." Her voice trailed off.

"Changes, Mamá?" I asked confused. "Bad changes?"

"Sí, bad changes, fearful changes. You have seen the ruin of the Moors and the Edict of Expulsion of all Jews. Now," she looked wildly around the room as if groping for the words, "it is as if the monarchs have given permission for hateful, angry, and fanatical people to become more bold and fearless in their spite."

"You mean others may speak to me as Doña Martinez?"

Mamá nodded.

"But what business is it of others, whether we are 'Old Christian' or 'New'?" I said indignantly.

"Unfortunately, it has become everyone's business these days, Isabel. Everyone judges their neighbor on whether or not they own the accursed limpieza de sangre," she said bitterly. "Isabel," she grasped my hand suddenly, "promise me you will not go to church without me or Papá or the marquesa. Promise me!" she said almost desperately.

"Sí, Mamá, I promise," I said looking away from her frightened eyes.

But I still did not fully understand. Not until the great Eastertime masses of that spring did I begin to understand. Mamá had been right. It wasn't only the shrewish Doña Martinez who spoke openly of Jewish taint and detestable Marranos. All during Holy Week the priest of Santa Maria del Popolo, Father Fuentes, who had been known for his long-winded and boring sermons, was suddenly preaching his most exciting sermons. They were called, "The Many Benefits of Expelling the Jews."

"First," said Father Fuentes, "after fifteen hundred years, we are finally avenging the death of our Lord and Savior, Jesus Christ. Not only did the Jews plot the murder of Jesus, but they stubbornly continue to reject the teachings of Christianity. I congratulate the monarchs Isabel and Ferdinand for the Edict of Expulsion of the Jews from Spain."

I looked around. The congregation looked only mildly interested. We had heard this all before.

"Second Benefit!" Father Fuentes held up two fingers to the listening congregation. "The plague shall soon be ended! Sí! In six more weeks when the expulsion of Spain's Jews is complete." The congregation sat up, grew interested, and alert. "My friends and fellow Christians, you must know that the Jews concoct poisons, the secret recipes of which are recorded in their evil Torah scrolls! Thousands of Jews sneak out and spill their poison into the wells of Europe and Spain! And this," shouted Father Fuentes, growing red-faced, "has been the cause for so long, of our deadly plagues!"

The crowd gasped at this news, though many around us shook their heads as if already knowing it. I looked at my parents incredulously, but could say nothing during the sermon. Yet I wished someone would stand up and say it is a lie, all a lie! Didn't all the physicians say that the plague was a sickness, that even the Jews caught plague, as readily as any Christian? Only ignorant people believe such things! But Father Fuentes sounded so convincing. And no one stood up to say anything.

"And thirdly," Father Fuentes said holding up three fingers, "without Jews in Spain, all of Christendom will rest easier in their beds at night. For who hasn't heard how the Jews hunt down innocent Christian children," the crowd gasped, "and slit their throats, and bake their blood into the Passover bread the Jews called matzah," he screamed.

A cry of indignation flared up from the congregation. But Father Fuentes, with a raise of his hand, halted the uproar and droned on against the Jews. Each weekly sermon was more hysterical than the previous one. All through Easter Holy Week, Mamá, Papá, and I cringed as Father Fuentes thrilled the congregation with his Jew-hating sermons. His hysterical voice rang in my ears, long after we left the grand cathedral.

○

I did not see very much of my beloved Teresa that spring, for Mamá and the marquesa could but rarely accompany us to Ladymass. And Mamá strictly forbid me from going alone with my friend. As that gloomy spring of 1492 moved fitfully toward summer, I yearned for the yearly carnivals and fiestas, which I hoped would bring people together again in happiness. And then came the day when I finally learned the truth. It was the fifteenth of June, my birthday, when Papá told me the secret that changed my life forever.

I had awakened before dawn awaiting Papá's knock upon my door; for it was our joyous yearly custom that Papá would arise early, before setting out for the day's business to give me birthday greetings and a special gift befitting the age I had reached.

Just after six and the tolling of church bells, Papá knocked upon my door, calling birthday greetings and summoning me to his room. I arose and donned my robe and entered the sleeping chamber of my parents, a beautiful room with ornate woven carpets and flowing draperies. Mamá had arisen even earlier, taking Manuel in his basket and had gone downstairs to instruct the servants concerning the evening feast to which our Sevillano relatives would attend in my honor. Except for Manuel, I was the youngest cousin left in our family and they made much over me at feast days and birthdays.

My father closed the door behind me. Though he was dressed for work, he looked uncommonly weary, as if he hadn't slept well. For a moment I studied the dear familiar face, the shock of dark, wavy hair falling across his forehead, the eyes lined with worry—no doubt for some obscure court matters of the men. "Papá, you have not slept well," I said reaching up to kiss him.

"Well enough, my pet," he dismissed my concern and pointed to an object sitting upon the velvet chair behind him. It was a smooth wooden box with metal hinges, not much bigger than the palm of my hand. As I approached, he smiled and bent down to open the box. The light that streamed in through the open shutters struck a shiny object within, a metallic object polished and bright. At first, the object, partially hidden by a piece of silk, looked familiar. I thought it was a tiny ornate cross, with the body of the crucified Jesus carved in its center. But as I reached in and took hold of it, I saw it was but a slender golden rod etched with arabesques. The carving in its center was no figure of Jesus, only an ornate lettering of some kind.

"It is beautiful," I said holding it up in the light. "But what is it? It looks like a crucifix missing its crosspiece." I looked up at Papá questioningly.

"No, *not* a cruciform. Not a Christian object at all, but a treasure of antiquity, a holy object of our family, handed down to me from my *abuela*, your *bisabuela*—your Great Grandmother Ruth."

Bisabuela Ruth. Family legend surrounded her name. Always she had been spoken of in the reverent tones reserved for the saints. Yet I knew only that she and my *bisabuelo*, my great grandfather, had suffered terrible misfortune on June the fourth of the year 1391. On more than one occasion I had heard Papá and his brothers utter that date in prayer. And the aunts would light candles yearly in church in their memory. But what that misfortune was, Papá had never revealed.

"Antiquity," I repeated in wonder. Papá knew I loved antique things. I had a fine chest beneath my bed holding many different objects of old—from a bit of knight's mail said to date from the age of King Arthur to small bronze animals of early Egyptian origin. "But this decoration and writing looks to be that of the Islamic people," I said, turning the rod over in my hand, "from the unfortunate Moors who lost the queen's war." Much of their confiscated kingdom was being sold now in the shops of Seville.

"Sí, it does resemble the Islamic style, but, actually, it is the artistry of another people who have lived in Spain since ancient times. Those three letters: Shin, Daled, Yod stand for the word 'Shaddai.' One of the most sacred names of God. It means 'the Almighty.'"

"Sha-dai," I repeated curiously. "But I have never heard that name being used before by the priests."

Papá stared out the sunny window. Newly blossomed flowers fluttered in the window box. He spoke distractedly. "No, of course you have not, my child," he said. "Indeed not." He turned back and looked me squarely in the face. "Isabel, it is the name employed in prayer . . . by . . . by the Jews," he drew the name out slowly.

"The Jews!" I said in confusion, astonishment.

"Isabel," he said pulling another chair up to sit facing me. "You must try to listen and comprehend. You have known already that we are New Christians, that once, long ago our ancestors were Jewish."

"Why of course, Papá, but that was more than a hundred years ago! A long, long time ago, Papá!" Talk of New and Old Christians always made me nervous.

"A long time, perhaps for a young girl, but not so long in the generations of a family."

"But we have been devout Christians ever since!" I protested, a feeling of panic rising in me.

"Isabel," he said gently, staring down at the gold piece, "this rod of pure gold is our family icon, handed down from my grandparents Ruth and Avram Cojano. You have reached the thirteenth year; and you must now know the truth."

I cringed, wanting to close my ears against truth, against the frightening undercurrents of secrecy in our family that were suddenly rising to the surface like hungry fish in water.

"Papá? Is not a birthday a day for light-heartedness, for pleasantries and special gifts and feasting and . . ."

"We are secret Jews," he whispered sharply, interrupting my harried words. His words pierced me like a swordpoint. I dropped the golden rod into its box, as if the sunlight had turned it hot. Papá might as well have said our house was struck by plague, so shocking and deadly were those two terrible words.

35

"Oh no," I shook my head, "not that, not that . . ." I stood up, set the box down, backed away. A worse set of fates could not befall a family—Inquisitors of the Holy Office, confessions under torture, financial ruin, dungeons, prison, the wearing of sanbenitos, public humiliations, and, in the end, sometimes, even *burning*. My mind ran riot with visions of doom.

"Please, Isabel," Papá caught my hand, "calm yourself. Perhaps when you know, when you understand . . ." he said. "Let me tell you our family story. Then it won't seem so sudden, so unnatural."

I nodded, reluctantly, trying to calm myself. I adored my father. There was little I wouldn't do to please him, but this . . .

"Sit," he said gently, pulling me down on the velvet chair.

"It was the year 1391," he said staring through me into some misty place of the past, "a year that shall remain forever in the mind of Jews as the infamous year of Jewish slaughter. It was at that time—a hundred years ago—that my grandparents, the Cojanos, from a prosperous merchant family and descendants of the sacred tribes of the Jewish priesthood, known as the Cojanes, were forced, along with thousands of Jewish people, to become practitioners of Christianity or be put to swift death by sword."

"Conversion by sword? Your grandparents?" I gasped. "But that is barbarous!" I exclaimed.

"Indeed, my child, it is. My grandparents, Avram and Ruth de Cojano, were newly married and sat worshipping one Sabbath morning separately in the men's and women's sections of the Jewish Temple of Seville. In joy, they prayed the *Amidah*, 'the Nineteen Benedictions of the Jewish prayer service,' for they were much in love and awaiting their first child to be born that year. But that day, joy was turned to horror. Jew-hating mobs had long roamed the cities of Europe bent on torture and murder of Jews, convinced that the Jews were responsible for every ill of society, especially for the plague. But few Jewish people knew that such mobs had arisen in Spain, in our very own Seville."

"Here, you say? Jews lived here in Seville?" I asked astonished. The idea of Jews in Seville was unheard of.

"But of course, my child. Jews lived in Seville for centuries until Christians hardened their hearts against us. Unfortunately, like many towns, Seville had its own fanatic archdeacon of hate, a Father Ferran

36

Martinez. He preached hatred and destruction of the Jewish people from every church pulpit in the city. His speeches inspired the ill-fed peasants and desperately poor city people to believe that all their hardships and starving children could be conveniently blamed on the existence of Jews in Seville." Papá's eyes stared out gloomily.

"Oh, Papá," I exclaimed. "It is no different now. Remember the Easter sermons?"

Papá closed his eyes and nodded his head grimly.

I swallowed hard. "What happened to Bisabuela and Bisabuelo that day, Papá?"

"Well, you see Martinez had invited another hate-filled Catholic priest known as Fray Vincent Ferrer to Seville. This priest Ferrer had already earned his reputation for roaming the cities of Spain, arousing angry mobs of people to follow him into synagogues with knives and swords and clubs, to convert the Jews to Christianity or commit sickening violence if they refused. Fray Vincent Ferrer loved to boast of converting or murdering thousands of Jewish folk in his unholy mission." Papá had begun to pace the floors, as if it calmed him a bit. "That day, while your bisabuelos worshiped in the synagogue, Ferrer, knowing it was Saturday, the Jewish Sabbath, revved up an angry street mob and stormed the Jewish Temple in the middle of Sabbath worship. Holding aloft a silver cross, he shouted 'Baptism or Death to the Jews!'

"Over half the congregation—men, women, and children, young and old alike—were mercilessly beaten and put to the sword. Only a small group of people managed to fall to their knees and beg conversion to the Christian faith. My grandparents, expecting their first baby, were among them. They were spared their lives because they begged for mercy and agreed to Christian conversion. Ferrer boasted of converting thirty-five thousand frightened Jews, in just this unholy manner, in towns all over Spain." Papá sat down, looking spent.

I looked at him, shaken by the violence of our family's conversion. If such hatred and violence had occurred a hundred years ago to my bisabuelo and bisabuela . . . and still the priests had not stopped preaching against the Jews in my own time . . . what did it mean? Did the Jews never escape the loathing and violence of the Christian world? I looked with questioning eyes to Papá.

"What has happened to the gentle preachings of Jesus?"

"Fanatics," he said sharply, "who preach of Christian love, but practice devilish hate. There is not much of Jesus left in Christendom today," he said bitterly.

"Then Bisabuelo and Bisabuela became practicing Christians?"

"Sí. Thereafter, Avram and Ruth gave up their proud Jewish names and took the names of Christian nobility—Juan and Rosa de Carvallo—and became outwardly devoted to the Church. But in their hearts they would not forsake the faith of their fathers and swore secretly to pass to their children and children's children the true faith in *Torah*—'the Hebrew Bible'—and in the One God."

We sat in silence as I tried to absorb the whole of Papá's story. Somewhere, back in the mists of time, we had been Jews. This I had always known. But I had thought our family had simply chosen conversion and had lived happily and prosperously as Christians for a hundred years. Papá had risen to the high court as a trusted Christian. Why now, when it was dangerous and detestable to be Jews, were we returning to the ancient faith of our Jewish ancestors? I sighed. The passions and changeability of adults was often unfathomable to me. At least I now understood at last why we had never had the limpieza de sangre like others, why we had become New Christians.

"You and Mamá are both secret Jews then?"

"Sí, Isabel. Your Mamá, a Caruso, is also a New Christian whose family had also been forced to convert at swordpoint in 1391. Such conversions became commonplace in Spain. But in spite of what the Christians believe, Judaism is not something one just gives up at the point of a sword! It is our birthright! Our belief in the One God! Our love of Torah, God's foundation of decent and moral behavior for all human beings!"

He turned and took my hands, "Isabel, it is up to you to pass on our family's true identity to your children and children's children. You and Manuel are our only hope for the future, for the salvation of our Jewish souls. It is your *birthright*, your Jewish *soul* which obligates you to do this." He looked at me, his eyes full of desperation.

I did not know what to say. I felt a whirlwind of emotions—shame, anger, shock, despair—as I looked down at this strange gift given in honor of my thirteenth year. "What exactly is the golden rod used for, Papá?" I said bleakly, trying to show my interest.

Papá sat down beside me, reached inside the carved box, held the golden rod lovingly before us. "It is called a *mezuzzah*."

"Me-zu-zzah," I repeated slowly.

"It is the signpost of the Jewish home, Isabel, a tradition going back to ancient times, when the Jews were slaves in Egypt. A bit of parchment with Hebrew blessings is sealed within. My grandfather once said that this holy mezuzzah has been in the Cojano family for at least five hundred years. This and their knowledge of the sacred and moral Torah laws are all that Abuela and Abuelo could save of their true identities."

"How did you get it, Papá?"

"Abuela lived to the great age of eighty-five," he said with a smile. "She asked me, on her death-bed, to keep the ancient golden mezuzzah as a secret link in a chain connecting the generations of the Cojano-Carvallos. I was only ten years old at the time, her only male grandchild. I still remember staring down at the tiny, wrinkled old lady who was known for her courage and valor. I loved her dearly and never forgot her words. 'At the thirteenth year of your own son or daughter, you must pass on the golden mezuzzah, sweet Paulos,' she said to me. 'You must not break the chain that represents thousands of years of our family's worship of the One God, *Adonai*.' I felt she had laid a great responsibility upon my shoulders, Isabel. Just as I do now to you."

"For a hundred years we have been secret Jews?" I asked in amazement.

"Secret Jews, sí, or as the Spaniards call us—Marranos—*swine, pigs, a thing that rolls in filth and vileness*," Papá said softly. I looked at him shocked that he used that word, an obscene street word that was said by Spaniards only in derision. Yet he had uttered the word not in shame, but strangely drawn-out in a tone filled unmistakably with love. "We are Mar-ra-nos," he said in that strange poetic way again, "the people who live the cross by day and the mezuzzah by night."

I felt both thrilled and frightened by those words. For even from earliest childhood I had been taught in church school that it was one thing to be a New Christian of devout character and quite another thing to be a Marrano, a secret Jew, a filthy defiler of the Christian faith.

Suddenly, the words of Doña Martinez came ringing back to me: *"They burn señorita, they burn, with all their wealth and fine possessions."*

As my father stared out the window, a new fear settled in the pit of my stomach.

"Papá?" I said weakly. "What happens to us now?"

He whirled around and looked me squarely in the face. "Isabel, I cannot lie to you. We are at terrible risk of being questioned by the Holy Office."

As long as I live, I will never forget my father's look of despair. It sent a new stab of fear through me as he spoke. For I knew that to be "questioned" by the Holy Office was the polite way of saying "tortured."

The rumors flew all over Seville of the goings on at such "questionings." Stories abounded of how the accused met unimaginable suffering and torture in old castle dungeons, stretched to tearing points on moving racks, drowned in forced drinkings of endless jars of water, tied by the arms and pulled to the ceilings of torture chambers, and dropped to the floor breaking and shattering bones!

If the accused were found guilty, which they almost always were, the unfortunate condemned ones were then burned before great raucous crowds on the castle grounds. But there had been few public burnings in recent years. The Holy Office worked in quiet, discreet ways so as not to arouse panic among the public. Many had come to believe the stories of torture to be mostly wild rumor.

"Papá, have you heard something? How can you be sure?"

"Through . . . through an informant. A person I know who is close to the workings of the Holy Office. He has informed me that all leading officials of the royal court with New Christian background are under close scrutiny by the Holy Office."

"What shall we do? How shall we act?"

"As if *nothing* has changed, Isabel. We must go on as we always have, in wretched secrecy. It can be revealed to no one! Not by word, not by deed. It is a dangerous, intolerable situation!" He got up and paced the floor wringing his hands. "That is why we must leave!"

"Leave?" I said confused.

Papá stopped in front of me. "Isabel, do you remember the Jewish ones fleeing after the Edict of Expulsion several weeks ago?" I nodded, remembering the heart-wrenching scene only too well. "Well, we—Mamá and I, and you and the baby . . ." he faltered.

"What Papá, what . . . ?"

"Soon, very soon, we too must flee the country . . . join our brethren . . . the expelled Jews. The . . . the informant I mentioned . . . he has told me that we are greatly endangered. That in a matter of days, a few weeks at most . . . we must take secretly to the road, blend in with the bands of Jewish people, carrying but a few of our belongings to the Port of Cadiz. We must melt into the crowd—the four of us—and begin to assume the identities of a Jewish family in the midst of forced expulsion."

"Leave our home . . . this house . . . Seville?"

"Leave Spain . . . forever," he said with grim finality.

"Oh, no! Oh, no! Oh, Blessed Mary, no!" I stared at my father, trying to grasp the meaning of the word *forever*. To leave everything, this house in which I'd been born, my beloved homeland, even, I realized, my own dear Teresa! It was unfathomable, unbearable! I threw my face into my hands and wept.

"Sh-sh-sh-sh, my daughter!" He came quickly to me, knelt down, took me in his arms. "I wish I could keep all this pain from you," he said his voice tinged with sadness and regret. "For too long we have cowered beneath the protective cloak of Christianity."

I looked up at him with a tear-streaked face. He handed me his kerchief. I blew my nose. Suddenly I thought of something. "What about Tomás?"

Papá looked at me sharply. "What about Tomás?"

"Have you not told him?"

"There is no need." He looked away.

"But he is my brother!" I said in shocked astonishment. "He is your son!"

"Since he joined the fanatic Dominicans in Toledo, he has not been much of a son to Mamá or I," Papá said bitterly. Haven't you noticed that he never comes home, not even to see his mother or his new baby brother? He has estranged himself from us. Isabel, your brother does not approve of our attachment to the Jewish faith," Papá said.

"Then he knows that we are Marranos?"

41

Papá nodded. "For eight years he has known, since he himself turned thirteen, the year I tried to teach him of the Jewish faith."

"He did not accept his Jewish birthright? He went to the Dominicans anyway?"

"Indeed. He rejected his birthright and gave himself to the most fanatical sect in all of Christendom! Even at thirteen, I had lost him to the Church. He had no interest in our Jewish heritage. He kept saying, 'The past is dead, Father. You should not try to bring it back.' No, I failed to bring my first-born son to the faith of his ancestors. I let my beloved Abuela Ruth down." Papá stared out into space, a look of bitterness and defeat on his face.

"Why did you not tell me sooner, Papá? Why did you wait all these years until I am almost grown, almost the age of betrothal?"

"Because the Marrano rabbis advise against it. They tell us not to reveal this until the thirteenth birthday, the year of Jewish adulthood, when a child is old and wise enough to accept the burden of this dangerous knowledge."

The year of Jewish adulthood, the words Papá had spoken to me that day in the carriage as we watched the fleeing Jews.

He leaned forward and took my hands. "I know this is a lot for you to understand all at once, my beloved. Your mamá has also taken the news of our impending escape quite hard. You must steel yourself and try to be strong and courageous, Isabel, for me and for your mamá." I looked up, nodded distractedly.

"What now, Papá? How shall I behave in church school or in Mass? For I have learned to pray as a Catholic and do not know the Jewish God."

"That is not entirely true, my love."

"What do you mean?"

He stroked the tops of my hands soothingly. "Do you remember, Isabel, the little prayer we taught you to whisper as a little girl upon entering the cathedral?"

"Why of course, Papá. Doesn't everyone say it? I have never stopped doing as you instructed—under my breath so that only God hears it."

"Do it now, Isabel. Do it now as I showed you," he said suddenly brightening.

"Sí, Papá," I said bewildered. I closed my eyes to quiet my thoughts in prayerfulness. And then I said: *Adonai, my God in my thoughts.*" I touched my forehead. *"Adonai, my God on my lips."* I lightly touched my lips. *"Adonai my God in my heart."* I touched the right and left side of my chest. "It is the prayer of the cross, Papá. But I never say the words aloud; Mamá says it would be disrespectful."

"No, it is *not* the prayer of the cross," said Papá, squeezing my hands. "All your life you have been saying a special Jewish prayer, the secret prayer of the Marrano, uttered to cancel the sign of the cross which we are forced to make."

I gasped aloud.

"You see, Isabel, Adonai is another of God's sacred names given to the Jewish people. It means 'The Lord.' We taught you to utter this prayer in the barest whisper because if it were heard it would place the Marrano in mortal danger. It is one of the little ways we Marranos have devised for preserving our Jewish souls in a world that would destroy us."

Stunned by Papá's revelation, I looked at the hand that made the sign of the cross in disbelief. For all the years of my childhood I had been making a secret Jewish prayer to nullify all my public Christian prayers. My mind reeled with the strangeness of it all, with the deception of my own parents. I looked at my father. Suddenly, anger flared in my heart.

"What if I do not want to follow the Jewish God, Papá?" I spoke fiercely, defiantly, more disrespectfully than I had ever dared before.

He turned and stared at me, his eyes boring into mine. I held my breath.

He sat down on the edge of his bed, in defeat, bent over. "I cannot force my daughter, anymore than I could force my son," he said despairingly. "Perhaps it is too late, too late . . ." he whispered hopelessly, covering his face with his hands.

He looked so undone, so wretched and alone, my heart ached to its very core. I threw my arms around him.

"Forgive me, Papá! Forgive me! I did not mean to hurt you! I will change Papá, if that's what you want me to do."

"No Isabel," he said gently, lightly stroking my cheek. "I am not hurt. I am in fact, heartened. For my daughter has shown me that she is strong and courageous, a young woman with a mind of her own. You must not do what *I* want you to do. Not even to please your papá. You must find out for yourself if accepting your birthright is the right thing for you. Tonight there will be a special ceremony in your honor with all of the Carvallo family. You will receive your true name, your secret Jewish name, given to you at birth," he said gently. "Perhaps that will help you understand and decide."

"My secret Jewish name? What is it Papá?" I asked astounded. Was there no end, I wondered, to the secrets of this family?

My father was peering nervously out the window onto the street below. "Dear One, the carriage awaits. We must speak of this later at your naming ceremony with all the aunts and uncles gathered around us," he said going to the door. "It will seem more natural then."

I followed him to the door. "I am so confused, Papá."

"Perhaps it will help to think of it as a little game, a charade or play perhaps. We must play our roles like the traveling actors we have seen at the yearly fiesta. It is strange, Isabel, but think, in playing the part of escaping Jews, we will most fully play our true selves. For too long our Christianity has been a cloak of protection. It must now be cast off."

"Sí, Papá," I said in a small voice. And then he was my old papá again, standing tall and erect, and looking very much the court official.

"There is just one last thing I must mention," he said slowly turning back to face me. "In the coming weeks you must never let one word slip about any of this to the servants. Or to anyone outside this house. Not to neighbor, nor servant, not even to Mamá's family—they are much too loyal to the Church. Not to any living soul outside these walls, Isabel. For there is *no one* trustworthy in a world governed by fanatics and the fanatical Holy Office."

I looked up startled. Not to anyone? Not even . . . No, he could not mean . . .

"Not even to Teresa de Rodriguez, Papá?" I asked imploringly. For the idea of not telling my dearest friend, in whom I confided *everything*, this most important thing about myself, was totally unimaginable.

I was to receive yet another unpleasant shock, for Papá recoiled with a look of sheer terror at my question.

"*Especially* not to Teresa de Rodriguez, Isabel!" was Papá's chilling reply.

five

I Learn the Meaning of the Friday Night Candles

Overwhelmed, I watched from the window as Papá left. My Bisabuela Ruth's golden mezuzzah was still in hand. I ran my thumb across the letters of the Jewish name of God where they had been etched into the gold. What was the name Papá had said?—Sha something—Shaddai. I shivered at the exotic sound of it, enthralled and shocked by all that Papá had told me. Yet another, more urgent thought interrupted the others. *Teresa, I may not tell you any longer what is in my heart and mind. I am not to tell you this new, most important thing about myself.*

I put the mezuzzah back into its box and solemnly carried the box back to my own room, pushing it deeply into the feathers of my mattress, where I hid things from the servants. Still on my knees, I lay my head down on my bed, drained of strength. In my mind whirled whispering, murmuring . . . secrets. Secrets kept by my parents . . . secrets I must never divulge . . . secret names I must remember not to say . . . secrets that brought shame and the scandal of the sanbenito to a family. Secrets that could lead to imprisonment or death. Shivering, I crawled onto my mattress, pulled the covers over me, trembled, and shook until I fell into the deep well of sleep.

Sometime later, something was trying to awaken me . . . *crawling back up . . . gasping for breath . . . I dream of drowning. . . . My face in the water, drowning. Suddenly the smiling face of old Doña Martinez floats by! She is smiling to see me drowning!*

"Mistress!"

"Sí?" I shouted, sitting up straight in alarm, gasping.

It was only Pascua, who had come in to straighten the room. She was staring down at me. I fell back upon the pillow.

"You are unwell, mistress?" she said, looking surprised to find me still in bed.

"I-I am well, Pascua," I said and slowly got up from the bed and went to the wash-pitcher. I threw cool water rapidly in my face and down my neck to shock the image of Doña Martinez from my mind.

"Are you sure? You don't look well. And it is so late in the morning! You never sleep so late unless you are sick. I think I should fetch your mamá to check for fever."

"No, Pascua, I am fine. I overslept, that's all."

"Ah, you skipped church to sleep late on your birthday, sí?" she said straightening the covers on my bed, plumping the pillows.

"Sí, that is it," I replied tiredly.

She watched me wash. "Mistress, I shall be more than happy to draw you a bath with rose petals. It will make you feel better."

"No, Pascua, not till later, when I dress for the dinner. Now, I must hurry and dress and go to help Mamá."

"As you wish, Mistress," said Pascua watching me from the corner of her eye.

When I had dressed, I went stumbling downstairs in search of Mamá. I found her busy and distracted with the servants, carefully measuring her precious spices into the cooking pots from special pouches around her waist and giving numerous instructions to the cooks. The entire household was in a bustle of kitchen activity, preparing for my birthday feast. But I waited, sniffing at the cooking pots and when she saw me, she came and kissed me. "Did you see Papá? Did he give you your gift?" she asked anxiously.

I nodded. "Mamá, may I speak to you . . . alone?"

She looked back at the servants. "Now? There is so much to do. . . ."

"Please," I implored.

She nodded knowingly and began to fill a breakfast platter of grapes and cheese and crusty bread. "Go and eat in the courtyard," she said handing me the platter, "and I will meet you there soon." So I went and sat upon the patio, among the fruit trees and potted flowers. I nibbled at the food without appetite as I watched a large bumble bee flit high and low erratically, among the orange blossoms. It suddenly struck me how uncertain the fortunes of a family could be—or the fortunes of an entire people, rising and falling like the bumble bee.

At last Mamá came out and sat down next to me on the stone bench. "Darling daughter," she put her arms around me, laid her head briefly on my shoulder. "I wish you happiness today and for all your days to come." There was such a note of sadness in her voice, I looked up into her face.

"*Gracias*, dear Mamá." Endless questions were swirling in my head. I did not know where to begin.

"Papá told you all about us, about your bisabuela Ruth?" she asked sadly, glancing furtively around to make sure no servants were about.

"Oh Mamá!" I whispered in anguish, "It is all so terrible—so *unthinkable!* To have to escape like common criminals! To leave our homeland! And then, not even to say good-bye to Teresa!" I couldn't help myself and began to weep again, stifling the noise with my hands.

"Oh my, oh my," she seemed at a loss for words as she held me close, her arms around me. I was glad we faced the courtyard walls away from the house, away from the eyes of the servants.

When at last I calmed down, she took out her kerchief and wiped my eyes and nose just as she had done when I was a small girl. I looked up at her dully. "It is all so sudden, so unbelievable, what Papá says."

Mamá looked down at the ground beneath our feet, twisting the kerchief in her hands. "Oh, Isabel, I could not believe it myself, that things had really come to this. When your father came and told me that he feared being brought down by accusers . . . I . . . I did not want to accept it. 'How could they do this to you Paulos?' I asked him. 'You are so highly respected. Never before have the royal coffers of Seville been as overflowing with taxes. How could they possibly throw the good services of such a man as you away?' 'Believe it, Maria. It is all too true,' your father said."

"They couldn't, Mamá, they couldn't! Perhaps he is mistaken."

"Isabel, I have told your father that we shouldn't act in haste, that things will calm down and all this business with the Holy Office will be forgotten. You know how people love to exaggerate the truth. Seville has always been filled with wild rumors about the Holy Office and its practices. Can we not wait, Paulos? I asked him again and again. They would have to arrrest half the city. Half of Seville has Jewish blood in their family lines. It means nothing. They wouldn't dare bother us. But your papá says that things have changed. That the fanatics and Jew-haters are on the rise. You remember what it was like at the Easter masses. They have been arousing the masses even from the pulpits.

"Then he said that he has already delayed many months, almost too long, hoping things would calm down. But now he says we have to go, while there are tens of thousands of Jews upon the roads. For it will be nearly impossible to escape after the Jews have all left Spain. He says we must go while so many ships await. While there is much confusion and people fleeing. While it will not appear unusual for a family of four with a baby to be walking along the roadways." She looked despairingly around the walls of our house and courtyard.

"I do not know how I shall ever bear to leave this house, the servants," she sighed deeply. "Isabel, my parents built this house in fourteen twenty-four. I was born here. My parents died here. You and Manuel were born here. And then to simply walk away from it all, to take the baby out onto the perils of the road . . . just like those poor pathetic people . . . the expelled ones. . . ."

She pulled the kerchief to her own mouth to stifle herself from crying.

"Oh, Mamá!" I whispered and stroked her cheek. "What will become of us?"

"I-I am sorry, Isabel. I do not mean to frighten you. I know we must trust Papá's judgment in these things. Whatever he says we must do—that is a woman's duty." We sat in silence for several minutes.

"It is so strange, Mamá, to think that we are Jewish," I whispered.

"Yes, it is strange to me also. In some ways—a dream—a dream I pray to awaken from," she said with fervor.

I stared at her. "You do not want to be Jewish, Mamá?" I was so surprised that I spoke too loudly. Mamá shushed me with a warning look, glancing around the courtyard. She stared out in silence. She seemed to be thinking how to answer. Finally she looked at me.

"Isabel, I want you to understand. It is not that I do not think the Jewish way—the way of our ancestors is not a beautiful way. It is a gentle way, whose laws not only sanctify God, but each and every human life. Perhaps it is even the superior way. So much of Catholicism these days has turned barbarian. It is just that your father feels more strongly than I do about our Jewish heritage."

I looked at her wide-eyed, stunned. I had never known her to think differently than my father.

"Oh, Isabel, I have grown so used to the Catholic forms all my life, my rosaries, my trust in the Blessed Virgin. This is not to say that I haven't also grown used to our beautiful Friday night candles. They bring on the Jewish Sabbath, you know. I have learned to appreciate both."

"What?" I gasped. "Our Friday night candles were not prayers for the Catholic dead?"

Mamá shook her head. "They are lit to bring on the Jewish Sabbath?"

So *that* was the true meaning of the Friday night candles! I should have realized—all the secrecy, all the late nights of going to the cellar after the servants had gone to bed. . . .

She smiled sadly. "Sí, Papá did not tell you? The Jewish Sabbath is what we have been celebrating all these years. The Sabbath begins Friday night after sundown and finishes Saturday at sundown. It is a beautiful tradition of candles and wine and braided bread set upon a table dressed in white like a radiant new bride. The Jewish Sabbath itself is called a bride. Everything in the home is supposed to be perfectly clean and fresh. We are transformed from careworn laborers of the work week into refreshed new beings of love and beauty, like a new bride on her wedding day." She looked at me so intently, groping for the right words to tell me all the things I had missed and never known. "It is a day of complete rest and renewal that has helped the Jewish people survive, don't you see? Every Shabbat brings a fresh new beginning for each and every Jewish person," she said, smoothing my hair.

"Then why do we never clean and scrub our home before the Sabbath?" I asked.

"Alas, Isabel, we have not dared to let the servants change the sheets and scrub on Fridays lest they grow suspicious of Jewish practices. But our little table in the cellar is clean and white. You will see, for tonight is Friday, and after your birthday feast, we will have a special Sabbath gathering just for you, my angel."

I stared at her in amazement. "You love *both* traditions. The Catholic and the Jewish, Mamá!" My words came out accusingly.

"I know this is strange, Isabel, but you see," she brought her rosaries from inside her pocket and began to finger them, "I do not care so much whether I am Christian or Jew. All ways of worshiping God seem good to me. But to be a Jew—it is so . . . so dangerous, so . . . misunderstood in the Catholic world. All I really want is to live my life in peace, to raise my children, to be with my beloved husband. If that means one must make oneself into a good Catholic instead of a Jew, then I do not mind so much." She dabbed at her own eyes which were filling with tears.

"We have become a strangely mixed up family, I fear. There is Papá's zeal for the Jewish faith, his anger at the Catholic world. Then there is my grown son, Tomás's zeal for Catholicism, his rejection and hatred of all things Jewish. And I? I am somewhere in between, wanting only a home of harmony and peace, seeing the good and the practical in both traditions," she said.

"And which should *I* choose, Mamá?"

She looked at me and I saw the worry lines and tiredness she tried to hide with her powders. "Oh, Isabel, don't ask me that. You will have to choose for yourself. I only know what Papá tells me, that we must somehow join the Jewish ones and get as far away from Spain as possible."

"But where?" I insisted.

"I cannot tell you that, my dearest. Even Papá does not know yet. It depends upon many things. I had so hoped it would be near Portugal, for the Portuguese are not so different from the Spanish and we could learn to master the language in time. They say many expelled Jews are going there. But Papá says no. He does not trust the Portuguese. Although they have not yet expelled their Jews, they are absolute Catholics, hating Marranos as much as the Spanish do here. The farther away the better, he says, a kingdom with few Catholics, perhaps Turkey. . . ."

"Turkey!"

"Sí, a Moslem nation, friendly to Jews. Oh Isabel, it is all so complicated, so confusing. I pray hourly to Blessed Mary for guidance." I laid my head upon her shoulder.

"Try not to worry too much." She smoothed the hair behind my ear. "Put your trust in Papá as I have. As long as we are all together— Papá and me and you and the baby—we will be all right. This is what I tell myself. As long as we stay together, things will work out— *somehow.*"

○

The next hours went by in a blur—stirring cooking pots, helping Pascua, laying the table. Somehow that evening I found myself bathed and dressed, greeting the relatives who came to honor me upon my birthday.

I remember how relieved I was when Tía Mathilde, my favorite aunt, arrived. She came bustling in with flowing silk and smelling of rose water. She sniffed the air, grasping her hand to her large bosom, and said, "Ah, cinnamon, mmmm, and nutmeg, and . . . oh . . . heavens, pepper!" She swooned with delight.

"Naughty girl," she said kissing Mamá upon each cheek. "We have been to the spice importer, no? Spending an arm and a leg, haven't we sister-in-law?" Tía Mathilde waved her fan rapidly as she spoke for she was of large proportions and exertion caused her to sweat mightily. Her large and cheerful presence diminished my fears. In her company, I thought, the terrible things happening to us didn't seem real.

The Carusos and the Carvallos feasted as kings and queens at court that night. I hadn't wanted food all day, but by then, even I was famished. Tía Mathilde was right. Nothing had been spared. Peppered hash of goose, delicate puddings of cinnamon and nutmeg, cakes of ginger, even spiced wine and pomegranate juice had been laid upon our table. I had a sudden foreboding thought that Mamá had prepared this feast, not solely for me, but for our last gathering together as one great family.

I opened my gifts: beautiful blue silk to be made into a frock from Tía Mathilde. From Tía Emilia an exquisitely painted fan with the image of an exotic ostrich in full plume stretched across its folds. A box from

Teresa, who had gone to Córdoba with her family, revealed a beautiful necklace made of tiny exquisite shells dyed to a brilliant blue color. From various cousins, I received flagons of rose and orange blossom waters, linen stationery papers held together with silk ribbon, a press for my dried flower collection, beautiful carved combs, and, most wonderful of all, from Mamá, a white lace mantilla, the head shawl that all Spanish women believe increases one's feminine beauty. I immediately set it about my head, causing everyone to exclaim and pronounce that I looked as lovely as an angel.

Finally, I opened a box from my older brother Tomás, sent all the way from Toledo. It contained a beautiful red glass rosary and my brother's careful writing, "To aid you in your daily prayers." I couldn't help myself from looking up at Papá, wondering what he thought of Tomás's reminder of our Christian duties. But he quickly looked away and said something humorous to Tío Carlos, my uncle.

○

After the feast, the relatives reclined around the sitting room. I sat upon the sofa between my aunts, Tía Emilia and Tía Mathilde. I called them the "funny aunts." For always they sat together and tried to make each other laugh. Tía Emilia had released my hair from the tight grip of its combs and was pulling it gently into a long horse's tail which reached below my shoulders. I was mesmerized by the long, soothing strokes of her hands on my hair.

"Naughty girl, your mamá," said Tía Mathilde. "She has been extravagant with the spice merchant again."

"Sí, Tía Mathilde," I said, "it was as if she was preparing for a wedding instead of a birthday."

Tía Emilia laughed behind me. And Tía Mathilde's eyes shown with mirth. "So," she said, "your mind is on weddings these days, eh? Has a gallant knight already asked your papá for your hand, little niece?"

I blushed deeply and shook my head.

"See how she blushes and turns as pretty as she can be," said Tía Mathilde. "We must find her a *caballero*—'a handsome knight' with shining armor and much property." She leaned forward and whispered in our faces, "A *Jewish* knight, of course."

My mouth fell open and I looked in complete amazement at Tía Mathilde, who also opened her mouth, mocking my own look of shocked surprise. Both aunts chuckled at my confusion. It had not yet fully dawned on me that my newly discovered Jewish blood extended to other than Papá and Mamá.

"Tía Mathilde, you cannot mean . . ." I began.

"Sh-sh-sh, my little plum cake," she said close to my ear. "Not so loudly that your mother's cousins, the Carusos might hear. Let us speak softly. They are not as proud of their Jewish blood as we are. This is a secret between us, the de Carvallos, sí? Your Papá has explained some things to you today, this important day of your thirteenth birthday?"

Speechless, I turned quickly and looked at the face of Tía Emilia, still stroking my hair. She only smiled in agreement with Tía Mathilde.

"Sí, Tía Mathilde," I said with growing excitement. The mere mention of our shared Jewishness was a revelation. I wished the Carusos, my mother's family, would go home. How I longed to pour out my heart to these two favorite aunts. But I cautiously said in a low voice, "Papá gave me something special this morning, something . . . that belonged to Bisabuela Ruth."

"It is a thing of great meaning and holiness," Tía Emilia said somberly. "It is not to be taken lightly. Bisabuela Ruth would have been so proud that her strong and beautiful great granddaughter now holds the family treasure. She was known and respected by her many friends and neighbors of the Church, yet she courageously kept the true faith of her fathers secretly alive. She did this knowing it could cost her her life. She lived to a great age and died with the Jewish watchword of faith, the *Shema Yisra'el*, upon her lips, and the mezuzzah—the one your papá has given you—in her hands. She was legendary for her wisdom, her courage, and her deep love of Judaism. I hope you will be much like her."

"Just wait," said Tía Mathilde, "after the Carusos go home, she will be given something that will make her even more like her bisabuela."

"Tell me, dear aunts! Tell me now!" I whispered excitedly.

"Sh-sh-sh, not even for another slice of your mother's cinnamon cake!" said Tía Mathilde mischievously, as she rose with some difficulty and moved her considerable weight across the room.

She sat down heavily near my mother's cousins and began a lively conversation, winking at us from across the room. Tía Mathilde was braiding my hair.

"Tía Emilia," I whispered softly, "are you sure it is a worthy thing to be a Marrano?" I had to risk asking, for my mind had been leaping back and forth from the moment I held Tomás's rosary, between admiration and revulsion for my family's secrets.

"My pet," said Tía Emilia, winding my hair into a coil, "it is an act of highest courage and deepest faith to be a Marrano in this town. It is for the strong-willed and proud, not for the meek of spirit. Which are you, dear niece, which are you?"

Six

J Am Given My Secret Name

Mamá's cousins, the Carusos, lingered on and on to talk and sip tea. I could sense the tension and silent aggravation in Papá's family, the way the Carvallo men drummed impatiently on the tables, the short furtive glances of the Carvallo women. I knew as the hour drew late that Papá's family wanted Mamá's family to be gone. It was the first Friday night I finally understood: we were Marranos, waiting impatiently to bring in the Jewish Sabbath with our secret candle-lighting and blessings. And then there was the matter of my naming.

I lay across the pillows of the sofa trying to stay awake, pondering the strangeness of having a secret name. For thirteen years I had been called Isabel, after the queen, the grandest of Spanish names, a name I had been proud of. Yet, to think that all along I carried a Jewish name sent shivers up my spine. What might it be? I struggled to think of Old Testament names. From my Catechism classes, I had learned of Eve, wife of Adam, but my mind drew a blank after that. For the Church dwelled little on the Old Testament, considering it an old and outmoded text of the Jews.

Somewhere in my musings I must have fallen fast asleep. For suddenly, I found myself being shaken. My eyes flew open. Tía Mathilde, her layers of silk swaying before me, looked mirthfully down upon me. She shook her finger chidingly at me for falling asleep. I sat up and blinked. The rooms were empty!

"Where is everyone?" I asked.

"At long last your mamá's cousins went home and the servants went to bed. As for the others, come," she motioned, "you will see."

I stood up and smoothed my gown and followed her to the cellar door. "I need your hand, little niece," said Tía Mathilde. "I shouldn't

55

. have worn such flimsy slippers." She clutched both me and the railing as she moved her great weight gingerly down the narrow steps in her velvet slippers. "Whooh," she fanned herself, "at least it is cool down here," she said as she released my arm. Then Tío Juan ran quickly up the stairs and drew the bolt across the door behind us.

Candles had been set about the wineracks. The stone walls were a mosaic of dancing shadows. Everyone stood in the glow, smiling at me around the beautiful table. It was as I had always remembered it, laid with a fine white cloth, an unlit candelabra of gleaming brass, pewter goblets, opened bottles of wine, and a braided loaf of golden bread under a lace cloth. For the first time, I saw what Mamá had earlier described: the table did resemble a beautiful bride decked out in pure white linen and lace.

I was rather embarrassed at all the eyes staring at me—Tíos Carlos and Juan, Tías Mathilde and Emilia, Mamá, Papá, and two of Papá's cousins—Pedro and his wife Susanna. How strange to see them all here in the flickering candlelight of our wine cellar! They had never joined us before. How strange to realize that they too must live Marrano lives with secret candles in wine cellars.

Papá filled the goblets and handed them around. Thirsty, I began to bring a goblet to my lips.

"Not yet, Cousin Isabel," said Cousin Pedro who placed a hand on my arm. "Not before the blessing." I looked around and saw that everyone was holding their goblet, not drinking. Then, as Mamá had so often done on Friday nights, she placed her own lace mantilla around her head and began lighting the ornate candelabra of seven candles. "Six candles for the days of creation, one for the day of rest," Papá said quietly as we all stared into the flickering lights.

With her hands, Mamá drew three circles in the air around the candelabra, then covered her eyes and began to murmur the blessing she always did—in the language I had never learned—Hebrew.

A hushed silence. Then, startlingly, came Tía Mathilde's rich, sonorous voice. Very low, very slowly, her eyes closed, she begin to sing a long, lilting hymn. Her large hand moved up and down with the rise and fall of the chants, as if to keep the notes both quiet and even. At the end, her eyes flickered open and she smiled.

All said "Amen," and Cousin Pedro said, "the *Kiddush*, Isabel, the blessing for wine. Now you may drink from your goblet." Then Papá tore the tender braid of bread, studded with dried fruits into large pieces and handed the platter around. This time a blessing was uttered by the men. And Cousin Pedro looked at me and said, "*Chamotzi*, Isabel, the blessing for bread." Then, as we ate the bread, Papá leaned over and kissed Mamá and me on the cheek. "Good Shabbat, dear ones," he said to the company. "Good Shabbat, Paulos," said everyone in return. Silence enveloped each of us as our eyes were pulled into the depths of the light of seven candles. A magical other worldly feeling fell across the crowd. I knew we all felt it as we stood wordlessly mesmerized in the light.

"Paulos," said Mamá, finally breaking the silence which had befallen all of us and tapping Papá on the arm. "It is late and we have not yet done the naming."

Papá nodded and picked up his goblet. All eyes turned upon me. I looked down and blushed.

"And now, my beloved daughter," Papá said, "the time has come to give you your original Torah name, and reveal to you your true identity, just as the Almighty Creator through Moses revealed the true identity of the Jewish people at Mount Sinai. Your Jewish name is who you really are in the sight of God. For the soul of each and every Jew was already known to God even before birth."

I looked at him surprised. "Before birth? How was it possible?" I asked, intrigued.

"You see, my child, when Adonai gave the Ten Commandments to Moses at Mount Sinai, the rabbis tell us that the souls of every Jew— living or dead—every person, of the past, present or future, were there. A thousand years is but a second in God's eyes. He sees and knows all, across the span of history. The soul of every Jew of the past, the present, or the future was present at Mount Sinai when Adonai gave the Ten Commandments to Moses. And God knew each and every Jewish soul by his or her name for all time. Mount Sinai is always happening. It is happening even now."

"You mean I was known, Papá? I, Isabel, was known?" I said enthralled at the strange and beautiful mysticism of the story.

"You, my beloved daughter, beautiful soul, yet to be born, were known to God as *Ruth*," said Papá his eyes never leaving my face.

"Ruth!" I said in astonishment, "the name of my great grandmother!" I said looking at all the faces surrounding me. The name of Ruth had never occurred to me.

"Sí," said Papá, "the name of my abuela Ruth—your bisabuela Ruth, of blessed memory. It is how we remember our beloved dead, by naming our children for them."

"Did I not tell you that you would receive something else belonging to your bisabuela?" said Tía Mathilde, nodding at me.

"Ruth is also the beautiful heroine in the Torah," said Tía Emilia. "And of course you know what the Torah is?"

"I learned about the Torah, today, Tía Emilia. Papá told me it is the book which holds the sacred story of the Jewish people."

"Sí! *Muy bien!*" she said approvingly.

"What is the story of Ruth, Tía Emilia?"

She blushed brightly. "Oh, mercy, I have never read a Torah before. Few of us would risk owning one. But your papá, he has one hidden away in this very cellar."

Before she had even finished speaking, Papá had gone behind the wine racks under a heap of filthy burlap that covered extra wood for the kitchen and brought from the wood pile a leather-bound book! It was shocking to think that the Torah had been in this house all along.

"It is actually not a true Torah, Emilia, for the Torah of the synagogues is a long scroll that unwinds as it is read. This book contains the words of the Torah in Spanish, including other sacred writings handed down to the Jewish people. The Marrano rabbi gave it to me years ago."

Mamá stood next to him as he turned its many pages with delicacy. "Alas, but for the prayers I have committed to memory, I read little Hebrew, but this Spanish version has served me well, all my life. Give me but a moment and I'll find the story of Ruth."

I tried to take in the hard sound of the name Ruth, so different from the flowing name Isabel. But it did not sound like me. Ruth, I said to myself fiercely. You are not Isabel. You are Ruth!

Aunts, uncles, and cousins, the fire light reflected in their eyes, held onto one another, swaying slightly, waiting expectantly for Papá's story, and sipped from their goblets. I looked at them all in astonishment, my mind racing, trying to decide how to feel. How could they all stand there so sure and serene when we committed the highest heresy in the land? When these simple acts of faith, this Jewish setting, could bring disgrace, ruin, and death? I felt ashamed, even as I thought such thoughts, wishing fervently that I could quell my nagging doubts. For too many years the Church had burned into my heart the terrible sin of Judaizing the Christian faith. In spite of the beauty of the ceremony I felt no better than a sinner and a cheat. Perhaps I deserved to wear the sanbenito. Perhaps old Doña Martinez was right. . . .

"Ah, here it is everyone," said Papá, mercifully interrupting my dark and troubled thoughts. "The Story of Ruth . . ."

Everyone's eyes were on Papá as he began to tell us about the story. "Ruth was the beautiful daughter-in-law who cast her lot in with the Jews, and was rewarded with a good life—husband, child, and prosperity, as well as the riches of God's love and approval for all eternity," he began. "For though she had come from the Moabites to marry a Jew, she chose to remain with her widowed mother-in-law, Naomi, when her own husband died young. Naomi entreated Ruth to return to her own people and told her she was free from further obligation to the Jewish people. But Ruth refused, professing her love both of Naomi and of the Jewish people. Over and over again, Naomi reminded Ruth how many were the Jews' laws, 613 in all, how stringent were their codes of conduct, how hard, in fact, it was to be a Jew whom the world often reviled."

"Sí! My God how the world hates us, in many times and places in history, not just this one! And here we are again in Spain, fleeing just like the ancient Jews of Egypt!" complained Tío Carlos in a voice of self-pity. He looked as if he had drunk a bit too much wine all evening, and Tía Mathilde patted him on the arm and said soothingly, "Sh-sh, Carlos, calm yourself."

"Did Ruth go back to her own people, the Moabites, after Naomi warned her?" I said to Papá impatiently, wanting to know the fate of this Ruth.

"No, my child. Time and again Ruth reassured her mother-in-law how much she honored and loved her, how she had become in her

59

soul, a Jew. It was Ruth's desire to cast her lot with the Jewish people, no matter how hard or difficult her life would be among them. Let me read the story to you."

And Papá read from his Five Books of Moses, his fingers following the script, his voice rich with feeling.

"'Return to your people,' said Naomi.

'Entreat me not to leave you,' begged Ruth.

'But you must renounce your former faith,' explained Naomi tirelessly.

"But Ruth responded just as tirelessly, 'Where you go, I will go. Where you lodge, I too will lodge. Your people shall be my people. And your God, my God.'"

We all stood silently at the finish of the story. Papá gently closed the book. Tío Carlos—still emotional—wiped a tear from his eye. It was a stirring tale, one I needed time to consider. Mamá had slipped her arm around my waist and smiled when I looked up at her in the candleglow of the seven-stick candelabra. A sudden, urgent question flew into my mind. I said, "Am I to be called Ruth now, instead of Isabel?"

Everyone shifted, eyes turned downcast, and throats were cleared uncomfortably. Mamá took a deep breath. With a nervousness in her voice, she said, "Alas this is one of the few times you may hear your beautiful true name. Like everything else in Marrano life, our Hebrew names may only be uttered in secrecy. Its use would be a telltale sign of Jewish knowledge. Good Catholics, you see, avoid Old Testament names like the plague."

I breathed a sigh of relief; I was not prepared for yet another great change.

"Let us now welcome our Ruth into the kingdom of Israel!" bellowed Tío Carlos, who turned and refilled his goblet and raised it in the air. Suddenly his voice was steady and full as he said:

"Shema Yisra'el, Adonai Elohainu, Adonai Ehad!"

"Shema Yisra'el, Adonai Elohainu, Adonai Ehad!" everyone echoed, adding Amen.

"What does it mean, Tío Carlos?"

"It is the watchword of the Jewish people, the most important blessing in Judaism for it commands all of the Jewish people to know and accept the One God over all creation. *'Here O Israel, the Lord Our God, the Lord Alone!'* " he said.

"The Lord Alone?" I pondered out loud.

"Yes, in the true faith of Judaism there is no Virgin Mary, no Jesus, no Holy Ghost, to come between humankind and God. Only the One God, Adonai Alone, is master of the universe, Isabel. To be a Jew is to accept God, alone, with no human helpers. Can there be any other way?" he asked me, his eyes challenging, blazing into mine.

I cast my eyes downward at the ground, my mind in turmoil.

"It is a lot to accept all in one night, Carlos," said my father, patting his brother-in-law's shoulder gently. "She needs time to understand the meaning of it all."

"Then like the great Ruth of ancient days, may you be granted much time, and a long and righteous life to walk humbly with Adonai, the One God, Alone," Tío Carlos said gravely, raising his goblet. He always had been the speech maker in our family. "Amen!" said everyone again.

Mamá gave me an urging look and I walked over and gave Tío Carlos a dutiful kiss upon his broad, bearded face. "Sí, Tío Carlos. Sí, everyone," I said looking from one beloved face to another. "Thank you all for your many gifts and kind wishes to me this night," I spoke in my most courteous, affectionate way. For I loved these people and realized with a pang that it might be the last time I would ever see them. But in my heart of hearts I couldn't tell them the truth—that I couldn't endure the idea that I was a Ruth, destined to cast my lot in with them, the hated, unwanted Jews.

Seven

I Eavesdrop upon the Men

I n the nights that followed my naming ceremony, I slept fitfully, awakening often in half-remembered dreams of shame and fear. Lying in the darkness, I couldn't help thinking: I am Ruth, a Marrano, a betrayer of Christianity, the one true faith! In the eyes of Seville, a sinner, deserving of bodily torture . . . spiritual hellfire. . . ."

Shadowy half-thoughts of shame and fear tangled with my waking life too . . . pay heed to the sanbenitos hanging in the hall of impurity . . . "Isabel, you are barely touching your food. It is your favorite—squab pie . . ." . . . *Judaizers who taint our glorious faith* . . . "Look! Manuel is smiling at his big sister!". . . *We are Marranos—swine, pigs . . . the people who live the cross by day and the mezuzzah by night* . . . "You have forgotten your Book of Hours again. Hurry . . . it is time for Ladymass.". . . *preserving our Jewish souls in a world that would destroy us* . . . "Mistress! Your mind has flown away! You are sewing the sleeve of your baby brother's gown onto your skirt!" . . . *Especially not to Teresa de Rodriguez!*

How I longed for the comfort and security of my safe, familiar life as a Christian! Once, when Mamá came to church with me, I tried to find solace in the Virgin Mary, uttering my confessions, my endless river of Hail Marys. "Hail Mary, full of Grace, The Lord is with thee . . . Holy Mary, Mother of God, Pray for us sinners, now and at the hour of our death . . ." Over and over I would mutter in desperation, trying to feel the old feelings of love and comfort she gave me. For so many years she had blessed me. But now, for the first time in my life, the statue of Our Lady, standing blissfully in the corner of the church, brought me no comfort. Her mild, unchanging face, seemed no longer to know me. Her hands held out in supplication seemed to reach out to others, but not to me. I felt forsaken. "Mamá," I cried bitterly, putting my head in her lap, "the Blessed Virgin no longer speaks to me nor fills my heart with comfort. She hates me for being a vile Marrano."

"No, no, never, my beloved," said Mamá, sweeping the hair off my face, "the Lady is incapable of hatred. There is a special place in her heart for the Jews always. She herself was a great lady of the Jewish people. She knows the turmoil in your heart and is merely letting you go now to your new life as a Jewess," said Mamá, kissing me, holding me, her own tears dropping onto my neck.

I could not speak of these things to Papá. He had become a man obsessed with Judaism. In the evening, before sleep, Papá had begun relentlessly to teach me everything he could about the laws, stories, and history of the Jewish people. Night after night by my bedside he spoke of Adonai, the one God over all creation, the Almighty one Alone who created the world and all that was in it. He explained about the secret ceremony of circumcision in which the Marrano Rabbi had brought my baby brother into the faith, the covenant connecting him to four thousand years of Jewish manhood.

"Can't we save some of my Jewish learning for later, when we have actually joined the Jewish people?" I finally asked one exhausted night. But he shook his head and pushed relentlessy on with that wild, desperate look in his eyes. He insisted that I must know as much as possible before we met up with the Jewish ones. "If you can recite a blessing, or recount a Torah story or a bit of Jewish history," he said, "then the Jewish people, our people, will accept you."

In spite of my fears, I found Papá's teachings compelling. I had not known before that the Jews were the first ones to perceive God beyond the physical world that could be seen around them. That Judaism was a tradition thousands of years older than Christianity or Islam. That the Torah and the Ten Commandments were the ancient roots of civility and decency and loving the stranger as much as ourselves.

Though he dared not bring his Old Testament upstairs, Papá tried to recount certain stories that had special meaning for Marranos, like the tale of Shadrach, Mishach, and Nebednego, the assistants to the prophet Daniel, who served as dream interpreter to the powerful pagan

King Nebuchadnezzar. In the kingdom of Nebuchadnezzar, Shadrach, Mishach, and Nebednego refused to give up their worship as Jews, their worship to Adonai. This enraged the king who had them bound up and sentenced to be thrown alive into a fiery furnace in the same way that many Marranos are burned at the stake, Papá said. Just as they were shackled and led away to the furnace, Nebuchadnezzar, who practiced black magic and believed in many false gods, taunted them: "See if your wonderful One God can save you now!" Yet to Nebuchadnezzar's shocked disbelief, Sharach, Mishach, and Nebednego walked through the fiery furnace and came out miraculously alive! They simply would not die. And the king was so dumbstruck by this that he forever after permitted them to worship as Jews and promoted them to high rank in his royal service. Never again did the king speak against worshipping of the One God over all creation. Papá said the story meant that the Jews as a people refused to die or go away or disappear simply because kings or queens or priests or angry Gentiles ordered them away.

By the last days of June, my head was bursting with it all. Days were filled with church-going, genuflecting before the cross, making all outword signs of Catholicism. Nights were filled with Papá's relentless Jewish teachings as I lay atop the mattress that concealed Bisabuela Ruth's golden mezuzzah.

Even while Papá filled me with Jewish learning, he tried to shield Mamá and me from the daily reports that trickled into the city of the expelled Jews, hungry, tattered people passing by the city, beyond the great walls, trying desperately to reach the boats before the date of Expulsion. They were not allowed to enter the gates of our city, not even to buy or procure food. Yet Papá did not realize how the gossip ran in church among the women. They spoke endlessly of the fleeing Jews. Of how the poor people of Seville, whose crowded hovels bordered the city walls, took pity upon the Jews, throwing pieces of cheese and dried bread over the walls to them. I felt dread to learn this, knowing we soon would be joining them. And I also felt shame. We hidalgos had been so protected behind our walled and serene courtyards and had been spared the nightly sounds of the tramping feet, the crying children, the pleas for food of the expelled ones.

65

During all these astonishing events, I missed the solace of Teresa's pleasing company. A week before my birthday, she bid me good-bye and went to Cordoba with her family to visit her recently widowed aunt. She was gone for nearly a month and I counted the days till her return. At last I received word that she had returned and that her father had invited my family to a return dinner, a grand banquet meant to impress the marques's wealthy peerage in Seville.

I had neither seen nor spoken to Teresa since becoming "Ruth de Cojano." Suddenly, I did not want to face her, fearing the pain of keeping my secret from her would be too great. "Please, Papá," I pleaded, "may I pretend illness and stay home?"

But Papá, in spite of my protests, insisted I must go. "We dare not avoid de Rodriguez now," he warned, "lest it raise any talk or suspicion about us. Besides, you cannot hide from the world, Isabel, least of all from Teresa. There is so little time to be with your beloved Teresa. Perhaps she will cheer you. It pains us deeply, these past weeks, to see how you have been staying quiet and alone so much in your bed chamber."

That was how I found myself nervously twisting my handkerchief in Teresa's courtyard that evening.

"So tell me everything that has happened since I've been away!" she said to me the minute we found a spot away from the crush of important people filling her house. My eyes rested warmly upon the sight of my Teresa sashaying among the elaborate statuary and fountains of her huge courtyard, speaking in her usual spirited way. I could think of nothing at all to say. My mind had gone as blank and empty as a new leaf of paper. What small and trivial things could I possibly think to say since all I yearned to say was the stunning truth? *"Oh Teresa, I am not who you think I am. My name is not Isabel Caruso de Carvallo at all, but Ruth de Cojano, the name of a Jewess! Sí, my friend, I am a hated, illegal Marrano!"*

"You're frightfully quiet, Isabel! And gloomy. Cheer up and tell me about your birthday celebration." She grabbed my hands and made me twirl and dance with her. She was in such high spirits. The dancing only filled me with more anguish. I bit back tears, and tried to get hold of myself, and tried to keep myself from sobbing in anguish at her feet.

"It was, it was . . . most interesting," I managed to choke out, feigning breathlessness.

"Interesting!" she said dully, dropping my hands. "Good heavens, birthdays aren't supposed to be interesting! Sermons in church, perhaps, not birthday feasts and presents!"

"Sí, well . . ."

"Silly goose, come sit down. What did you receive? Many presents? Tell me everything!" We sat down upon the wrought iron bench which surrounded a large tree growing in the center of her courtyard.

"Oh, the usual things. A lovely mantilla from Mamá, silk and ribbons, and perfumes. Oh, and I *loved* your necklace with the tiny blue shells. Gracias *mi amiga*," I said staring down at the carefully swept ground. "Your gift made me very happy."

"Well, you're very welcome, but you don't sound very happy. Hmmm, maybe your birthday was interesting, like a sermon, instead of a fiesta, after all?" she said looking at me sympathetically.

"It was actually nice, with all the relatives around," I said, avoiding her careful gaze. "I just missed you, Teresa, that's all."

"Gracias, señorita. You do me a great honor!" She leaped up and bowed low, like a gentleman, grabbing my hand and grandly kissing it. I actually brightened and giggled. Often we played "The Unmarried Lady and the Courting Gentleman" and because she was the taller one, it was she who usually played the courting gentleman.

She giggled too. "Well, I sure enjoyed myself, Isabel. While we were in Cordoba, my father bought so many things for us, I can't even remember all of them to describe to you. The soldiers have been sacking what is left of the Moorish kingdom of Granada and all the Spanish markets look like an Arab treasure chest!"

In spite of myself, I laughed. In her high spirits, she almost made me feel foolish for the darkness of my thoughts. At least until I heard her next words.

"So," she sighed, "it was a wonderful journey, except for all those Jews! They were everywhere, blocking all the roads from Cordoba! They slowed our carriage down dreadfully. Papá kept cursing. But with soldiers around to protect and move them along, we could do nothing but creep slowly for hours on end. Papá got so riled. I thought he would split his waistcloth! It was so very tedious and inconvenient. It nearly ruined the journey for us. Those Jews made it take days longer to get home, Isabel!"

My heart sank. I felt a sudden wave of nausea.

"Teresa, let's go inside," I said. "I-I'm feeling a bit ill. It's too warm here, the air is so heavy and damp."

"Are you serious? It's worse inside; you'll suffocate. There are so many people in there. They're even standing in the pantries!"

"Please?"

"Well, if that's what you want, let's go," she said putting her arm around my waist.

She scrutinized me.

"You do look a little pale. Perhaps your womanly time of the month, is coming on, no? I always feel nauseous right before then, myself."

It was not my womanly time of the month, but I didn't tell her so. I merely nodded as we walked across the courtyard together.

Teresa's house had grown warm and humid, but I was glad for the distraction of the noisy crowd and no longer had to hear about the terrible inconveniences of Jews.

We found a place under the cool stairwell, where we sprawled on pillows we had snatched from the library. On the wooden floors it was cooler than the rest of the house.

"Isn't there anything good to report while I've been away?" she pouted.

"I wish there were," I shook my head, "My days have been filled with sewing and waiting despondently for your return. It has been quite uneventful without you."

"I cannot believe that! Things are never uneventful for you, Isabel Caruso de Carvallo, not for the daughter of Don Paulos de Carvallo, chief financier of Seville! Why your house is always filled with gay and important people and glorious food. And, did I not hear that at your birthday feast your mother cooked with a king's fortune in rare spices— cinnamon and nutmeg and pepper?"

How like Teresa to generously point out our family's wealth and importance, though, in truth, it was her father, who had the greater wealth, land, and title, if not the learning and wisdom of my father.

"That is true, Teresa," I relaxed a little, finally thinking of something safe to say about my birthday celebration. "My entire family, including all my aunts and uncles, celebrated my birthday as if it were a wedding day feast!"

We giggled at the mention of "wedding day," for we had both reached the age of betrothal. The very thought of matrimony, as yet to be arranged by our fathers, filled us both with indescribable excitement and dread.

"There is one thing . . . ," I ventured.

"What?" she leaned forward eagerly.

"Well, since you were gone, many have started saying that Seville has become a place of secrecy and whispers behind closed doors. Even at church, they notice this. It is all because of the Holy Office."

Teresa was looking at me quite curiously. I knew I skirted dangerously close to truthful things, but in my anguish I could not help myself. "Papá says Holy Office spies are everywhere. They skulk about in friar's cloth and priestly vestments, looking for heretics and . . ." my voice dropped to a whisper, ". . . Marranos."

I watched carefully for Teresa's reaction to that word, but she showed no sign of particular interest or surprise. Her head went down as she suddenly began to adjust the silver comb that held her long and silky brown hair rolled tightly to the nape of her neck.

"Isabel, you goose," she said, "you're always taking life so seriously, worrying so much about the little people. That's what I love about you so much. Such a tender heart. Why should you fret about them?" You must stop listening so much to your papá's court talk. It is the men's concern." Her head came back up when she finished her hair and she stared at me. I blushed deeply. She opened her fan and waved it energetically in my face. "See, you're flushed and overheating inside. I told you it was warmer inside than out."

"But don't you feel just a tiny bit sorry for the sad lot of the Jews and Marranos?"

"Perhaps a little sorry for the Jews." She paused and frowned in thought. "At least they practice their strange religion in the open, even if they do reject Jesus and his teachings. But I don't feel so sorry for the Marranos. They defile Christianity like cowards, in secrecy. Still, I do not like violence of any kind, not even my father's hunting parties. I would much rather just expel the Marranos like the Jews instead of sending them to torture and burning by pompous Inquisitors! Pray, what if the wrong people are accused and burned? That's not unheard of you

69

know." She fanned herself and me once again. "All right, if it will make you feel better, we'll pray for the souls of all the poor unfortunates deserving of attention from the Holy Office tomorrow in church, but not tonight. Sí?"

"Teresa, I . . ." I said with such force that she turned.

"Sí?" she said, her eyes lighting up.

"I am in need of a drink." My heart was beating as fast as the hooves of Teresa's racing stallion. For I had so wanted Teresa's assurance of love and approval that I had nearly disobeyed Papá and started to confess.

"Drink and eat too!" she finished for me. "Don't be shy. Let's go to the food tables. Besides, I have been wanting you to taste the spiced pomegranate juice. Your mother gave my mother the recipe and you must tell me how it compares to yours."

"Sí!" I breathed a sigh of relief. Somewhere up there, the Blessed Virgin, or maybe one of the Jewish angels Papá had spoken of, looked down upon me and kept me from opening my mouth and bringing destruction on our lives.

She pulled me downstairs into the dining hall where the food was laid. We squeezed through the humid rooms overflowing with velvet suits and flowing gowns. The walls nearly rang with the clamor of shrill laughing and booming voices.

"Point to what you want and I'll get it," she said pulling me between two layers of people hovering near the food.

"I only want something to drink," I said loudly over the din.

"Go back to the stairwell," she called back leaning over a platter with a fork. "I'll bring it to you. The crowd is too thick for both of us here."

I returned dutifully to the stairwell and sat on the bottom steps, leaning against the open wall and listening to the many voices rising and falling around me. From a few feet away, just behind the wall, I heard the loud, distinctive voice of the Marques de Rodriguez. I pressed myself close to the wall and pulled my skirts close about me, not wanting the marques to know I was there for I hated the way his arrogant eyes swept over me when Teresa wasn't with me.

"So, Don Paulos," I heard him suddenly say, "has it not been a victorious year for Seville and all of Spain itself?" Papá! The marques was speaking to Papá!

"First, the glorious defeat of the infidel Moors in Granada," he was saying, "who have sullied Spanish life for nearly a thousand years. Let me tell you, I have not stopped celebrating since January when the great victory was announced by the queen's trumpeters. I even traveled down to Granada to watch the queen's troops bombard much of the Moorish cities to crushed rock. Any Moors not smart enough to have left by then were quickly run through by sword or sold into slavery. How I relished the sight! Did you hear, Don Paulos? They are still celebrating in Rome and praising the genius of our great Catholic Queen Isabel for ridding Spain of the cursed Moslems."

I held my breath, wondering how my father could possibly reply to the marques. How well I knew that he did not share the jubilation of the marques over the fall of Granada!

"Perhaps we should not revel over the destruction of a gentle and ingenious people who brought the Spaniard his olives and silkworms and adorned his southern kingdom with ancient beautiful buildings, fountains, and minarets." Papá answered in formal, calm words.

"A paltry sum—olives, silkworms, spouting water, for God's sake—for having put up with filthy Moslems on Christian soil for seven centuries!" said the marques, with a note of disdain and amusement. I had seen him enjoy angering Papá on more than one occasion. "Fortunately, the queen has confiscated all the gold and treasury of the Moslem Caliph and has vowed to turn all the mosques into churches!"

In the awkward silence that followed, I could imagine Papá's mustache twitching—a tic he had when restraining his anger. I longed to peek around the wall, but dared not. "Let us not forget the queen's most recent Christian victory," piped in another loud gentleman, "the expulsion of the Jews, perhaps the greatest feat of all in rescuing Spain from the infidels!"

I sucked in my breath. Shouts of "Here! here!" went round the group accompanied by the clink of glasses, except for Papá's I was sure. I squeezed my eyes shut and prayed he did not lose his temper or say something we would all regret. But it wasn't my father who spoke next.

"Yes, just so," said the marques, "it's certainly a good start in rooting out the Jewish taint, but much more is needed, I fear."

"More? What more can possibly be done beyond shipping them overseas?" said another.

"Well, Don Pedro," said the marques, "expelling the damnable Jew is the part that can be seen. It is the unseen part carried on in cowardly secrecy that is so revolting! We all know that a Marrano spirit infiltrates the converso population of Spain and threatens the souls of our children and grandchildren right here in Seville. Let us praise the good work of the Holy Office. I've heard the Castle of Triana is stuffed full with Marrano infidels awaiting their turn at burning. There are so many, in fact, that tomorrow afternoon there is to be a great *auto-de-fé* on the castle grounds, complete with troubadours and food tents. Fanfare, feasting, and fire—my favorite kind of fiesta! And of course, the entire town will be coming, from peasants to princes."

I held myself stiffly behind the wall as the men murmured and chuckled agreeably. I knew of what they spoke. The auto-de-fé, was the great "act-of-faith" in which all discovered Marranos and heretics were publicly tried and condemned, then burned before the cheering throngs. They had grown common in many towns in Spain, but had been more rare in Seville, a town with so many influential New Christians. Though Papá had been required to attend such public spectacles before, he had shielded me and Mamá from ever going to one.

But the marques hadn't finished toying with my father. "And you, Don Paulos?" he quipped in a note of loud amusement. "You, no doubt, can't wait for tomorrow, can you? I know how eager you are to watch all the heretics burn, no? Surely even my tender-hearted neighbor Don Paulos de Carvallo cannot deny the words of Jesus: *If men abideth not in Me . . . Cast them into the fire and they are burned!*"

I gasped, then threw my hand over my mouth, in hopes they did not hear me. How I hated the Marques de Rodriguez for taunting my father. I could only imagine how Papá would keep his composure now. I prayed that Papá's face remained completely impassive, except perhaps, for that slight twitching of his mustache.

But I was never even to hear his reply! For at that moment, Teresa reappeared, having come through the very room with the men, her hands loaded down with food and goblets.

She rolled her eyes toward the wall. "Here take this. Let's go back out to the patio," she whispered. "I cannot stand to sit here and endure the dull talk of men."

Reluctantly I followed Teresa, the voice of my soft-spoken father lost, swallowed up in the laughter and harsh din of men's voices. But I could barely tear myself away from the terrible, spellbinding talk of Marranos and burning.

I did not know how soon I would be forced to witness first hand the execution of those cruel words: *Cast them into the fire and they are burned.*

Eight

I Am Prepared for a Horror

My heart ached to see Papá trapped with the arrogant marques and his guests. I hoped we would all soon be going home. But later, when I caught sight of a servant refilling the wine goblets, I knew Papá would not be coming with us. He would be compelled to stay as late as the marques wanted, as was the custom with the men. I hoped we might stay late and travel home with him. But Mamá would not hear of it. Not with the marques entertaining so many drinking men. I had no choice but to bid Teresa an early good night and depart with Mamá in the carriage, for home.

"You might not see me for a few days, Isabel," she whispered, kissing me at the door. "Not until my annual summer party for girls. I'm trying to convince Papá to take me to the country tomorrow, to visit El Rápido."

I remembered the auto-de-fé that her father had so gleefully mentioned and felt sorry for her. The marques would never agree to leaving tomorrow.

"I hope you convince your Papá to take you away, Teresa," I said before kissing her back.

Upon our arrival home, Mamá rushed upstairs to check on Manuel. I followed close behind her. We found Marta, Mamá's oldest servant, who was now too frail for heavy labor, snoring peacefully in a chair beside the cradle. Manuel, his tiny arms stretched high overhead, slept serenly, a half-moon smile upon his little face. Mamá put her hand on her heart and smiled at me, relieved that all was well. Marta was quite elderly and Mamá was always worried leaving Manuel with her. But she was the only servant Mamá dared trust with baby. Not only was she devoted to Mamá, but her aged eyesight was so poor that she could not see the unmistakeable evidence of his circumcision when she changed the baby's swaddling.

Mamá gently awakened Marta and helped her to the servants' quarters. I stayed to watch Manuel sleeping in his cradle, stroking the little wispy hairs on his head. I never grew tired of watching him. When Mamá returned, she gestured for me to sit with her as she prepared herself for bed. As she slowly pulled combs from her hair at her dressing table, she turned to me with eyes of fear and sadness and said softly, "Soon. Very soon, Isabel darling. . . ."

She spoke so quietly, I wasn't sure I had heard her correctly.

"You mean . . . ?"

"Sí," she began to whisper, "the escape. Your papá's informant has said it is a matter of days till we leave, no more. It must be quite soon. There is less than a week left on the expulsion edict, even after the extension." She bit her lip with a worried frown. "At least we are fortunate to be so near the Port of Cadiz. We can get there in but a day or two."

"The Port of Cadiz!" I whispered. "You mean where we go to spend days by the seashore, to eat freshly caught fish and walk among the shouting fishmongers?"

She nodded somberly. "It is where the ships for the Jewish folk are docked. And there is another queer thing about the Port of Cadiz we have heard. It is the very same place where the boats of the great explorer Cristobal Colón are also docked, the Niña, the Santa Maria, and another . . . I have forgotten the name," she shrugged. "Anyway, they say Colón will be sailing the same week as the last ships of Jews! Perhaps it is good luck."

"Cristobal Colón," I said dully.

Mamá, brushing her hair in long thoughtful strokes, stopped and saw my glum expression and put her hand tenderly under my chin. "Isabel, my love, perhaps it will help if we think of our journey abroad as a great and exciting sea voyage, an exploration. We can all be little Cristobal Colóns, embarking on a great exploration, sí?" she said hopefully.

I nodded, trying to cheer up for her. She continued to stare at my image in the looking glass. "You know Isabel, I think when things calm down in Spain, we may even return home one day. Wouldn't that be wonderful?"

"Sí, Mamá, very wonderful," I said without conviction. It was so like Mamá to try to cheer us up, to envision a happy ending to our sorrows. But my mind was elsewhere, preoccupied with a question that had begun to inch its way more and more into my thoughts.

"Mamá, who is the informant? Papá and you have spoken of him several times."

"Well," she said, "I only know he is someone Papá knows well and trusts to tell the truth. More he will not tell me."

"Not even you, Mamá?"

"He says the less we know of the details, the safer it is for us. I don't even want to know too much. As long as Papá knows what to do, that is all that matters." She returned to brushing.

"But what happens if . . . ?" I blurted and caught myself, just in time.

"If . . . ?" she looked up sharply, her eyes wide with concern.

"Never mind," I shook my head. I had nearly blurted out, "What happens if . . . if we cannot reach the port of Cadiz in time? If the informant has made a mistake? If . . .?" I had too many questions from my nightmares. Questions Mamá would refuse to consider. Asking them would have only upset her.

I slept fitfully that night half-listening for Papá's reassuring tread upon the stairs. In the small hours of the morning, I awoke to heavy thudding sounds. Papá! I jumped out of bed and went to peer into the dark hallway. I felt a wave of relief to see his head emerge at the top of the stairs. But as I began to shut my door, I saw his shadowy silhouette swaying wildly, grasping the rail for support.

"Papá?" I ran out and grabbed his arm, thinking he had been injured.

"Isabel," he swung toward me, jerking his arm away from me, with great irritation.

"Why are you up at this hour?"

"I thought you were unwell and might need help," I said, stung by the rebuff.

"Help," he said dully. "Well, I need only one kind of help and that you can not gifme," he slurred. "An' it is found in a wine bottle . . . er . . . maybe two."

"Papá, you've drunk too much wine!" I said throwing my hand up to my mouth in shock. Never in my thirteen years had I seen my father intoxicated. The marques, sí, many times, but my father, never.

"Sí, sí. How else could I endure half the night with that pompous Rodriguez and his boot-licking cohorts?" he asked, swaying dangerously at the top of the stairs and squinting at me.

I shrugged and stared, distressed at my father's pain. Without another word, he strode across the hall, pushed open the door, and stumbled into my parents' bedchamber, shutting the door in my face.

☙

We slept quite late the next morning. The moment I awoke and felt the blazing sun bearing down on me through the open verandah windows, I knew it was eight o'clock or later. If I did not hurry, I would miss the last morning Mass. Mamá was going to accompany me this time, for it was important that we be seen often by our neighbors and friends at Santa Maria del Popolo. I began to wash myself at the basin on my washstand. No time to be bathed by Pascua in a tub strewn with rose petals today. Through the bed curtains I saw that the servants had brought my morning meal when I had not appeared for breakfast: a hard roll, a square of cheese turned soft in the heat, and an orange. But my thoughts flew immediately to Papá, to the vision of last night's encounter in the dead of night.

I dressed hurriedly and went to knock on my parents' door.

"Sí?" came my father's groggy voice.

"Papá?" I called timidly.

"*Uno momento.* I'll be right there."

The door opened abruptly and I caught a glimpse of Mamá lying down, a cloth upon her forehead.

He closed the door behind him and ushered me back to my room and sat down in my chair, still in his nightclothes and robe. His eyes were red, his face haggard, his expression grim. "Mamá has a sick headache, and I, unfortunately, do too though for very different reasons, I'm afraid," he said sheepishly. "I am sorry, Isabel, about last night. I hope I did not upset you too much. I know I was not . . . myself."

78

He slid down in my chair, leaning his head back and closing his eyes. "Oh, my poor Papá." I knelt beside him and gently stroked his forehead, "Is the headache bad?"

"Sí, a headache of overindulgence, both from the wine and last night's company." He finally opened his eyes and took a long look at me. "Oh, you are dressed, already."

"Papá, it's late. I was just on my way to late morning Mass."

"Never mind church today, Isabel," he said sitting up and wincing with the exertion. "There is an unpleasant duty before us. The carriage has been ordered. Mamá, you, and I will leave in an hour. Today there is to be a great auto-de-fé in Seville. I had hoped to go myself and save Mamá and you from the ordeal. But the archbishop sent over a special invitation this morning. He has set aside special seatings and may come to greet us. More heretics and Marranos, I fear, to be relaxed."

The auto-de-fé! I had forgotten all about it! I looked at my father in horror, a sinking feeling in my stomach. I knew as well as he did, the meaning of this term relaxed. It is the sly, "polite" way that the Holy Office refers to the burning of condemned ones—alive on the stake in a public square in front of throngs of people.

"Oh, Papá! Don't make me go! I could not stand the sight of it. You have never before asked me to go. Please, Papá, let me stay and help Marta with the baby?" I begged.

Papá got up in spite of his pain and began pacing the floor. "Isabel," he said gently, turning to face me, "it would be a dangerous mistake for the three of us not to appear. All of Seville's chief officials and their families have been summoned for the ceremonies. At the very least, it would be considered a grave and suspicious slight to the archbishop if I, the royal tax collector, and my family, did not appear."

"But how can people stand it, Papá? How can they?" I twisted my hands together nervously.

"They have convinced themselves that an auto-de-fé is a fine day's entertainment! That's how!" His voice was low but he brought his fist down upon my bureau. "Ages and ages hence, they will call the Spanish not Christians, but barbarians!"

He looked away from my expression of horror and aversion and ran his hand through his tousled hair.

"Isabel," he said, his voice cracking, "you must steel yourself and find a way to bear this. At this moment your mother is lying ill with the very thought of going. My own head feels as if it were pounded by cannon balls. If you fall apart now too . . ." his voice trailed off in despair.

I wanted to say, I will be strong for you Papá, I will accept all the horror and pain of being Jewish. But it would not have been honest. And I had always spoken the truth to my father.

"Is there no chance. . . . ?"

Papá looked at me sharply.

"No chance. . . ." I rasped out, ashamed, yet unable to stop myself, that we could return to the Church? He walked to the window and stared out. He did not look me in the eyes. But I saw that his own were suffused with pain.

I weakened and went to him, grabbed his hand and appealed to him as a very small child does. "Oh please, Papá, may we not return to the Church?" I implored.

"What is it exactly that troubles you, Isabel?"

I groped for the words to express precisely what was in my heart.

"Oh Papá, I-I just feel a shame—the shame of being Jewish. What if everyone is right, that it is a terrible sin to forsake Jesus and Mary?"

"Ah, that is what troubles you," he said and looked away tiredly for several moments with the effort of finding an answer. "Isabel," he finally said, "what if it is a terrible sin not to return to our Jewish faith? What if it has been a grave sin for our families to have left the God of Israel, the Torah, the Jewish people this past hundred years? To have lived in comfort behind the mask of Christianity? It is one thing to convert at the point of a sword, another to choose Christianity again and again, as Mamá's family and mine have done for several generations. Even the family of the most famous Spanish Jew of all time—the great Moses Maimonides, a revered Rabbi and physician in the eleven hundreds—was forced to convert to Islam at the point of Islamic swords. But as soon as he and his family could return to the faith of their fathers, they did so. That is just what my conscience tells me, that I have forsaken the One God, and with it, my own people and must now with my family repent and return!"

To think that we had been sinners all along by practicing Christianity! I had so well absorbed the Church's hatred of all things Jewish, had so swiftly accepted shame and guilt for my Marrano background, it had never occurred to me that we might have sinned against God to have left the Jewish faith to begin with!

"I never thought of it that way. Truly not, Papá."

He went back to the chair, sat down, leaned over, and put his aching head in his hands.

Now I was the one to pace back and forth. "It's all so confusing," I said. "If only . . . if only being Marranos, being Jewish, didn't mean we had to leave our homeland . . . like criminals."

He looked up. "But Isabel, even if we were the sincerest of Christians, it would make no earthly difference to the Holy Office. They have their eye on the wealth and properites of all New Christians. My informant here in Seville says it is only a matter of time before the Inquisitors of the Holy Office hunt down not only us, but all New Christians in Spain. The Holy Office is greedy and will spare no one."

"Papá," I said after some silence.

"Sí?"

"How does this informant know so much?"

"He knows because he and his kind make up the very fabric of the unholy Holy Office."

"He is an Inquisitor?"

"He is young and ambitious to be appointed one, I believe."

"Then why does he help you and warn you?"

"Because he finds it very lucrative to help the Chief Royal Tax Collector of Seville," he said with disgust.

"Lucrative? You mean you give him money for his help?"

"Precisely."

I was stunned.

"But how can you trust him?"

"Because he and I are linked together in unavoidable ways," Papá said mysteriously.

"I don't understand."

"I cannot explain everything to you now, Isabel. You must accept some of this on my word. You know I have many friends and informants at Court. That is the nature of my business. Aren't you going to eat that cheese and bread?"

I shook my head. "It's been sitting too long. The cheese is soft and the bread stale."

"It doesn't matter. I need something to settle my stomach."

I handed him the plate. He chewed on the food, gazing toward the open window. We sat in silence, each in separate islands of thoughts. I broke the silence at last.

"I suppose it is just as well we are leaving," I said dejectedly. "In church they blame the Jews for everything, for the death of Jesus, for keeping Christians from being good Christians, for poisoning the wells of all cities and causing the plague, for stealing the wealth of the nation, for murdering little Christian children and baking their blood into Jewish food. They have begun to teach us these things in church school, just as they do the catechism."

"What a pity we must leave," Papá said sarcastically. "I would like to stay and see whom Spain finds to blame when it has rid itself of all the Jews and yet the plague and the ills of the world remain!"

I watched as Papá tore savagely with his nails into the flesh of the orange.

"Would you like some?" he asked, holding up an orange section.

I took the section and ate distractedly.

"Oh, Papá, why do our monarchs want a kingdom with no Jews and no Moors, only Christians? Why do they preach, one nation, one people, one religion?"

He looked wistfully toward my window where flowers fluttered on the open verandah. "Spain was once a realm of many flowers, Isabel— the flowers of Judaism, Christianity, and Islam blossoming together. Three brilliant colors all in the same garden. But no longer," he said in a bitter tone. "For some perverted reason, the monarchs have decided they no longer desire a garden with flowers of many kinds. They now want only one kind of flower, an endless field of one flower, overtaking all others. It is unnatural; it is not God's way. Look around you. God Himself created the fields of varied flowers. Human beings are God's flowers. We are many colored, richly varied. God is One, Alone. But we, like the flowers are supposed to be many."

Papá left and I went out onto my balcony, waiting wretchedly, for my parents to dress. I tried to distract myself but could think of nothing but the terrible scenes of the day to come. I picked up the little watering can, which the servants kept filled upon my verandah, and watered the brightly colored flowers in my window box. They released their sweet perfume in the morning sun. I had planted and nurtured them all. I could not conceive of ripping out all the red and yellow ones, leaving only the white ones.

As I stared at the flowers, a vision flashed through my mind, a vision of two gardeners insane with hatred. They were out in their garden swinging their scythes, cutting down flower after flower in their very own garden. It was shocking to think that the mad, hysterical gardeners were our very own king and queen! That I, in my Christian life, had been named for such a queen.

Rage crawled up from the depths of my being. I wanted to scream into the streets, "Queen Isabel, you are a stupid, stupid queen! Why do you destroy your own garden?"

So loud was the scream inside my own head that for one second, I wondered if I had screamed aloud. But I peered down on the street below. People and horses moved along as usual. It was almost strange to think that on the day of a great and terrible auto-de-fé, the life of the street unfolded as usual. There was the smell of the bakehouse almond cakes wafting toward our windows, the clop-clopping of horse's hooves over the cobbles, dogs barking in the alleyways of the tradesmen's shops, the gay voices of the late-morning Mass-goers bustling through the streets clutching their prayer missals. I was struck by the terrible realization that today I would see condemned ones—people just like me—who would never know the pleasures of mornings again!

Suddenly my thoughts were interrupted by different street sounds. I cocked my head and leaned far out and stared down the street as a company of town criers marched up the street, shouting and singing. A crowd followed them. I could see them but could not yet hear them. It must be an announcement of a wedding or birth in an important noble's family, I thought. But I sensed something else as I watched the restless, jeering commoners gather on the streets. And then . . . I heard the criers, aligned in the middle of the street, singing as they read from their unfurled parchments: a cordial invitation from the archbishop for all to join the spectators at today's burning of heretics. An auto-de-fé! The street commoners hooted and cheered as the criers promised them entry into some of the refreshment tents. "Come and watch the cleansing of evil souls in the baptism of fire!" finished one crier in a shrill voice that was swiftly swallowed in the cheers of the wildly excited crowd. Trembling, enraged, I quickly withdrew myself and slammed my window mightily against the ugliness below.

Before I had time to catch my breath, Papá now fully dressed had flung open my door, grimly beckoning. The carriage had arrived. Mamá, a look of worry and concern in her eyes, carried Manuel slowly downstairs and handed him over to old Marta. I floated down behind them as if in a dream. The three of us in our finest clothes climbed inside the coach.

Mamá looked up toward the nursery window, fanning herself rapidly and dabbing at her eyes. I knew how it frightened and upset her to leave the baby once again. He would have to be fed on goat's milk all day. Mamá had never before been gone so long and unable to nurse. I heard her give strict instructions not to let any other servants change or bath him, flattering old Marta that she was the only one who could properly care for baby.

Papá looked bleakly through the curtains of the carriage opening, a damp rag held to his head. The headache still lingered. As I settled in, I squirmed with the heat of so much finery on so hot a day.

When we were all settled in, Papá stuck his hand out the carriage opening and snapped his fingers sharply. The driver of the coach, aware of his official mission, set his horses at a rapid clip toward the gates of town. He knew well our destination just outside the city walls, the grounds of the crumbling Castle Triana where the accused meet suffering and unimaginable torture in the castle dungeons before an almost merciful burning. The castle had once been a place to show the splendor and majesty of the crown. Now it was known for torture and death—the appointed place for the terrible auto-de-fé.

Nine

We Attend the auto-de-fé

As we rode toward our grim destination, I gazed cheerlessly out the coach for distraction. Many commoners walked jauntily in groups, laughing raucously. I realized they were going gaily to the auto, as children go to a puppet show.

Mamá said that it was the promise of so much food and drink being given away that attracted them. But Papá said simply, "The ignorant masses consider it great sport to see the humiliation and burning of heretics. It makes even the poorest human beings feel lucky and superior."

The coachman let us out on a grassy meadow, as close as he could get to the entrance of the castle grounds. Dozens of other coaches clogged the way, letting out their passengers helter-skelter. They were all wealthy folk, like us—hidalgos—in elegant dress and velvet jackets, chattering with gaiety. Many had brought along young children, who paraded themselves proudly in their finery, as if it were a great treat to come. I realized it wasn't only the poor ignorant masses who considered the auto an entertainment of pleasure and sport.

As we followed the crowds, I realized I could never find Teresa in such a crowd, even if she hadn't convinced her father to take her to visit El Rápido.

Jostled and pushed through the gates, a sense of revulsion for my fellow Sevillanos washed over me. I vowed not to smile, nor speak in pleasantries to them, nor eat, nor enjoy myself in any way. I would hold my rosaries all afternoon and pray Avé Marías for the souls of the condemned ones until the moment they were brought out, strapped to the stake, blindfolded and helpless, and the fiery torches placed . . . Dios . . . I could hardly bare to think of it! How, I wondered, would I endure it? How, I wondered, could the unlucky condemned ones?

As we finally entered the castle grounds, grand music—fanfares with trumpets and coronets—welcomed the people as if we were entering a tournament of jousting or a royal ceremony. A young page led us to one of the many wooden platforms reserved for families of noblemen and court officials. As we sat down, Papá and Mamá played their parts, smiling and nodding at the others already seated on the platform. But I looked away and refused to curtsy politely. Behind us, in the back of the stand, a young lady and gentleman laughed and giggled with such abandon and delight that I turned and gave them a cold stare to remind them of the tragic solemnity of the occasion. Each time their voices rose in gaiety, I turned and repeated the stare. Finally, the woman rose and said, "Come Marcos, let us go to the wine tents where the company will be much gayer and more charming than it is here." As she haughtily passed by, I was surprised to see that she hardly looked older than I.

After the late morning hours of eating and entertainments, the afternoon proceeded with fits of both drama and tedium as the guards trotted out various prisoners in sanbenitos for public confession. With a shock, I realized that it was the first time I had seen sanbenitos on real people, not merely hanging in the church hall. I gazed at the ugly garments of shame, shifts torn from rough yellow flaxen cloth. They had come horrifyingly alive upon the wretched bodies of the condemned ones standing slumped before us, heads down, hands tied behind their backs. The prisoners looked as if they had been beaten down in torture chambers. Each time a group was brought from the castle dungeon, the officials allowed the crowd to roar and jeer and shake their fists before the portly archbishop raised his hand in a sign of silence.

These were the lucky ones, I learned. They had been spared death. They had been given a severe flogging instead, then a public shaming in which the repentant man or woman was forced to parade through the town stripped to the waist while a town crier proclaimed his or her offense.

Late in the afternoon, the trumpeter's clarion call alerted us that the final tribunal of the day was about to commence, the one the audience had long awaited. Soon we would see the final group of heretics, the

86

ones who had committed the most serious crimes of Judaizing the Catholic faith. Some of them, we knew, would be "relaxed." How genteel the Holy Office's term "relaxed" sounded instead of the truthful one, "burned at the stake."

A churning in the pit of my stomach began when ten people, seven men and two women, and . . . a boy, who could not have been older than I, were led out by three soldiers. Balls and chains bound their hands and feet. *Dios mío*, I crossed myself. "Papá?" I said and gestured toward the young boy. My father looked at me with eyes of despair and said in a hoarse angry whisper, "No, they do not even spare the children."

For another hour we were forced to bear witness to the long tribunal of the Inquisitors. I could barely take my eyes off the young and frightened-looking boy. Several times his knees sagged as if he might collapse, till the soldier near him gave the back of his legs a fierce thwack with a leather strap, which made the boy stand straight. Tears welled up in my eyes while a cheer rose from the peasants. The queen's soldiers were sent to stand amidst the crowds of peasants to ensure silence and decorum while the interrogation of the ten people standing in the blazing sun proceeded.

When watching the boy became too painful, my eyes swept the other nine condemned ones. Even in their pitiful sanbenitos and conical hats, I could see that they had once been people of culture who looked hardly different from us. I was especially drawn to one of the two women, a handsome lady of advanced age, a shock of white hair hanging beneath her conical hat. She held herself with remarkable dignity in spite of being barefoot beneath her immodestly short sanbenito and standing before the jeering crowd.

We were told that six of the accused ones had committed only minor offenses. I prayed that the boy and the dignified lady were among them. The first, a well-known Christian poet, confessed to getting ideas from the Jews' Old Testament stories. Another had scrupulously cut away all the fat of the meats in his household, which seemed to be a suspiciously Jewish habit. A third man had cursed and interfered with a soldier separating an accused Marrano woman from her child.

I held my breath, only three of the "minor" offenses to go. The fourth was the other woman, a mother of several young children, who had not shown up in church after the birth of her last child, long after the forty-day confinement of childbirth. I gasped. What would become of her children? But I had no time to think of it, for they had begun to announce the the fifth—my heart thumped—not the boy or the dignified lady, but a man, who had uttered the psalms of the Old Testament without adding the Catholic *Gloria Patri* at the end, a possible sign of Jewish blasphemy.

There were now five people standing—three men, the boy, and the dignified lady. We were down to the last minor offense. "And number six," said the pronouncing priest, "this man, Juan de Suarez"—my heart sank in terrible despair— "for warning a New Christian neighbor of his impending arrest." The entire six were dispatched back to the castle dungeon for a mere flogging and five-year imprisonment!

Now I knew the bitter truth. The boy and the lady were among the remaining four, condemned to die at the stake!

My mind burned with angry curiosity. What could they have done to warrant death by burning? I counted my rosaries almost without stopping, unthinkingly, when suddenly, I caught myself. How easy it was to forget who and what I really was! A secret Jew, Ruth de Cojano, saying her rosaries! Neither Christian, nor Jew, but a heretic in the eyes of the Holy Office. How easily it could be me standing between the lady and the poor trembling boy! Papá, noting my distress—for I sat on the edge of the chair—laid a calm hand upon my arm.

The light was beginning to fade as the workmen built the pyres before the eyes of the crowd, before the eyes of the condemned ones. People got up and stretched and wandered in and out of the food tents. Mamá and Papá grew faint with hunger and were forced to go for brief refreshment. Though Mamá tried to insist I accompany them, I stubbornly refused. In spite of the pangs in my stomach and the smells of roasted meat, I had decided that if those standing before us must be deprived of life, I must be deprived of food.

Not until nearly nightfall of that dreadful day did the final phase of the ceremonies begin. Torchlights were lit up all around the square and the eager crowd was finally allowed its long-awaited thrill, its show of fire. I sucked in my breath and leaned closer to Papá as we heard the final accusations of the remaining prisoners. Don Filipe de Perez was first—accused of not kindling fires for a year of consecutive Saturdays. Don Felipe's house had been watched by the sentinels of the towers whose duty it was to record houses without fires on the Jew's Sabbath day.

Second was an old and doddering man, Carlos de Lopez, whose hands shook from the tremors of his great age. He cried softly as his accusation was read: failure to eat pork for the last five years, claiming the flesh of pig upsetting to his digestion, as reported by two of his devoted servants.

After each accusation, I sucked in my breath in a gasp. How small and trivial seemed their crimes to me!

And then, alas, came the boy. *"Young Diego de Himenes. You have been found guilty of engaging in detestable Jewish burial, according to the reprehensible laws of Moses. Upon the death of your mother, you were witnessed by many servants of turning her face to the wall at her death and ordering her corpse to be washed in warm water and then, for seven days following, wearing the torn and rended garments of mourning Jews. What say you, boy?"*

"Steel yourself, Diego!"

We were near enough to hear the white-haired woman shout next to him. The guard swiftly approached her, and with the back of his hand, slapped her savagely across the mouth. Her head hung to the side a moment but she raised it defiantly and spit at him. He raised his hand to strike her again. But this time the archbishop raised his hand in a halting gesture.

"What say you boy? You have been found guilty. But if you beg forgiveness and walk to your death holding this crucifix, then, after you are burned your soul will be restored to heaven. If you do not, your soul will go to Hell along with all the Jews of this world. What say you?"

The boy shook so hard, his chains rattled. The defiant woman held her gaze upon him as if trying to give him courage. He said only two unforgettable words in a small thin voice, "No, sir."

The woman shook her chains and stamped her feet in a strange kind of glee. The noise of the restless crowd began to increase.

Then came the defiant woman's turn. The priest read her name aloud: Maria de Torres. She was accused by her very own cousin of making bread in the Jewish way. When kneading the dough, she would throw particles of dough in the oven fire, the small sacrificial ceremony "the detestable Jews perform when making their *challah* or 'Sabbath bread,'" the archbishop explained aloud with much fervor. After noting this suspicious behavior, the cousin, a loyal Catholic, had begun to watch Maria ever more closely. She saw that Maria had been washing and cleaning the house and bathing herself every Friday before sundown. Finally, the cousin was shocked to see Maria lighting a candle in a pitcher in her cellar, saying an incantation over a cup of wine and moving her head backwards and forwards as Jews are known to do in prayer. "She displayed nothing less than all of the reprehensible habits of Jews," proclaimed the priest, "polluting all of Christendom!"

I tried to hide the shock and fear on my face. Was it not the very same "reprehensible habits" that I had seen for years in my own home? I dared not look squarely at my parents, but glanced at them sideways. Mamá leaned on my father's shoulder; he held her hand tightly in his grasp. Though Maria de Torres stood barefoot, filthy and beaten in her sanbenito and conical hat, she never for a moment lost her look of fierce anger and dignity. When the priest asked if she would repent of defiling the glorious Catholic faith with her "Jew bread and Jew habits" she shouted angrily, "As I said during the tortures in your filthy castle dungeon, I answer only to the One God, Adonai, the Holy One Blessed Be He! He tells me it is you—you filthy beasts parading as Christians, who will go to Hell!"

Only privileged ones like us, placed so near the elevated platform of the ceremony, could hear the bold reply, or see the gleam of triumph spreading across her face. The archbishop was a model of patience. He showed no reaction to her angry speech.

A ripple of excitement stirred the crowd. Suddenly, I heard a low, steady chanting growing louder and louder. It came from the audience and I leaned forward to catch the words.

"Listen Papá, they're chanting Maria, Maria, Maria!" I said heartened by the crowd's support. But my father turned, and with stricken eyes, shook his head, and I cocked my ear and listened again.

And this time it sounded different. It sounded . . . oh merciful God in heaven! Papá was right. It wasn't Maria they were shouting, but *Marrano! Marrano! Marrano!*

I threw my hands up to my ears, not caring who saw me. The horrid chanting seemed to go on ceaselessly. The archbishop stood there patiently letting the crowd rant a long time before his hand went up in that familiar gesture to bring silence. Finally, the noise died down, and the archbishop was shouting, "Filipe de Perez, Carlos de Lopez, Young Diego de Himenes, and Maria de Torres, baptized Catholics all, who have allowed Satan to defile their souls by the evil practice of Judaism. As it is written in John, chapter fifteen, verse six, in the words of our Savior Jesus: *If anyone does not abide in Me, he is thrown away as a branch, and dries up; and they gather them, and cast them into the fire, and they are burned!* All three of ye are relaxed to the secular arm of our glorious government!" The archbishop's arms reached to the skies in a drama meant to excite and the thrilled audience took up their cries once again, which echoed around the square: *Fire! Fire! Light the fire!*

Without the slightest prayer or comforting word to the condemned ones, the archbishop simply nodded to the soldiers to begin their gruesome task. The guards began to push and shove the prisoners toward the *quemadero*, "the burning place"! From our elevated seats, we could see and hear it all. The old man was pulled like a small docile pony. The other man walked silently, his head bowed low. Maria put up great resistance, kicking, yelling, and shouting obscenities to the guards, forcing them to drag and curse her. But the boy, Diego de Himenes, collapsed weeping and crying, and begged for mercy! My heart felt like it would burst, as the guards dragged the boy by his arms and feet, his knees scraping the ground! Suddenly, Maria de Torres caught a glimpse of the boy. She turned and shouted with all her might, "Diego, say the Shema! Say it over and over and do not stop! It will carry you to the other side where your ancestors will greet you!" she shrieked till the guard kicked her forward.

Then, saints be praised, the boy stopped weeping and stumbled to his feet—and began to recite the Shema. He had drawn courage from Maria de Torres!

The mob roared again. I watched, terrified as the prisoners were thrust upon the quemadero and the guards lashed them to their individual stakes. The tension of the audience rose; the roar of the crowd was deafening.

"Papá!" I yelled above the din, the sound strangling in my throat.

He reached for me, pulled me close, pressed his mouth to my ear and whispered, "Say the Shema Yisra'el under your breath!" Then, aloud, he commanded "Say your Avé Marias for the souls of the three wretched ones, daughter. It will still your nerves. And say, even as the prophet Jesus said, 'Forgive them Lord, they know not what they do!'"

I turned to stare at him, realizing he was referring not to the victims, but to the Holy Office that carried out such horrors in the name of Jesus. His eyes were pointed straight ahead, as if he could not or would not look away from the horror-filled scene. Mamá bent over and covered her face with her hands. "Don't look, Isabel, look away!" she cried.

Yet I could not stop myself from looking. I felt compelled to watch the sufferings of the condemned ones, almost against my own will. It was as if time stopped. For eternity we seemed to watch the executioner blindfold each one of the four. In that endless moment I felt sure the executioner could not do what he finally did. He took his blazing torch and brought fire to the straw of each stake: one for Don de Perez, who dared not to kindle his fire on the Jew's Sabbath, one for Don de Lopez, a frightened old man with shaking hands, who couldn't tolerate the heaviness of pork, one for Diego de Himenes, a young boy in mourning, who buried his mother in accordance with Jewish law; and one for defiant Maria de Torres, who had barely hidden her many acts of Jewish cleanliness and Sabbath prayer, and who now struggled and squirmed in her ropes, even as the executioner brought the torch to her pyre! I thanked God we were too far away to hear their cries now!

How swiftly the four condemned ones were engulfed by the flames as the crowd roared madly on!

"Oh, Papá! How can they bear it?" I cried. "How can they bear such suffering?" My voice was lost in the deafening noise. Around us, people leaped up from their seats, some in horror, some moved to shout and shake their fists in support of what they saw. Desperately I tried to think of a comforting thought, any thought at all. I tried to say my Hail Marys, but for the first time in my life the words of Blessed Mary gave me no comfort, no hope whatsoever.

When I thought I could stand the horror no more, a strange, comforting thought flew into my mind. I remembered how I had once heard Teresa's father, who loved to regale his dinner guests with the details of violent death, say that numbness set in when people were put to the sword as well as burned at the stake. After the first bright hard stabs of terrible pain, the body's sensations shut down, no longer capable of feeling the searing pain of steel nor fire. For once I wanted to believe the gloating words of Don de Rodriguez! Dear God, I prayed, may it be so.

I glanced around, breathing hard. Even the haughty young señora and her husband who had laughed so gaily in the beginning, clung to one another, subdued at the sight of the four human bonfires exploding toward the sky. From behind us a gentleman came and whispered into Papá's ear, and Papá in turn whispered into Mamá's ear. I saw people here and there whispering into each other's ears. The gentleman returned to his seat as quickly as he had come. I looked at Papá questioningly. He leaned toward me, his voice urgent and compelling, "Isabel!" he whispered.

"What Papá? What?" I shouted anxiously above the din.

"Word has traveled up from the crowd that all four died a martyr's death uttering Shema Yisra'el!"

I looked at Papá bleakly and nodded, trying to find comfort in that.

Again he put his mouth to my ear and whispered. "We are not alone, Isabel. There are many among us, right here who know the Shema, many courageous Marranos, like us. That gentleman who spoke to me heard all four condemned ones—even that poor, young boy—utter the Shema as they died on the stake. Isabel, they are in God's safe-keeping now!"

He pulled away and looked at me for a sign of understanding. Awed by the horror before me, I could only nod. I was wrestling with a sudden new emotion that I could not yet put into words.

The heat of the great fires had begun to reach us. Our eyes stung with smoke. Around me people coughed and fanned themselves profusely.

Behind my fan I tried to remember the words: Shema Yisra'el . . .
Adonai . . . Adonai . . . Discouraged I realized that I could remember no
more of the Hebrew. But undaunted, I began again in Spanish: *"Hear O
Israel!"* I said fiercely under my breath, *"The Lord Our God, the Lord
Alone!"*

◌

We sat there, along with most of the crowd, mesmerized by the
glowing firelight long after the bodies had been consumed by the
flames. Women here and there could be heard weeping, the shock of
such gruesomeness too much for them to bear. We all sat dumbly as
the putrid smell of burning flesh and wood enveloped the square, as
ashes began to fall gently on everyone, like dry, dark raindrops.

Many in the crowd were making the sign of the Cross and
murmuring, "Father, Son and Holy Ghost," the Christian benediction,
quietly to themselves. I too, made endless signs of the Cross. Or so it
appeared outwardly. Yet under my breath I was actually saying with a
burning passion, "Adonai, my God in my mind; Adonai, my God on my
lips, Adonai, my God in my heart." Defiantly, the way María de Torres
would have done it.

Transfixed by the dying blaze, I realized that I, too, had endured a
baptism of fire and was reborn—a Jew.

Ten

We Prepare for Escape

J awoke the next day, my nose still inexplicably filled with the sickening smell of burning flesh. Desperate for fresh air, I leaped up and threw open my verandah shutters. The morning was dark with rain, tiny streams flowing through the cracks of the cobbles below. The rain and all its darkness pleased me—as if tears were being shed for those who suffered and burned at the stake. Nobles and peasants alike had reveled in yesterday's fires. But the heavens knew better and wept.

Staring out into the rain, I realized that anger had dispelled my melancholy. I felt as if the fires that had burned in the quemadero yesterday now burned angrily inside of me, Ruth de Cojano, the *Jewess*. By candlelight, in a fever of anger and rage last night, I had taught myself the Shema—in Hebrew. Never again would I be caught unprepared to say it.

I closed the shutters against the pouring rain and donned my robe. I realized that few people would make it to church that morning, between the rain and the late hour most had returned from the auto.

Not wanting to be alone with my thoughts, I went to the door of my parents' chamber and knocked.

"Pascua?" I heard my mother call nervously.

"It's me, Mamá."

I heard the muffled sounds of a scraping chair.

"Thank God, it is you," said Mamá ushering me in and bolting the door behind me.

Papá held baby Manuel in his arms, rocking him tenderly. Mamá hurried back to her table. Clothing was strewn before her. I was surprised to see all our traveling clothes. "After last night, we thought you would be sleeping quite late," she said.

"I couldn't, Mamá."

She nodded and took up her sewing, moving the needle in a hasty, almost frantic way. I looked curiously over her shoulder and understood why she kept the door closed. She was sewing small pockets up and down the insides of our undershifts. Into these hidden pockets, she explained, we would carry away what we could in small treasures, gold and silver coins, dried fruits and meats, stockings and caps for the baby, jewels that Mamá could not bear to part with. She handed me a shift and swiftly set me to the task beside her.

Papá put the baby gently back into his trundle and gestured for me to pour myself tea. Already he had rung to have a breakfast tray brought up. He sat down at his table and, with a sigh, went to work on his account ledgers while Mamá and I sewed and the baby slept. We stayed together nearly the whole morning, saying little. We drew quiet comfort from one another, each in our own strange island of thoughts. There seemed little to say the morning after an auto-de-fé. Finally, I broke the silence with the question that was in all our minds.

"When, Papá?" I asked in a small voice. "When shall we be leaving?"

"In four days. Saturday," he replied, matter-of-factly from his writing table.

"Saturday? Why Saturday?"

He put down his quill. "Because it is the Jewish Sabbath day, the day of worship and rest when Jews would never work, nor travel."

I looked at him with confusion.

"Don't you see? A Saturday will be the least likely day to arouse suspicion among any Christians. We will set out, the four of us. First I will gather the quarterly collections from the local farms. Then we will set out for a picnic in the country, our first long drive with the baby. And then . . . escape. Just as my cunning informant has advised."

"Will we get to meet the informant, Papá?"

Mamá stopped sewing and looked up.

"No," he said sternly and returned to his accounts.

I was wildly curious about the mysterious informant, but I knew from the tone of his voice, it was useless to ask Papá. He would tell me no more. Suddenly I remembered something.

"Teresa! Teresa holds her yearly summer party for girls on Friday! I usually stay the night with her afterwards. But if we are to leave the next morning, what shall I do?" I looked from one parent to the other. Mamá looked to Papá, deferring to his judgment.

He thought for a moment. "You must go, Isabel. Only you may not stay the night. You must tell her that we are planning a trip to the country the next day, just after my collections, and may not sleep there this year."

Papá closed his ledger and explained our plan of escape: the four of us would set forth in the carriage, appearing carefree, with baskets of food and wine. We would accompany him, resting and eating in the carriage, while he collected the royal taxes from four farmers and landowners in the south district as he does every quarter year. The district was usually but a half-day's work for Papá. The driver, who was never permitted to wander far from the carriage, would not know Papá's exact business with the landowners, lest he be tempted to rob Papá of the money he collected. Once Papá had gathered his taxes, he would order the driver to take us in the direction of the sea, as if we wanted to enjoy a cooling drive to catch the sea breezes."

"Does the plan make sense to you both so far?"

Mamá and I nodded. Many times we had accompanied Papá on his rounds, turning the day into an outing.

It would be just past midday. Papá would say to the driver, why not take the road to Cadiz? He would wink and say, "I shall show my wife and daughter the sight of all the departing Jews." The driver, given his own generous food basket and wine, would doubtless take little note of such a commonplace request. People often journeyed to that road just to gawk at the traveling bands of Jews running to meet the boats in time.

But in truth Papá had arranged that along this very same road an "old acquaintance," a man known as Don Estaban de Gomez, dressed as one of noble birth and also traveling by coach, would catch sight of our coach and insist we pull over. Mamá and Papá and I were to greet him as old and dear friends. He would admire the baby and insist that we come home to show him to his wife. We would then be cordially invited to his country villa and olive grove, only two or three leagues south, where indeed the countryside was sprinkled with hidalgo villas. Don Estaban de Gomez, however, did not really own a villa, nor have a wife.

Our own driver and coach would be generously paid and dismissed. We would enter the carriage of Don Estaban. And there, in the cramped confines, we would begin our transformation into Jews— removing our fine aristocratic garments and exchanging them for the clothes of simple Jewish folk, which Don Estaban himself would be bringing. They were to be plain cambric shifts, head scarves for Mamá and I; a tunic and Jew's hat for Papá.

"Oh Papá, you don't mean one of those dreadful pointed hats?" I protested. How dignified and courtly my father always dressed. I could hardly bear the thought of seeing him in the hat of a ridiculed Jew.

He answered quite mildly. "It is of little consequence, Isabel. Such hats are decreed for all Jewish men in Spain."

Most importantly of all, he said, we must relinquish all our jewels and religious things—Papá, his large silver cross, Mamá and I, our rosaries. Every item of our New Christian lives must be handed over to Don Estaban. We may take only what we can carry with us—food baskets, blankets, gold, medicinal herbs, all things which fleeing Jews themselves carry.

Mamá and I looked at each other with our mouths open. "Who is this Don Estaban?" she asked suspiciously.

"A trustworthy man," Papá said, "made even more trustworthy by the clink of many coins."

"Is he the informant you have spoken of so often?" I asked. Mamá too looked curious.

"No, Estaban de Gomez is most certainly not my cursed informant. I trust de Gomez more. He is an old acquaintance who for a considerable price, helps frightened New Christians like us disguise themselves as Jews and escape to the awaiting ships at the Port of Cadiz." Papá reminded us that New Christians of any kind, however sincere their Christianity, were strictly forbidden by law to ever leave the country. This was the queen's assurance that New Christian wealth and talent would find their way into the coffers of Spain.

For saving our lives and taking great personal risk himself, Don Estaban would extract a small fortune from us in gold, jewels, and fine clothing. He would then carry us nearly ten leagues, two day's journey, to a juncture in the road where many paths converged. The four of us, God willing, would have but a single day's journey by foot, to the ships' harbor. When the moment was right, we would step out of Don Estaban's coach, no longer privileged Caruso de Carvallos, but de Cojanos, fleeing Jews. In our plain and simple dress we would step among the long lines of Jews journeying in haste these last days of July to the Port. From that moment on, Papá and Mamá must address one another as *Saul* and *Merriam*, baby Manuel as *Mica*.

"Saul? Merriam? Mica?" I said with wonderment. "Are these . . . "

"Our true, secret names from the Torah," Papá said. "Just as Ruth is yours."

I looked from Papá to Mamá to my brother and tried to burn their new names into my mind: you are Saul and you, Merriam and you, baby brother, Mica.

"What then, Paulos?" said Mamá anxiously.

"When we leave Don Estaban," Papá said lowering his voice to an urgent whisper, "we must play the part of humble, grateful Jews given a ride by a kindly hidalgo who takes pity on an expelled family with a baby and who carries them a few leagues closer to the ships. You see, the queen's soldiers have been ordered to ride up and down the roads to assure the Jews safe passage to the ships. They will be watching everyone. They will notice if we behave like nobles and not poor Jews. If all goes well, it will be July thirty-first, no later, giving us only one extra day to reach the port. I have learned that the edict has been extended to August first. That, dear ones, will be our last day to board ship because on August the second the queen's soldiers are ordered to put to death any stray Jews not departed from Spanish soil." Papá looked at us anxiously for understanding.

Mamá sighed deeply as she forced the needle through several thicknesses of cloth.

"Where will the great ships carry us, Papá?" I asked nervously, trying to imagine a place that was not Spain.

"To Turkey and the great city of Istanbul where the Turkish king, known as the Sultan, is overjoyed to have Jews bring their wealth and talents."

For the first time, I heard hope and assurance in Papá's voice. The kingdom of Turkey! Even the name sounded foreign and far removed from my own land.

"Is it cold there, Papá?"

Though the morning was warm I shivered. How I dreaded a cold and frozen land such as France where I had heard stories of people rummaging for food much of the year and where many folk without shelter died frozen hideously to the ground. I had only known the south of Spain, and its beautiful Mediterranean Sea and the warm embrace of its winds and sea breezes.

"No, not cold, but perhaps not so hot as here. I am uncertain, Isabel, but it does not matter. Hot or cold, there we must go."

I sighed and leaned forward to stroke the soft, feathery hair of my brother's head, my brother who was soon to be called Mica, not Manuel.

"Then, there is the greatest challenge of all, which I have not yet explained, Isabel."

Another? Already my mind was a whirlwind of dangerous challenges.

"Even if we manage to elude all Christian authorities, the hardest part will be convincing the Jewish ones themselves that we are truly Jews."

"Sí, perhaps the hardest part of all!" Mamá said looking up, her needle poised in mid-air.

"But I do not understand, Papá. We can simply tell them we are escaping Marranos, that we are Jews, like them. How could they reject us, their own secret ones?"

"To understand that, Isabel, you must understand the thinking of Jews. First of all, even to bring a Marrano on board the ships is an act of unlawfulness, imperiling the Jews and leading to their own arrest by the Holy Office. Aiding and abetting New Christians is as bad as Judaizing the Christian faith. But worst yet, you see, Jews consider Marranos to be traitors, even heretics to the Jewish faith."

I gasped, "But why?"

"They consider it a grave sin to be secret Jews, living in comfort as New Christians. They would have condemned your bisabuela Ruth, saying she should have chosen death over conversion to Christianity."

"Death? But then you, nor I would have been born!" I protested.

"Indeed. It is easy to judge how others behave at the point of a sword. Even in the Torah it states, 'Therefore choose life.' Remember I told you even the great Maimonides was forced to convert to Islam. This has been the fate of Jews for most of history. Convert or die. Then, having converted, to live condemned for having done so. Condemned for having Jewish blood to begin with! Condemned if we do and condemned if we don't! Even now, our Catholic monarchs bargain for a few Jewish souls, offering any Jew who wishes to convert to Christianity the right to stay in Spain and live as New Christians."

"How many do convert, Papá?"

"Hardly any. They nearly all refuse to forsake Judaism. It is just as well. They would find no security these days as New Christians. I am sure the monarchy is careful not to mention its charming Holy Office."

"So Jewish folk hate us Marranos even as the Christians hate us?" I asked with dismay. All this time I had been picturing the Jewish people welcoming us, with open arms!

"We must earn their confidence by our humbleness and sincerity, learning and imitating carefully all that they do."

A dazzle of light lit across the sky. Lightning. Then the long low rumble of thunder, like a growling beast. I looked bleakly into the dark skies and felt homeless already. So now there was to be danger from the Jewish world, as well as the Christian one. The world had turned into a place of turmoil, fear, and suspicion on all sides.

"Papá, couldn't Don Estaban de Gomez take us all the way to the ships? Then we wouldn't have to try to convince the Jewish folk until after we board the boats."

Mamá stopped sewing and looked up hopefully at Papá.

"That, dear ones, is out of the question. Don Estaban dares not transport us too close to the port. He is much too squeamish to come so near queen's soldiers and officials of the Holy Office. Besides, it would hardly seem natural for poor Jews to be chauffeured in a noble carriage all the way to the port. He has agreed to leave us five leagues from Cadiz. That will give us only one day's travel by foot. Besides, this will give us time to blend in with the Jewish ones." He sighed. "Then we must worry about finding space on a ship. The ships will be filled to overflowing as it is."

"I am not looking forward to taking baby on a cramped and filthy sea voyage," Mamá said firmly.

"Thousands travel by boats every day, Mamá," I tried to say assuringly. "Teresa has sailed abroad to Italy twice."

"Sí, those Old Christians come and go as they please," she said bitterly.

"Don Estaban will also bring us identification papers, falsified but authentic-looking, I hope," said Papá. "They will have our Jewish names on them." He thought for a moment. "We will each hold our own, just in case we should be separated."

"Oh, Paulos, never that!" Mamá protested in alarm.

"No, no, beloved, fear not." Papá said gently. "But Maria, we must try to think of every possible complication. I cannot deny that this is a dangerous undertaking. I have tried to think of anything that would harm the safety of my family."

"Or you, Paulos," Mamá said gazing into his eyes worriedly.

"All of us," Papá agreed, smiling wanly to her. "Perhaps it will help us to picture in our minds the road to Cadiz crowded with Jewish travelers." Papá closed his eyes and spoke as if he could truly see it. "We will be just like them, not only in our simple dress but in manner and religious action. And in name—Saul and Merriam and Ruth and baby Mica—who would never utter the name of Jesus, nor Blessed Mary, nor any of the saints nor Church blessings, nor Avé Marías."

Mamá and I, so faithful to our daily rosaries gasped and stared at one another. Even I had not considered giving up my rosaries, or my many Catholic prayers and habits so abruptly. Surely I would forget sometime and ruin everything.

"My rosaries, my rosaries . . ." said Mamá in despair, "I had so hoped to bring my mother's rosaries with me into the new kingdom. What harm could a small strand of colored beads do? In rememberance of the good parts of our Christian lives?"

"Beloved," Papá said gently to Mamá, "to let slip even so much as an Avé Maria will endanger us all. That is why Estaban de Gomez will take them from us."

Mamá looked down wordlessly and took up her sewing. Then I did too, returning to the shift in my lap. There seemed to be nothing more to say.

Papá went back to his ledgers. The scratching sound of his quill on the thick parchment was the only sound in the room. Something was scratching at the back of my mind, too. Papá had said that Estaban de Gomez would extract a small fortune in gold and silver from us. And Papá would be collecting large sums of money from the landowners. A small fortune meant for the royal treasury of Seville. Yet we would not return from that tax collecting trip! The money would not go back to the royal bursars in Seville. What if Papá did not appear at the royal bursar's by Monday morning with his collections, having taken out only his commission? Blessed Mary! Suddenly, it all came clear, like finding the last missing pieces of a puzzle. My father, known far and wide for his trustworthiness, intended to rob the royal treasury!

"Papá," I set down my sewing and whispered. "Will you not be stealing from the Royal Treasury?" Papá looked startled. "I-I mean, you will not be taking the treasury's portion back on Monday as you always do. Will they not think you have stolen it?"

"Isabel!" Mamá looked up, shocked.

But he lowered his eyes. "Sí," he said. "She is quite right, Maria. I, Royal Tax Collector over all Seville, a man who has served the Royal Treasury with honesty and honor, not even so much as losing one *marivedo* of the royal taxes in fifteen years, shall be known henceforth as the royal embezzler of Seville." Papá slumped forward and leaned his head in his hands.

"But Papá, you do not mean to steal the royal portion!" I whispered in alarm.

Without uncovering his eyes, Papá said. "Oh yes, Isabel, I do. What do you think I will use to pay Estaban de Gomez—sausages?"

"But we have money in the great bank in Seville. You have said so many times. Couldn't we just get the money from there?" I said almost accusingly to my father.

"Not such a vast amount. It would attract too much attention. Besides, there is not much left there anymore. I have had to pay my informant hefty sums from there already," he said despairingly.

"Paulos, it cannot be helped." Mamá hearing the accusation in my voice, laid down her sewing and went and put her arms around Papá's back. "She does not understand it all. Even I barely understand it." Then she turned to me.

"Isabel, dearest, the despicable Holy Office will seize ten times that amount in this house!" Her voice trembled a little. She swept her arm around the chamber. "All our servants, clothing, the carriage and horses, our carpets and furnishings and family heirlooms. They will take everything, Isabel, every copper pot, every gown of silk. They will steal from us and fill their own greedy pockets. We will bring a handful of coins, blankets, some food, and the clothes on our backs from home. But the gold and silver from your papá's Saturday collection will be all that we have to escape with. We'll be borrowing against the vast fortune we are leaving, that is all." Mamá fluttered around us both, trying to soothe, trying to comfort. It was so like her to try to keep our home peaceful at all times.

"Guess what?" I asked, eager to change the subject.

"What?" Papá said.

"I learned something that might please you both a little," I said shyly.

"You please us always, already," said Mamá, picking up her needle and thread.

"Sí, it is just that I have learned the prayer by heart—in Hebrew. Remember, Papá, how you wrote the Hebrew letters in Spanish for me so that I could say the Hebrew words? Well, last night after . . . after the . . . the auto, I studied and now I want to recite it for you in Hebrew."

"The Shema?" he said, a genuine smile crossing his face.

"Sí, the Shema. From now on I will say it every morning and every evening before I sleep."

"Oh, Isabel!" Papá said with pleasure, looking at Mamá who smiled and nodded.

"Since my birthday, I have had it written down and hidden away, even though the servants cannot read. Now I have torn up the note and thrown it into the kitchen fire."

"Excellent. Safe inside your head. That is where it belongs."

I put my hand over my eyes as I had seen Papá and the uncles do at my naming. Slowly, and very quietly, I said, "*Shema Yisra'el, Adonai Elo. . . Elohainu, Adonai Ehad. Here O' Israel, the Lord our God, the Lord Alone. Baruch Shem Kvod Malhuto L'olam Va-ed.* Blessed be the Name of God's Glorious Kingdom Forever and Ever!" I took my hand away and smiled.

"Amen," Papá said.

"Amen" echoed Mamá softly.

"And just like the first Ruth, where you both go, I will go; Your God is my God too."

My parents gazed at one another from across the room. Their faces filled with a bittersweet sadness.

"Am I not your Ruth, now?" I whispered.

"Our Ruth . . ." Papá said, his voice cracking.

Mamá picked up her sewing again and said matter-of-factly, "Sí, like the first Ruth and Naomi, we will all be wanderers together."

Eleven

I Bid Adiós to Teresa

hose last four days went by in a flurry of sewing. Mamá and I sewed such long hours that our hands began to ache and our eyes reddened from the endless repetition of pushing needle through cloth. We sewed countless hidden pockets inside our thick cotton undershirts, even into the cambric shirt Papá would wear beneath his vest. We mended and brushed out our traveling suits. We debated for long hours over which small treasures to put into the pockets. Then we inserted and sewed the chosen ones into the pockets themselves. When all that was done, we had yet to finish sewing the blue silk material that I had received from Tía Mathilde on my birthday. It was to be made into the frock that I wore to Teresa's annual summer fiesta for girls.

Papá stayed many long hours in town attending business and court affairs as usual. Then Friday, the dreaded Friday, arrived. We were not to leave until the next day, but for me Friday was the true beginning of our departure. It was the day of saying good-bye, yet not saying good-bye, to Teresa.

We barely finished the dress in time. I stared with a small bit of pleasure into Mamá's looking glass as she brushed my hair into long silken strands and caught my hair at the sides with silver combs. After she scrutinized the dress a final time, fluffing the sleeves, straightening the hem, she finally pronounced me a true *hermosura*—"a beauty." It was at that moment that we caught each other's eyes in the mirror and saw the stark fear laid bare. All the week's harried activity was finished. Suddenly we had time to dwell on the grim days ahead. Mamá sighed deeply and looked away.

I turned and grabbed her around the waist. "Oh, let me stay home with you Mamá. I don't want to leave you alone. We could just send word that I am ill and cannot go. Anyway, I am not in the mood for a party."

"That is kind, my pet, but no," Mamá said, pushing me gently away from her. "That would only bring Teresa around with questions. Besides, you would be heartsick later not to be with her this one last time."

The bells tolled the hour of noon. The party would be starting. With a downcast heart, I started down the stairs. Mamá followed behind me. As I reached the bottom, I turned and ran back up, taking the stairs by twos.

"Isabel, what? You'll get yourself into a sweat . . . !" she protested.

"The gift! I forgot the gift!" I ran into my chamber and picked up the small ribboned package left on my bed. But then, on a sudden impulse, I was down on my knees lifting the many layers of my bed linens. There it was . . . the slit in the mattress. My hand probed inside and brought out another little box. Inside lay the golden mezuzzah. I slipped it into the deep pocket of my skirt, pushed the box back into the feathers, and pulled the linens back in place. Stuffing both into my pockets, I ran downstairs.

"Isabel," said Mamá, brushing my arm in dismay, "however did you get goose feathers on your sleeve?"

"I will be late Mamá," I said kissing her quickly.

Mamá waved her kerchief to me from the doorway. I knew I had done a daring, unwise thing, taking Great Grandmother Ruth's golden mezuzzah with me. But I told myself I needed something to touch, to give me strength, to remind me of Maria de Torres and young Diego de Himenes. Something to keep the fire burning within when I faced Teresa.

At Teresa's, the girls chattered endlessly of trivial things—new silk dresses, new ways to adorn their hair, impudent slaves, and young hidalgos who came to call. I realized that I would never have knights or hidalgos call on me. Not in the kingdom of Spain.

The marques had hired puppeteers to entertain the girls. All my life I had adored the tiny theatrical world of puppets, but for once the brightly colored stage and life-like puppets did not amuse me. As we watched the little adventures of the fair damsel Susanna and her suitor, the silly stumbling Ramón, the faces of the other girls lit up in ecstasy. Yet I sat there unmoved. How old it made me feel to realize that puppets could no longer amuse me.

After the puppet show, Teresa told amusing stories of her horse El Rápido and danced around, swirling her silken skirts. I longed to have her all to myself, to spend our last hours together alone, knowing I wasn't even to spend the night this time. The kindly marquesa, Teresa's mother, sensed my sadness. She came up and put her arm around me, and said, "Isabel, I know you told me you cannot stay the night, but could you not stay a while after the others have left? Teresa, I know, would want that."

I nodded gratefully to the marquesa. Heartened, I mingled a bit more with the girls, pretending as we ate dainty treats and drank spiced juice that all was normal. I pretended that I, too, had no more on my mind than a handsome rich suitor to come courting and the dress I would wear to receive him. Yet, as I bit into the spice cakes, I could not stop the swirl of dark thoughts darting in and out of my head: *Here in the midst of luxury, we are surrounded by horror. It is all around us, everywhere in Seville, like the air we breath. But like the air, we cannot see it. For some strange reason, people choose not to. Just as they sit at the auto-de fé and cheer, seeing, yet not seeing the true horror and pain of it.*

As if knowing the very thoughts in my head, Carmela de Sanchez, a spoiled and haughty girl who I had never liked, said, "Did not simply everyone attend the auto-de fé this week? All except Teresa, poor thing. She just had to go to her Papá's villa to visit El Rápido and miss all of the thrilling excitement right here in Seville!"

My heart skipped a beat. I could not believe my ears. Usually not even Carmela spoke so boldly. The girls began to speak at once, their voices rising in excitement. Teresa looked politely interested, but I could not read her thoughts. Carmela, who did not like to have the attention taken from her, spoke up loudly. "Was it not one of the most thrilling events ever in Seville? Better than a joust, I should think, much better. This was my first. I felt so grown up to go. My father would not let me go before. You see," she said leaning in to whisper to her circle of listeners, "he thought I might throw up during the proceedings. And you know why, don't you? All because of the horrid smell!" she said, pinching her nose for emphasis. The girls all gasped and disolved into laughter. Carmela looked triumphant, the center of attention.

"We were so lucky," said Carmela, raising her voice to normal again, "for an outrageous sum my parents rented one of the upper windows of the old castle. We were able to see and hear the condemned ones as they were dragged to the quemadero in their sanbenitos. Do you know those disgusting Marranos, including the boy, never even repented? They kept right on saying their detestable Jew prayers all the way to the end. I sat next to a most handsome gentleman. He and I cheered together when they lit the pyres. . . ."

Rage grew inside me, and sent my heart beating like the hooves of a runaway horse. Against all wisdom, all caution, all sanity, I stood, wanting to smack her hard across her cruel, arrogant face.

"Mamá!" said Teresa, looking up embarrassed.

I spun around. The marquesa, had come up softly behind us, looking distressed.

"This is much too vulgar talk for genteel young ladies. Why don't we go outside for the patio games now?" she said giving a stern look to Carmela.

As we passed outside to the courtyard, Carmela stopped beside me and said, "What, pray tell, was bothering you, Isabel? You looked about to explode!"

But my rage had cooled considerably. I looked her in the eye and said calmly. "Why nothing, Carmela. I was just surprised to hear how you relished the sight of so much violence and cruelty. We heard many ignorant peasants speak much the same at the auto," I said walking away, satisfied with the ugly scowl that had settled across Carmela's face.

How relieved I was when the party was over and Teresa was saying good-bye to her guests. It would finally, mercifully, be Teresa and I, alone. She came back into the sitting room where I waited and flung herself down on the sofa. "That Carmela! Hasn't she turned brazen now that her father has been promoted to chief saddle-maker for the queen's soldiers in Seville?"

"Brazen and wicked," I said a bit too passionately. "She was always like that, Teresa."

Teresa nodded. "Oh let's not talk anymore of her. What I want to know is . . ." She suddenly leaped up and grabbed my hands pulling me up and swinging my arms to and fro."What is it? What is it? I know you brought it! Pray tell!" she insisted.

I laughed. Of course I knew what she meant. For I had already whispered in her ear that I had forgotten to bring the little gift I had wrapped, then teased her with what it might be.

We tussled, laughing, and I escaped and ran behind the sofa, then outside to the patio and back. Back in the parlour she caught me from behind. Before I could stop her, she had plunged her hands into both my pockets.

"You musn't!" I gasped aloud, trying frantically to pull away from her. My golden mezuzzah was in one of those pockets. Though I finally wriggled free, she had already come up with the treasures from deep within both pockets.

"See? I knew you were hiding gifts," she said triumphantly, looking first at the ribboned box, then, to my horror, at the golden mezuzzah.

I felt the blood rush to my face. My heart beat rapidly as she studied the unfamiliar golden rod. And then I said in as light a voice as possible, "Here, give it back, Teresa! It's just a trifle I had in my pocket. Yours is the ribboned package." She handed it back, but looked at me questioningly. I slipped it quickly into my pocket.

"What was that?" she asked.

"Oh, just something I found."

"Where on earth would you find such a thing of gold?"

"Out . . . upon the road once . . . with Papá, I think. Yes, with Papá," I lied.

"But it is something of a foreign religious nature, is it not?" she persisted, her voice tinged with alarm.

"Perhaps a medallion or coat of arms. Papá said I should have it melted down and remade into a bracelet," I said, amazed at how quickly I fell into the thinking of a liar.

Teresa looked at me for a moment as if she were about to say something, but she changed her mind and looked at the small package in her hand. The moment of tension was gone. She untied the ribbons and slipped off the small piece of blue silk left over from my dress.

"Oh, Isabel! It is stunning," she said running her hand over the glossy lacquer box with raised Chinese flowers. Oh! And look at this— inside!" Teresa gasped slightly and stared at the beautiful object inside. It was a small silver cross, with a tiny, exquisitely carved body of Jesus polished to a high shine, attached to a delicate silver chain. She looked up at me sharply. "Haven't I seen you wear this before? Around your neck?" She touched my neck. There was nothing there now.

"Well, it is one of my many crucifixes. But it fit so perfectly in the little box. I just thought perhaps you would like it."

"Like it! Why I have never seen anything so beautifully carved before. It looks very rare! Are you sure your mamá approves?" Teresa looked at me, her face flooded with surprise and confusion and gratitude all at once.

"Oh yes, she approves," I said with assurance. And this time I did not lie. Indeed, Mamá had helped me decide to give Teresa my most rare and beautiful crucifix, for I would no longer be needing crucifixes.

"Why thank you, Isabel! I shall cherish it always," she said, then handed it to me so that I could clasp it around her neck.

We stood staring at one another, only for a second, then, suddenly, she was my old Teresa again. She grabbed me and began twirling me around until we both tumbled to the floor cushions.

"You know, Isabel," she said when she had gotten her breath, "you needn't have brought me something so fine. You should have brought a small trifle like the other girls. You know my birthday's not for three months!"

"I know . . . I know. It's just that you're my best friend and you have given me many things."

"Like what?" she challenged.

"Like happiness and companionship. And loyalty. You always stand beside me. I'll never forget how you defended me from old Doña Martinez, " I said winding a pillow tassel around my finger.

"Oh silly thing! Who listens to that old hag? Not even the priest! He sees her coming and he turns and hurries the other way! Otherwise, she just fills his ear with gossip about everyone in church." She suddenly grabbed my shoulders and shook me, making me look at her. "What has come over you, today, Isabel? Making such long speeches!

Giving me your prize crucifix. You act like you're leaving the country!" she said merrily.

"What a silly thing to say," I tried to say nonchalantly.

"Well, then, what is it?"

"Nothing . . ." I raised my eyes and shrugged. "I was just lonely while you were away this past month. You spend so much time at your father's country villa with El Rápido."

"Do you know why I convinced Papá to take me to our villa this week?"

"Because you missed El Rápido, no?"

"No! I could not bare the thought of another auto-de-fé. I went once before and was sick to my stomach. So I begged and cried and threw such a tantrum that finally Papá agreed. But he was greatly put-out with me. He insisted we go to the country because no self-respecting Christian could stay in town and not attend an auto-de-fé. I was so relieved. And so was Mamá."

"Oh, Teresa, I am glad you did not have to go; I am proud of you for not wanting to see . . ." my voice cracked.

"Was it bad?"

"Horrible!" I whispered. "I have nightmares every night."

"Poor, dear Isabel. I am so sorry. But don't tell me about it. I heard enough from Carmela," she sighed. "I won't be able to avoid it next time. Papá has threatened to sell El Rápido if I refuse to go again."

"Oh, Teresa!" I said in sympathy.

"We will sit together at the next auto, sí? And hold tightly to each other and close our eyes."

"I hope . . . sí," I said despondently.

"Look at us." She sat up. "We are both suffering from the melancholy!"

"What?"

"The melancholy. Sadness. My mother suffers from that a lot and has to take to bed. There is too much melancholy in Seville these days—autos-de-fé, wars, expulsions. This town has forgotten how to be gay. Isabel, we must think more of bright, happy things. That's what my father always tells my mother. She thinks too much of the sad and tragic in life, and not enough of gaiety."

"I will think more of you, then," I said. "That will cheer me. You have made me feel cheerful and happy all the years of our friendship."

"There you go again, Isabel, adding up!" She turned and threw a pillow at my head.

"Adding up?" I said, catching the comb from my hair that the pillow had shaken loose.

"Sí, you know, when people say good-bye and journey off to war they add up all the things they like about each other. And then say, 'Adiós, Adiós, my beloved.'" She got on one knee and pretended to kiss my hand, playing the courtly gentleman again.

"Must you go home tonight?"

"Sí, I must," I said softly.

We heard footsteps outside the room and looked up to see the Marques de Rodriguez. He had just returned home, having gone to a tavern as he always did whenever the females invaded his house. He swaggered across the room and stood over us, scrutinizing me with a long bold look. I shuddered and smoothed my skirt and looked at Teresa. Even she seemed to shrink in her father's presence. We both started to get to our feet.

"No, sit, sit," he gestured us back down as he lumbered over to the windowseat and sprawled out. "The party was a success?" he asked Teresa.

"Sí, Papá. The girls all had a wonderful time, didn't they, Isabel?"

I nodded my agreement.

"And the puppet show?"

"That was especially wonderful!"

"At least, those puppeteers earned their exhorbitant fee," he said and turned to me.

"And you Señorita de Carvallo?" he said looking at me. "You also enjoyed yourself?"

"Oh sí, Marques. It was the most splendid of Teresa's summer fiestas yet."

"Ah, Señorita, always as gracious and polished as her father. How are all the upstanding members of your family these days?"

"Quite well, thank you, Marques," I said. My heart began to beat more rapidly.

"That is good to know. You all must have been quite stimulated by this week's auto-de-fé. We were forced to miss it, alas." He glared at Teresa. "But I heard what a great conflagration it was."

"S-Sí, Don de Rodríguez."

"Papá!" said Teresa, "what a cruel thing to say."

"You see?" said the marques, gesturing toward his daughter. "This is what I heard all week. How terrible and cruel the auto is. I am sure Isabel will tell you it was no worse than a bullfight."

I sucked in my breath and cast my eyes downward, but said nothing. Again, Teresa, knowing my discomfort, came to my rescue.

"We hate it when you say such things, Papá," Teresa pouted.

"Ah, well," the marques waved about a thin reed he had held in his mouth. "You are both too young to appreciate the qualities of a good auto-de-fé. Those of us a bit older value its cleansing effects. Your own father, I gather, felt equally cleansed, Isabel?" He assumed a look of innocent curiosity.

"He said it was a great education for the masses," I blurted, hoping I said something harmless.

The marques threw his head back and laughed. I bit my lip and looked at Teresa who had sullenly turned to picking threads on a cushion.

"Did he now? Well that is good. I can see he considers an auto-de-fé to be a good balm for the Christian soul. It is indeed an education for us all to see blasphemy burned away so completely. For too long, the New Testament teachings have been ignored. And what is the result? Christian Spain has become polluted by Jewish blood. Finally, the queen's great bishop, Tomás de Torquemada, has shown her the way to end the Jewish threat with the Holy Office of the Inquisition and its grand auto-de-fé. And the Holy Office promises more frequent autos. A practical measure, of course. The Christians are digging out so many Marrano infidels that the dungeons of Triana are over-stuffed like a goose at Christmastime."

His eyes pierced through mine accusingly. I hoped the fear in my heart did not find its way to my face. I stood. "I believe you are right about everything, Marques. And now I must take my leave. My parents will be waiting. Gracias, Teresa, for the wonderful fiesta, for everything."

My heart ached at the idea that this was my final good-bye to Teresa in the presence of her intimidating father.

But she jumped up. "You are leaving, already? Can't you stay at least an hour?"

The Marques de Rodriguez looked at me curiously. "You needn't rush off, Isabel. There is no merit in ending a fiesta too soon," he chuckled agreeably and slapped his protruding belly.

"Oh, but I must go. There is much to do. We're off tomorrow on a little country outing, after Papá finishes his farm collections."

"Tax collecting on Saturday? He makes all of you wait for him to go on a little outing? Does your poor, hard-working papá not even take Saturday for rest?"

I immediately caught the sly, taunting meaning of the words. "N-no, never on Saturday, a very busy workday for Papá, Marques. Only on Sunday does he allow himself to rest."

"Ah, a wise and thoughtful man, your papá. He covers his tracks shrewdly."

"His tracks?" I blurted out in alarm.

"Now, now. You needn't look so serious, Isabel Caruso de Carvallo. I wish your papá well. We have been neighbors and acquaintances many years. What do I know about the trials of the work week? Everyday is the day of rest for me. I have none of your father's interest in hard work, or personal ambition. But I wish him well. His earnestness, his devotion to work—it amuses me," said the marques, his eyes wide with sincerity.

But I did not trust him. I knew he was toying with me.

"Sí. Sí. He thinks much of you too, Marques," I said. Again Don de Rodriguez threw back his head and laughed.

"Indeed, he thinks how much he'd like to be rid of me!"

"Oh Papá," said Teresa in disgust, "stop teasing Isabel!"

"*Buenos noches*, Don de Rodriguez," I curtsied and backed away, eager to be rid of him myself.

"Good night, Señorita de Carvallo!" he boomed out in a mocking tone and bowed crisply.

By this time, Teresa had arisen and joined me. With her hand around my waist, she walked me to the door.

"Will I see you Monday morning—at Ladymass? After your—your little trip?"

"Ladymass, sí, I . . . I think. I hope." I stammered.

"Should I get one of the servants to walk you home? It's nearly six o'clock."

"Oh, no, Teresa. Such a short walk across the plaza and around the corner. There is still so much light. . . ." We stepped out onto the front walk together, dragging out our good-bye as long as possible.

"Then . . ." she reached out to hug me and we fell into each other's arms.

Suddenly she was whispering. "Isabel, should anything happen . . . anything at all. . . ."

I pulled back and looked at her suspiciously. My heart pounded. What had she heard?

"What could happen?" I said casually.

"Oh," she held her hands upwards, groping for words, "I don't know. There are just so many rumors flying around Seville. About New Christians. I-I worry about you. . . ."

We stared hard at one another, our eyes locked in agonies of unspoken thoughts. Were we thinking the same thing?

"You know there's always a home for you here. . . ."

"Oh Teresa, I'll be safe enough," I said, sure that we spoke on two levels at once.

"I pray so. *I do.* Every night to Blessed Mary. *Keep my Isabel safe.*"
Tears welled up in my eyes.

"Adiós, dearest friend!" I barely managed to sob out.

"*Vaya con Dios*—'God be with you,' Isabel!" she whispered fervently.

I stumbled down the long walk, tears blurring my vision, then picked up speed until I was half-walking, half-running through the wrought-iron gates and crossing the plaza, looking back several times. Teresa remained standing there, her hand frozen in mid-air, a salute good-bye. As the house of de Rodriguez fell out of sight, I remembered Teresa discovering my golden mezuzzah! And questioning its purpose!

Then, picking up speed, I thought, Oh beloved best friend, who prays for my safety, have you guessed that we are Marranos?

Twelve

I Am Accosted by a Friar

When I could not run any longer, I slowed to catch my breath, my eyes still streaming with tears. As I crossed the large empty plaza, I wondered how I could possibly endure my last hours in Seville knowing I would never see Teresa again. The melancholy sound of church bells sounding the evening Vespers only deepened my sorrow. Wiping my eyes and nose, I took deep gulps of air and vigorously fanned my face to dry the telltale signs of crying. I did not want to arouse curiosity among the servants nor increase the worry of my parents.

I had gone halfway across the plaza before I noticed a figure in friar's vestments, the hood drawn up, the familiar sash and prominent cross hanging about the waist. He was standing alone on the side of the square with a small stand of trees, his hands hidden in his sleeves. I glanced around. Except for a stray pedestrian well ahead of me, the square was deserted. Seville had become a place of secrecy. People rushed about their business and went quickly home. Even the grand houses around the square gave a sense of concealment. Their shutters were closed, their curtains drawn. Should a thief in friar's cloth assault me, there would be no witnesses.

The face inside the dark hood was staring in my direction. Papá had always instructed me to walk briskly, head held high if I ever sensed the presence of danger in the streets. It was better to show no fear of mischief, he said, for if a woman seemed unafraid and likely to resist, the thief might reconsider his assault. Then something even more chilling occured to me than the idea of a thief dressed in friar's cloth. I remembered the auto-de-fé and that friars had become the "hand" of the Inquisition, serving as spies for the Holy Office.

I quickened my step and cut a wide diagonal to avoid the friar. I had nearly made it to the corner and considered myself out of danger when a stern, imperious shout rang out: *"Señorita, Señorita, por favor"*—if you please! I turned with dread. Was it to be an Inquisitor or a cutthroat? If it was an Inquisitor, could Teresa have possibly had time to. . .? I was ashamed to finish the thought even as I had it.

The friar was running towards me! My feet froze on the stones; my heart galloped with fear.

"Señorita, I must know—you—your name is Isabel is it not? Isabel . . . Caruso . . . de Carvallo, daughter of . . . Paulos and Maria?" he said trying to catch his breath. I looked fearfully into the dark recess of his hood. A thin, hard face peered out, the face of a surprisingly young man, despite the sternness of his voice.

"How do you know my name?" I demanded, taking a backward step.

"Isabel," came the arrogant voice, "it is I, Tomás, your brother, back from the monastery in Toledo."

I gasped. How could I not have known him? Of course, I had not seen my brother for five years. He would be twenty-three or twenty-four now, as this young man could be. But I only vaguely remembered my brother's face. The last time I had seen him, he had worn a mustache and a thin fringe of beard around the jaw line. This face was clean-shaven with the short cropped hair of the abbey.

"Show me," I ventured cautiously, trying to picture the dark black beard on the sides and chin.

He yanked down his hood and I saw clearly a thinner, more gaunt version of Papá.

"Oh, Tomás! It *is* you!" I ran up and threw my arms around him. "How wonderful you have come, dear brother. You won't believe what is happening to us. Dear, blessed, Tomás . . . you've come just in time."

But he reached up and pulled my arms away from him and stepped awkwardly away from my embrace!

I backed away stunned and hurt.

"I am a man of God now, Isabel. It is not proper to embrace." As if to prove it, he actually brushed off the places where I had touched him!

But I was desperate, so sure his sudden appearance was a sign sent by God Himself. I ignored the rebuff and simply saw it as a sign of my brother's purity as a servant of God.

"Oh, Tomás, thank God you have come," I cried. "Mamá will be beside herself with happiness. Papá will no longer be so alone in his plans. And baby Manuel. He is so beautiful a baby. You've not even seen him yet."

My earlier spell of melancholy was swiftly replaced with joy. For despite all that Papá had said about Tomás, that he rejected our Jewish ways, he was still my brother, my parents' son. He would want to help us. Perhaps Papá had written him after all and he had come to aid in our escape. Perhaps, as a man of the cloth, he had some special influence to intercede for us. Perhaps, we might not have to depart from Spain! My mind raced through the many joyful possibilities.

"No," Tomás interjected brusquely, "I have not. I was not invited, as I recall, to the baptism."

The baptism! I had a sudden flash of memory: Papá wiping the tiny forehead clean of the priest's holy water and uttering the Hebrew blessing behind the curtain. And the secret circumcision of Manuel in our wine cellar. Surely, knowing that we were Marranos, he wouldn't expect us to make a great celebration of the baptism.

Confused, I replied, "But you were so far away in Toledo."

"Not far enough," he said.

I heard the coldness in his voice and wondered what I had said to offend him. It did not occur to me to wonder why he waited to see me in the middle of the plaza, not around the corner at our home. But it did not really matter. It was thrilling to have my brother back on the eve of our terrible escape. I lost all inhibition and began to unload the burdens of my heart in a burst of anxious relief.

"Tomás, I am so desperately sad today. I have just had to say good-bye to my best friend in all the world, Teresa de Rodriguez—you remember the daughter of the Marques and Marquesa de Rodriguez, Papá and Mamá's oldest friends?" I dabbed at my eyes with a kerchief, the tears threatening to spill again.

To my dismay, he said harshly, "I did not come to talk about your girlfriends!"

"But don't you understand Tomás? We shan't see them again. At least for a long, long time, perhaps forever! But of course, you must not know. We are fleeing, Tomás, fleeing the country!" I waited for the drama of my words to sink in, to show upon his face. Instead, he stared hard and unblinking as I continued. "We are joining the expelled ones, you know." I lowered my voice to a whisper, though the square was still deserted. "You know, of course, that we are Marranos. Papá said you learned at the age of thirteen, like me. That you used to watch the candle lightings in our cellar to bring in the Jewish Sabbath, just as I have. Of course, I know you do not join in our attachment to the Jewish faith. Papá told me this also. But you are still part of our family, Tomás. Oh, I am so glad you have come! Isn't it the greatest coincidence that you have chosen now to come?" I paused looking up at him.

"What else has Papá taught you about the Jewish faith?"

"Oh, much more. He has taught me about the Torah. He has read and told me many stories and lessons from a Spanish Bible that he keeps in the wine cellar. He has told me the beautiful story of Ruth who adopted the Jewish people. Tomás, did you know my true Jewish name is Ruth? Not Isabel, for the hateful queen who wants to get rid of the Moors and the Jews." Suddenly, in my enthusiasm, a thought occured to me. "Tomás, what was your original Jewish name?"

He did not answer, turning away to stare out into the empty square.

"Oh, it doesn't matter. Only that you've come, dear brother. Now you will help us get well away from the danger. Did you know a cruel auto-de-fé was held here several days ago? It was horrid. And then, with enemies and court spies everywhere about, Papá has been planning our escape and . . ."

"Isabel!" he interrupted my nervous chatter with a voice of fury. "You tell me nothing . . . nothing I do not already know."

I was astonished. "But how could you? Papá did not plan to tell you!"

"Is that what he told you?" he replied coldly.

"Sí," I said, a confused look crossing my face. For a moment I was stunned and simply gaped at him.

"Let us walk," he said. "I don't want to stand in one place too long." We began to walk slowly in the direction of the house. Tomás brought his hood back up again, concealing himself.

"Tomás, you have grown so tall and handsome since I saw you last," I said, wishing that he would show some brotherly warmth to me. "It is such a great comfort to see you again."

"Perhaps it won't be when you know my errand."

"Why did you come all the way from Toledo?" I said smiling up at him.

"To procure information, you might say, that will better aid your escape," he said the word disdainfully.

"How could you know about our escape so far away in Toledo?" I asked in amazement.

"Because I have been living *here* in *Seville* for the past six months."

His words jolted me. I gasped. "You have been here in Seville for six months?"

He nodded and I stared stupidly at him from the shock of this revelation. "And never once did you come to see us? Not even at the birth of Manuel?" Now it was I who spoke coldly, angrily. "How do you think Mamá would feel if she knew?"

"I neither know, nor care."

"Tomás!" I said shocked. "Then why have you come?"

"I told you, to aid your escape. Let us just say that Father and I have been engaged in negotiations for some time. I have kept him informed of certain indisputable facts about his present situation," he said cryptically. The word "informed" leaped out at me.

"*You* have kept Papá informed, did you say? *You* have been his informant?"

"Precisely."

My mind was suddenly swirling—the memories of my parents conversations of the past weeks, the many times Papá spoke of his secret informant, Mamá not knowing who the informant was, Papá telling me how he was forced to pay off the informant with vast sums of money! It all come rushing back with sickening speed.

"So you never intended to come see Mamá or me or Manuel?" I asked with dismay.

He blushed. "I have been meeting with Father at a nearby abbey. I have been under the strict instruction of my Dominican superiors. I do nothing without their consent."

"Then you won't be coming with us tomorrow to meet Don Estaban de Gomez . . . ?" I said loudly in a rush.

"Isabel!" Tomás whispered sternly, looking all around the square, "stop babbling. Get hold of yourself."

"I-I am sorry," I said and lowered my voice to a whisper.

"I have already seen Father numerous times these past months. The two of us have been engaged in formulating the plans, but our mother knows nothing of my involvement. And you must not, *must* not tell her either!"

"Not tell Mamá? But why not?"

"It would unnecessarily upset her, that's why. She would insist upon seeing me. She would grow hysterical. She cannot be trusted not to blurt things out, don't you see." In spite of his earlier reluctance to be touched by me, his hand was suddenly squeezing my wrist hard. "She is not to know of this meeting. Do you understand?"

"Tomás, you are hurting me," I protested.

He dropped my arm and looked away with disgust.

"At least you have been helping Papá with our plans. That is a loving act of a son for a father." I said feebly.

Tomás winced at my praise. "You're a fool, little sister."

I looked at him, trying to understand him. He had once been such a quiet, earnest boy.

Now, as a man, he was more than earnest. He was intense. Intense with a smoldering arrogance I'd never seen before. But I told myself that it only mattered that he was helping us. He and his Dominican superiors.

"Oh, Tomás, don't be impatient with me. I am just so glad to see you, to know that you have been helping and planning with Papá. I won't tell Mamá because I know you don't want to hurt her feelings. That you have been doing important work and that you have been helping us plan our escape in secrecy and . . ."

"Isabel!" he said angrily, nearly shouting.

Instantly, I ceased talking.

"You must stop your incessant jabbering. Listen to me with utmost care now. I have a message for our father. There has been a sudden change of plans concerning your . . . departure . . . and there is no time to arrange another meeting—to speak to him away from the house and away from Mother. I hoped to see him myself and have waited here most of the day to see him. But I have seen him neither leave nor return to the house. Finally, I saw you come out today. I followed you hours ago to the Rodriguez house and I have waited all this time for your return," he said irritably.

"Oh, Tomás had I only known . . ." I said contritely.

He ignored this. "You must convey the change of plans to Father. You alone. Do you understand Isabel?"

I nodded, wanting to please him, to show I was worthy of being taken into his confidence.

We began to walk slowly again. Tomás held his arms inside his sleeves and turned his head ever so slightly towards me.

"About the ride with this friend of Father's, this Jew-helper—what did you say his name was?"

"You mean, Don Estaban de Gomez?" I asked.

"Estaban de Gomez," he repeated carefully. "Well . . . it must be delayed by one entire day. Do not, I repeat, do not attempt to meet de Gomez on the road to Cadiz tomorrow," he said firmly.

"Delay?" I said my heart sinking. Terrible as it was to leave, I was eager to start, to get safely underway. Delay meant a whole extra day to worry and fret!

"But Saturday was perfect, Tomás," I protested. "Don't you see, Saturday is one of Papá's big collection days. People would see that we work and ride on the . . . the rest-day of the expelled ones."

Somehow I could not bring myself to saying "Sabbath" and "Jews" around Tomás. His eyes seemed to forbid it.

"Be that as it may, it would be exceedingly dangerous for you to leave tomorrow. Just tell him this"—he paused gathering his thoughts—"this Estaban de Gomez has been delayed and will not be there until Sunday. Now repeat the message," he ordered.

"I am to tell Father that we must not leave Saturday as planned before. It would be exceedingly dangerous. Instead, we are to depart on Sunday. Estaban de Gomez will be delayed. He will not take us to Cadiz until Sunday. Is . . . is that correct?" I looked up at him.

Tomás looking ahead of him, merely nodded his head.

"And one other thing, Isabel. You must relay this message to Father. Under no circumstance, to Mother. To bring her into this now would be disastrous."

"Of course, Tomás, I understand." I added hopefully, "You will be joining us on our journey to the Port of Cadiz, on Sunday?"

He looked at me with great irritation. "What do you take me for, a Jew?"

Shamed, I lowered my eyes.

He tapped his foot impatiently a moment. "I must go now. I have been hanging about this square most of the afternoon. I have many pressing matters to which I must attend in the service of the Lord."

I looked up and nodded somberly. "I understand, Tomás."

"Now go, Isabel. Go quickly and find a way to give the message only to our father. Try to keep in mind that the success of escape now rests on your shoulders," he said ominously.

I stared at him wordlessly. And then he gave me a small shove towards the street. Another strange physical contact from the friar who was too holy to hug his sister.

In a last parting attempt to revive our sibling love, I clasped his arm and squeezed it affectionately. Even that mild gesture made him tense and pull back.

"Oh, Tomás, I know I'm not supposed to. It's just that we might not meet again in ever so long."

My mind flashed back to the age of eight when I had wept at his leaving home. Seized with a wild impulse, I reached deep into my pocket. "Look!" I drew out the family icon. "It's the family mezuzzah," I said softly, "the golden mezuzzah of Bisabuela Ruth. See here, carved upon it, one of the sacred names of God in Hebrew." I looked at him intently, trying to show him the wonder of our mysterious shared past.

Instantly, I knew I had made a grave error. He stared hard at it, his lips curled in a look of total disgust, and backed away several steps.

"I just thought you might like to see our heirloom. . . ." my voice trailed off.

"Isabel, go home now and put that ungodly thing away!"

Stung, I stuck it hastily back into my pocket. Ungodly yes, to most of Seville, but not to Marranos who loved the One God over all, I wanted to say in protest. For once I restrained myself. "Is that everything, Tomás?"

"That is everything."

"But Tomás . . . didn't you . . . didn't you say that you came not only to give information but also to get information from Papá?"

"Oh, I have procured all the information I need," he said, backing away.

"But what . . . ?" I started to ask what information he meant. But he had already turned and was moving swiftly away from me in the opposite direction.

As I stared at the retreating figure, he looked like any monk, moving purposefully down the streets of Seville.

Thirteen

We Are Betrayed

P ascua, who was sweeping in the parlor, heard me return home and came to the hallway. "Buenas noches, Mistress!" I answered breathlessly. "They are upstairs? Mamá, Papá?" I lifted the skirt of my blue silk and started up the stairs by twos, not waiting for her answer.

Pascua was surprised at my haste. "The party of Señorita de Rodríguez, it was not pleasing?" she called after me.

Pascua liked nothing more than to hear the details of my comings and goings. My life seemed little more to her than a gay stream of amusements and fiestas. How astonished she would have been by the truth, that it was I who now envied her. She was safe from the terrors of expulsions, burnings, and dangerous secrets. The Holy Office seldom troubled servants or slaves, who owned nothing to confiscate—who were themselves valuable properties. After our absence was discovered, the servants under our roof would all be sold to another house of wealth, where they would be taken care of in return for their labors.

I paused impatiently at the top of the stairs, and called down, "Teresa's party was *buena*, Pascua. I . . . I shall tell you all about it later."

Mamá pulled me inside before I even knocked upon the door. "Oh, thank heavens, Isabel," she said. She had been waiting anxiously for my return, wanting all the family safely around her in the final hours of our preparations. I watched as she brought the bar down across the door. How strange to see my mother act so guardedly. She had always created a feeling of such openness and trust in the household.

I stood breathless inside the door and gaped. Our traveling possessions were strewn about everywhere. The floor, the bed, the chairs, Papá's writing desk—all were spread with coins, jewelry, swaddling and clothing for Manuel, vials and small pouches of medicinal herbs, nuts, dried fruits, and aged summer sausages from our pantry. I shuddered to see Papá's dagger, the one he carried to his tax collections as a safety measure against robbers. So that would be going too. Even Mamá's precious pouches of cinnamon and pepper were there. I realized that spices could be sold for a hefty price, like jewels. The sheer volume of items that Mamá had put out so hopefully would never fit into a few tiny pockets and two large food baskets. She flitted to and fro in a state of confusion, picking up and examining items only to put most down, shake her head, or throw her hands up in despair. I could see it was a terrible ordeal for Mamá to decide which few things from our large and grand household must be chosen for our journey.

"Papá, where is he?" I asked.

She put her finger to her mouth in a gesture of quiet and pointed across the room. In the little alcove by the open window, Manuel was sleeping peacefully in his basket. And then I heard the sound of light snoring. Papá! Behind the bed curtains, Papá was sleeping soundly. I was glad, for I knew he was exhausted from many nights of uneasy sleep. But with a sinking heart I realized my urgent message from Tomás would have to wait.

So, I began to help Mamá. For several hours we sewed pockets and quietly discussed the things we must take. She forgot to ask about Teresa's party; I did not bother to tell her. I realized such things were no longer important to our lives.

I watched anxiously for any sign of Papá's awakening. As the early evening slipped by, my excitement at seeing Tomás faded, replaced by the memory of his cold and forbidding face.

Mamá and I slipped downstairs for a light supper laid by the servants. The cook and the scullery were about so we spoke only of the pleasantries of Teresa's party, the puppet show, and dainty sweets.

We returned to the bedchamber and still Papá slept. Mamá urged me to go to sleep early, but how could I sleep with so important a message to relay? Wearily, I took up needle and thread once again, while Mamá nursed Manuel. It was well past dark and the candles were lit when Papá at last roused himself awake. He greeted me smilingly, stretching, looking more refreshed than I'd seen him in days.

"Papá," I said eagerly, kissing him on the cheek. "You're awake at last."

"Awaking, my pet, to your sunny face, is better than the morning sun," he said smiling sleepily, noting the darkness outside the window.

"Papá?" I got down on my knees and gently shook his shoulder. "I want to tell you about Teresa's party. There is much to tell. Come downstairs and I'll fix you something to eat. You even slept through supper!"

He nodded and yawned but made no move. Instead, to my dismay Papá asked me to bring him Manuel, which I did reluctantly. I watched restlessly as he talked and cooed to him, showing no sign of rising from his bed.

Wild with impatience, I shook his arm. "Please, Papá, let me lay your supper for you. You must be so hungry. There is mutton pie and ale," I said imploringly.

"Go Paulos. Isabel's right," Mamá said from the other side of the room, biting off the end of a thread. "You haven't eaten since noon."

Papá yawned. "Oh, all right; perhaps in a few minutes, when I get my appetite back." He kept on smiling at Manuel, who smiled and blew small bubbles back and held Papá in his spell.

Desperate, I tried dropping a hint of what I had to convey without arousing Mamá's interest. But it came across as a string of barely coherent babbling.

"Papá, do you think Manuel will look like his brother, Tomás? Of course, I haven't seen him in so long and have forgotten what he looks like. But even if I did, I hear that they change the look of a person at the abbey, shaving the face and cutting the hair in a circular way. Still, the baby's face is so fat and the face of a man so thin and angular . . ."

My hint at last took root. Papá looked up sharply and stared at me. "How do you know so much how a monk looks?" he asked.

I leaned close and whispered, "Because I have *seen* one who resembles him, greatly."

Papá, looking distressed, glanced across the room at Mamá, who was humming to herself, oblivious to our low talk.

He got up swiftly, laid the baby back in his basket, and said aloud, "Well, I do need a stretch, after all. Come, Isabel, I think I'm ready for that supper you promised. We shall return soon, Love, to help you." He picked up a candle. Mamá nodded distractedly and we pulled the door shut, waiting for her to get up and bar it again on the other side.

We crept downstairs to the deserted kitchen. As Papá checked carefully to see that all the servants had gone to bed, I cut a large slice of meat pie and poured the ale.

"Well?" he whispered as he picked up the fork and began to eat.

In low, excited whispers I told him everything—my shocking meeting with Tomás on the plaza, the sudden change of plans, the revelations that he was the informant, that he had been in Seville six months secretly helping Papá. Even in the half-light of the candle I could see the change in Papá's face. It was no longer full of restfulness and hope, but grim. He pushed the half-eaten plate away, slumped forward, his head in his hands.

"No, no, Mío Dios, no!" He pulled and tore at his hair.

"What is it, Papá?"

He looked up, a wild, desperate look on his face. "Isabel, Tomás lied to you. He could not possibly have changed any plans with Estaban de Gomez, nor delayed our departure for a day."

"Why not?" I said my heart skipping a beat.

"Because I never told him!"

"You never . . . ?" I did not fully understand.

"Isabel, he never knew that we were actually leaving tomorrow. He never even knew the name of Don Estaban."

I thought back to the conversation. " . . . This friend of Father's, this Jew-helper—what did you say his name was?" Tomás had asked. I remember the sly face, not meeting me full in the eyes as he asked. And I had answered, "Estaban de Gomez." A sickening feeling hit deep in the pit of my stomach. Something was wrong. Terribly wrong.

"But Papá," I laid a hand upon his bent back, trying to assure him, trying to assure myself, "it is our own Tomás who helps us, no?"

"Help?" he said looking up dazed at me. In the candlelight I was shocked to see that his eyes were brimming with tears. Then it all came starkly clear: Tomás's cold, unfeeling gaze, the refusal to face Mamá, the sly questions about Don Estaban, about Papá and his teachings. The way I told him everything—everything about our escape plans. It was *I* who had betrayed all those things to Tomás, told him things he did not know, watched him gathering his bits and pieces of information just the way the Holy Office spies did before condemnation. Tomás—my own brother—had turned evil, had become one of them—the torturers, inquisitors, lighters of human pyres!

"Oh Papá! Forgive me, forgive me, what have I done!" my voice rose in panic and terror.

"Sh-sh-sh, Little Queen, you'll rouse the servants." He took me in his arms. He stroked my hair as the tears flowed from me. "Sh-sh-sh, it's not your fault. You could not have known. He would have found another way if you hadn't come along . . . Little Queen, sh-sh-sh. . . ." Little Queen—a name I hadn't heard in years. The name he had called me when I was small to teach me I had been named in honor of the great Spanish Queen, Isabel of Castille. The queen who now wanted Isabel Caruso de Carvallo out of Spain.

"What will he do to us, Papá?"

Papá took a deep swallow of ale. "I am afraid he means to bring the Holy Office to our doorstep. His message of a change of plans was only a ploy, an excuse to accost you, to come and question you. How wickedly clever my son has become!"

"You mean that is why he came home to Seville?" I said, wiping my face on my sleeve. "To hurt us, his family?"

"I fear so. Months ago, he showed up in Seville. He had come all the way from Toledo to tell me that it was bad enough for him to live with the knowledge that he was tainted with the blood of Jewish ancestors, but even worse to live with the shame of knowing his present family were Marranos. He told me he was reporting me to the Holy Office and that only if I begged public forgiveness for embracing Judaism might I save all of us from arrest."

I looked at Papá in horror. "What did you say?"

"I begged him to consider your innocence, the love of his mother whom he once adored, the well-being of the baby brother who is his own flesh and blood. I reminded him of my long and loyal service to our Catholic Majesties, the honor of our—and his—family name. For months I have secretly met and tried to negotiate with him," Papá said with despair.

"Did he not once reconsider?"

Papá took another gulp of ale. "Tomás, he-he was completely unmoved! He told me that the salvation of our souls was more important than the salvation of our bodies—that in fiery death, we would be purified, our souls cleansed in purgatory." I held a trembling hand over my mouth, to keep myself from crying out.

"All the time we met, he showed not the slightest interest in seeing his own mother, sister, or infant brother. Indeed, he seemed to want to avoid it like the plague. I can imagine how ashamed he would be to face his mother as he truly is. No, he would prefer to work from afar and avoid his own painful confrontations with his conscience. The Dominicans have worked their will very well on my son," my father said bitterly, his face set hard and grim. "They have earned their nickname *Domini-Cannes.*"

"What does Domini-Cannes mean, Papá?"

"It's Latin for 'dogs of the Lord.' They are called that because they have become the most fanatical sect of monks in Spain, sniffing out victims for the Holy Office like dogs. I had hoped, prayed, that the money would change his mind."

"The money?" I said, confused.

"Sí. I began to offer Tomás large sums of money—more and more of my personal tax commissions. Suddenly my son had a change of heart. He began to declare how merciful the Holy Office would be, how indulgently they would judge my 'minor offenses.' As the months passed, more money went from my hands to his. Finally Tomás said that the Holy Office had agreed to allow Mamá and you children to go free. The only question remaining was what to do with me. My freedom, he said, was less certain."

"Papá!" I grabbed onto his hand.

He shook his head. "I thought, perhaps, more money, my personal fortune, could secure my freedom, too. Each time he came to speak to me, I handed over to him more and more of my fortune in silver and gold. Each time he took my money, he said things looked brighter and that the Holy Office was considering total leniency for me, for all of us.

"Oh, Isabel, I walked away victorious, emptied of nearly all my worldly fortune, knowing they would take my house and servants. But I thought let them have it all if they will let us all go. I realized the time had come to leave—before the Jews are all gone from Spain, before

Tomás and his superiors in the Holy Office grew tired of our negotiations. I knew from my old acquaintance, Estaban de Gomez, how many Marranos simply melded in with the Jews and escaped with them. Tomás must have become suspicious that we might try this too." He ran his hand through his hair in despair. "Now I know the truth. I am too great a prize for them to let go. . . ."

"Oh no, Papá." A queer sensation seized my stomach—spasms.

"You have always been my strong daughter. You must be strong for me now. . . ."

Suddenly, I was sick, horribly sick. I ran to the scrap barrel and began retching, my knees barely holding me as I braced myself upon the edges of the barrel.

Papá was quickly at my side with cool rags wet from the water jug. When the worst of the sickness passed, he blotted my face and neck and helped me to a chair. "Take deep breaths, Isabel, bend over for a moment. It will pass," he said soothingly.

The next hour went by in a fog, my head aching. I remember Papá helped me up to bed and pressed more compresses to my head. He sat with me, soothed me. Mamá came looking for us. She entered my bedchamber and stared down at me. "Tomorrow of all days we need our rest, Paulos," she chastised, unsuspecting of the truth. "Time enough for long talks when we're on the road."

"You're right, Maria dear. Isabel has just been a trifle ill. It is overtiredness and too much food at Teresa's," he said. "Go on to bed. I will be there in a moment."

As soon as she closed the door, Papá leaned toward me and spoke in a soft caressing voice, "We will try to proceed as planned, my dearest, just before dawn. It's as early as we dare depart, without arousing suspicion. But if something . . . should . . . by chance, happen to me, you, my brave daughter, must be strong. Like your namesake Ruth, you will help your mother and Manuel take refuge among the Jews. Where the Jewish ones go, you, my family must go."

"Oh, but nothing must, Papá!" I sat up, tensed again, but he soothed me back down on the pillows.

Then he said with eyes full of love, "I am going in to speak to your mother, now, to tell her all that you've told me. You will rest and gain back your strength. In a little while, I'll be back to awaken you. . . . There, there." I tried to resist, tried not to be lulled to sleep, "Relax, my pet, relax now. I will send for a carriage at dawn. Sleep now, my blessed daughter, Ruth. All will be well. All is in Adonai's hands. . . ." He was stroking my forehead . . . gentle, mesmerizing strokes . . . smoothing the hair back from my forehead . . . lulling me . . . till I found myself plummetting into the dark, cool abyss of sleep.

○

I was dreaming a dream of many sounds: First I heard the soothing, lilting sounds of nuns singing the Ladymass, then the chanting of monks in prayer, the sounds of their high, gentle male voices lifting my spirits and my eyes upward toward the heavens. I was in church looking into the carvings of angels and cherubs on the chapel walls. Suddenly, I was standing in the hall of sanbenitos. Staring into the hideous yellow shrouds that I had seen on the living condemned ones! It was the dead shrouds themselves from which the chanting emanated!

I ran out of the church into the churchyard and the sounds changed to bells, deafening shattering bells, threatening to shatter my ears, as if I were trapped in the bell tower. I ran through streets of fire and smoke calling "Mamá, Papá, Teresa!" like a lost child looking for loved ones. Once again the sounds changed and I heard screaming and angry shouting. Where was I? It was the roar of a mob, a sound of piercing hatred and mayhem. The auto-de-fé! I heard a voice shout: "Burn the Jew!" I turned to see the speaker and found myself staring into the face of old Doña Martinez! She looked thrilled and overjoyed at the sight of the fires!

I followed her gaze and in shock beheld the burning of Maria de Torres! And then the sound of fire became a deafening crackle in my ears!

I must awaken or drown inside the deafening sounds.

Then, "Little Queen, Little Queen where are you?" It was Papá's voice. He could not find me.

"Papá, Papá. I am here! I am here!"

○

"Huuuuuuuh!" I gasped. I had come awake in a cold sweat. I sat up, putting my hand on my chest, feeling the frantic beating of my heart, wishing my room was not so pitch black. I cocked my ear to the night. There was only the peaceful creaking of the walls, the slight rustling of leaves outside my window. I relaxed back onto the pillows, my heart steadying, sleepiness reclaiming me.

I could not see the sand trickling in the hour glass by my bureau, but I doubted if it was more than two or three o'clock in the morning. Soon, very soon, Papá would come in to wake me for leaving! Drowsiness dragged me back towards the cavern of sleep. How long I stayed there I do not know. But something brought me back. My eyes fluttered open. I listened in the dark. It came from the open window. A passerby, a distant dog bark? No. It was something else—the sound of horse hooves upon cobblestones not far away.

I sat up, wide awake, my body knowing more than my befuddled brain. Strange, they were not the usual leisurely clop-clop of carriages being pulled slowly towards the plaza. I cocked my ear. These were brisk hooves, horses being sent swiftly along the street—clip-clop, clip-clop, clip-clop—as if the rider hastened towards his destination with urgency.

Then I heard not one, but several riders on horses, moving forward, growing closer. I sat up stiffly as the horses trotted up the street towards us. Could it be business at this hour of the night? A doctor fetched perhaps, on horseback, and coming to tend someone sick in the barrio? But this was three, four horses. Unless . . . unless . . .

And then I was up, pulling the silk screen away from the window, leaning out into the darkness, staring with a mingling of fear and uneasy premonition. Shadowy figures on horses! Torches held high! As my eyes adjusted to the night, I counted five horsemen. They had stopped at the very gate to our house! Was I awake or was this, I prayed, still my nightmare?

One torch-bearer looked up. I pulled back fearfully lest I be seen. What now? Some urgent court business summoning Papá? It had happened on occasion. I tried to calm myself. But it could be that other thing with the Holy Office. Oh please, not this day. Not this day of days!

Then there was sharp rapping at our door. Dear God!

"Open up in the name of the queen's soldiers!"

I ran out into the dark hallway. I told myself these were just impatient court guards sent to fetch my father on royal business. But a chaos of voices arose around me—stamping feet, the servants running upstairs from below, Mamá and Papá scuffling in the dark upstairs hallway, donning robes, Papá shouting, "Maria, go back, go back to the children!"

"No, Paulos, don't go, do not, I beg you!" Mamá was shouting back.

My eyes, adjusting to the dark, saw that she grasped Papá's arm. Manuel left alone in the midst of the uproar, shrieked in terror.

"Maria, whatever happens, my wish is for you to go with the children as planned." He held her tightly, and kissed her face a half-dozen times.

Mamá, slid to the floor and grasped his knees. "No, Paulos, please no!"

Papá saw me frozen with terror in the hallway.

"Maria," I heard him say, "it is no use. There is nowhere to go, nowhere to hide. This way you and the children will go. It is destined to be. I have known it was coming. I have hoped and prayed it would not. But it has been arranged by forces beyond my control," he said in a strangely calm voice.

"Oh, Paulos, you have known? You have waited? You have let them come?" She was weeping.

"If I had not tried to deal with them, they would have come for all of us, even the children!"

At last I awoke to the grim truth. Not royal business, not a dream, but the hideous arrest of my father! Papá had known all along it was hopeless. He could only hope that in giving himself up, Tomás would honor his promise to let his mother and siblings go. He never even told Mamá last night after putting me to sleep. He had simply gone back to bed and laid down next to Mamá and waited for the Holy Office of the Inquisition to come!

"Papá!" I ran to him.

"My Ruth!" He held me tightly to his chest. "Go with your mother and baby brother to the Jews. Get to the carriage and find de Gomez on the road to Cadiz! Live. Live the life you were destined for as *Ruth*. Promise me! It is the only thing that can help me endure what is coming!"

"Sí, Papá! I will . . . I will. Oh, I love you."

"And I love you my only daughter." He drew me to him, squeezing me till I could barely breathe.

Then it began again . . . the pounding of doors, glass shattering somewhere, the sound of the servants crying, shouting, and moaning below the stairs!

"What shall we do, Master?" someone shouted up to us.

"I am coming!" He bent down and pulled Mamá, weeping uncontrollably to her feet, giving her a last full kiss on the lips before she slumped back to the floor and wept, her head and hands bent to the floor. I tried in vain to comfort her. And then, before we knew it, he was gone from us, down the stairs. Mamá held her hands out towards the stairs, her mouth open, screaming, "Paulos! Paulos!"

"Open the door!" Papá shouted.

On the other side the soldiers were pounding, trying to break down the door! A servant fumbled with the latch. And then came the dreaded sound of the heavy door swinging open followed by the clunk of boots, the rattle and clank of heavy metal. Shaking, I perched at the top of the stairs and stared down. Five men crowded into the entryway. My father stood tall, his head high, shoulders squared. A monk unrolled a scroll and began to read as three soldiers surrounded Papá, and another monk, head down, shoulders slumped, stood in the open doorway.

"Paulos de Carvallo," a high voice began to intone without emotion as the servants wept softly, *"in this month of July and year of Our Lord fourteen ninety-two, you stand accused of Judaizing the Holy Christian Faith, practicing the demon faith of Moses for many years while professing the faith of Holy Jesus. You have been witnessed corrupting the young by despicable teachings of said faith on the premises of your very own home. It has been reported that for years you have lit candles and uttered blessings in your hidden cellar on Friday nights—a practice associated with the execrable Sabbath of Jewdom. On numerous occasions you have been seen washing the hands before eating and after, as the practice of the Jew, and putting on clean and new clothes to be seen on your person upon Saturdays and other days associated with execrable Jewdom. In addition, as Chief Agent of Tax Collections, you have disrupted the collecting of the king's taxes every year for five years on the Jews' holiday known as Yom Pikker."*

"Yom *Kippur*, you stupid Dominican backside of a goat!" Papá shouted in a voice reeking contempt. A guard moved forward as if to strike him, but the other monk standing quietly in the doorway, held up his hand to halt them. Even so, the soldiers seized him and chained his hands behind his back.

The monk looked up, glowered at Papá, unraveled a bit more parchment, and continued to read. *"And finally, it has been discovered by highly reliable sources within the Dominican Order that you have plotted to illegally leave the country with said queen's taxes, for the purposes of engaging freely in more Jewish abominations. . . ."*

I listened to the very things I had revealed yesterday to my brother and regarded the quiet monk, who stood stiffly in the doorway. As the reading continued to drone on, Mamá moved trembling down the steps, watching in horrified fascination. Manuel had quieted down or fallen back to sleep in exhaustion. I stared intently at the shadowy figure of the other monk. He was tall and slim, his head cocked a certain way under his hood. Something about the figure and the way he held himself grabbed my full attention. But in the dimness I wasn't sure.

"You are here ordered to appear before a Tribunal of the Holy Office of the Inquisition, Friday next and to be bound over immediately for imprisonment in the Castle Triana."

"No-oo-oo," Mamá cried out and hastened the rest of the way down the steps until at the bottom a guard moved forward to stop her.

Papá's head jerked up. "Who accuses me?" he demanded.

It was then that I saw the head of the thin monk jerk ever-so-slightly upwards also. In spite of the guard, Mamá moved towards the thin figure of a monk. Staring at him, she snatched down his hood. Even in the dim light after five long years, Mamá knew who it was.

"Tomás!" she began, "Tomás, my own son!" she screamed with a rage I had never before seen in her. All eyes were riveted on her. "You have turned your very own father in to the Holy Office of the Inquisition!"

"Mother," my brother said, unruffled, looking away and replacing the hood over his head.

"Maria, go back, it is no use!" Papá implored.

Mamá looked back and forth between father and son and then collapsed at my brother's feet. "No, no, I beg you my son, Tomás, let him go!"

Tomás winced at Mamá's screams. The other monk watched with interest, as if the scene were a diversion, an entertainment. Angrily, Tomás spat out, "I have no father on earth. My only Father is in Heaven, *Jesu Cristo*, the one true Father, the Son of God! And in this world, he who does not love the One True Father, burns. As it is written in John, chapter fifteen, verse six . . ." Mamá stood there in shock, looking aghast at the face of her son, a face composed of hatred and violence.

"Spare us the Sunday sermon!" my father broke in. "We have made a bargain, Tomás. To have me, instead of them. I have kept my end, now you do yours. Let us be off. I cannot wait to begin my imprisonment. I spit on your false father. I spit on you, my false son!"

The soldiers dragged him out the door.

"Papá, oh dear, Papá!" I called out, weeping.

Mamá and I ran out the door as they bound his arms behind his back and hoisted him up on a horse behind a soldier.

"Oh Papá, I will come and see you in prison!" I shouted.

"No Isabel, no! It is useless! Promise me you will go! Maria! Take the children and go! To the boats, to the expelled ones! I beg of you! Promise me. . . ."

Those were the last words I ever heard him say. A mounted soldier trotted up next to him, stuffed a thick gag in his mouth, and tied a scarf around his head. My heart shattered like glass into a million smashed shards!

I ran beside the horse, crying, "Oh my Papá!" And I stroked his leg until the soldier in front of him thrust his sword menacingly in my direction. I leaped back and turned to Tomás.

"I hate you, Tomás!" I shouted and spat in his direction.

Tomás lifted himself easily onto his horse, never even acknowledging me or meeting my eyes. Then Mamá ran to him and grabbed onto his boots. "Oh please, my son, please! Have mercy!"

"Do not touch me, again! I am a man of the cloth!" he said savagely as he booted her roughly to the ground.

In anguish, I ran first to Mamá, who lay weeping on the ground, then back towards Papá, whose horse was being led away. But when I tried once more to approach him, a mounted soldier blocked my way.

My heart about to burst I thought, what final words, dear God, could I say to my beloved father? As if God heard my plea, the answer flew instantly to mind.

"Papá!" I shouted with all my might, all my heart: *"Shema Yisra'el, Adonai Elohanu, Adonai Echod!"* I said it again and again until he turned his head in my direction and nodded vigorously to me, even bound and gagged as he was.

"Don't press your luck, little sister," Tomás said with disgust.

The older monk leaned sideways and said something in the ear of Tomás.

Then my brother—may God damn him to eternal hell to match my earthly one—without so much as a glance in our direction, called out a harsh, "We got what we came for. Now let's be off!"

And all five horses turned and galloped dreadfully away.

fourteen

We Begin Our Escape

Grief-stricken, Mamá and I staggered up the walkway. From the house of the kindly old hidalgo couple next door, I heard a creaking shutter. I looked up hoping the sound of my weeping mother would bring their help, a kindly word of sympathy, a pronouncement of their horror at the terrible thing that had been done to Papá. But we were met only by silence and I realized the noise had been the firm closing of shutters. The Caruso de Carvallos were now to be shunned. We had become a house of dishonor, a house to which the damning Holy Office had come.

Mamá dragged herself up the stairs to Manuel who was now wailing. I was too much in shock to follow her. Instead, I paced downstairs from room to room stepping over shards of glass where the soldiers had broken a window. I called out the names of several house servants, "Pascua? Alonso? Consuela?" But they refused to come out of hiding. I heared their muffled cries in different parts of the house.

Suddenly, out of the gloom, came dear old Marta, carrying a candle, hobbling towards me like an angel of mercy. She set down the candle and held out her arms. In agony and relief, I ran to her, throwing my own arms around her and sobbing. We hugged and embraced, weeping in each other's arms. "Oh my poor mistress!" she said stroking my back with her bony hands. I held onto her in desperation until at last she pushed me gently away. Wiping my eyes, I looked at her imploringly.

"Marta?" I said in a weak, pinched voice.

Tears streaming from her eyes, she stood before me, ringing her hands. "What will become of us Mistress?" she sobbed lightly, "Oh what will become of us?" And she wrung her hands over and over, her bent back shaking.

Stunned, I stared at her. Dear, frail Marta was as lost and confused as I! In a flash, I understood: she had never known any other home but Mamá's. She faced her own terror, the prospect of old age, without the loving care of my mother and father, without knowing what would become of her. Now *I* was her mistress and she looked to guidance from me.

Better than a slap in the face, it was Marta's woe that brought me back to myself. She had made me realize that there was no help for me, except my own. I had never done anything alone without the instruction and protection of many adults. Now I was truly, utterly alone. My father's words, "the age of Jewish adulthood," had an urgent, new meaning.

With a calm I did not feel, I put my arm around Marta's old bent shoulders. With as much assurance as I could muster, I said, "Do not worry, Marta. There are many days of food left in the larders. Mamá and Manuel and I . . ." I thought for a moment. "We will go to the family of my father's sister. Some officials, perhaps monks . . . will soon come and take you to another nice house. Sí, all will be well for you and the others." Although I knew this brought her little comfort for the sting of losing her home, she stopped weeping and wringing her hands, and I was calmer for having calmed her.

"Gracias, good Mistress," she said simply. Sniffing, she picked up her candle and tottered slowly back down the hall towards the servant's quarters.

I went upstairs. Manuel was still wimpering. Mamá, lying down in shock and grief, seemed not to hear him, so I picked him up and rocked him until he mercifully fell back to sleep.

While Mamá and the baby slept, I paced the floor of my bedchamber trying to think what to do. At first, I thought that we might stay in the house, for a day or two to recover. But quickly I realized we could not, dare not, stay. All came clear to me: We were being left alone—at least for the moment—because of a bargain Papá had struck with Tomás. His life in exchange for ours!

How long would my brother or the Holy Office honor that bargain? I knew that if I shut my exhausted eyes, I might awaken to find the Holy Office coming back to claim our house, our servants, all our valuable worldy possessions, Papá's tax routes, even ourselves! We must go today—now—this very day. But where? To my father's sisters, my aunts? After the betrayal of my own brother, could I trust my aunts and uncles? Would they still welcome us with open arms? And would not our sudden presence endanger them with the Holy Office? One thing I knew, I could not possibly return to my old life as a Marrano. No, it was clear that I, Ruth de Cojano, must do as Papá said. I must get us to the Jewish ones!

The Jewish ones! In all the chaos, I had forgotten. If we were to leave the country at all . . . I tried to figure in my head . . . today, Saturday was the twenty-eighth day of July, the day we were to meet Esteban de Gomez! What if we didn't manage to meet up with him after all? Could Mamá and I and the baby reach the port in time on foot? The Jews had been granted one final extension till August second. That was five days from now. Five days to reach the Port of Cadiz before the ships set sail. But Papá had warned against trying to find space past July thirty-first. With a baby, the crowd would be crushing. We *must* find a way to meet up with Esteban de Gomez as planned!

In a rush of frantic activity, I tiptoed into my parents' bedchamber and threw on the thick cotton shifts that held all our sewn-in pockets, followed by my petticoats, my traveling suit, my boots. I hadn't realized how hard the task of dressing myself was, without Pascua. With Papá's dagger, I mercilessly ripped apart his traveling clothes to get at the coins and jewels Mamá had sewn into his shirt and vest. When I had emptied everything out and saw the torn and cut garments, I was again overwhelmed. I buried my face in Papá's dear clothes and started to weep again. But I forced myself to stop crying, reminding myself that Papá's last wish was for our safety. This fueled my determination to get Mamá and Manuel and myself to the boats. "Be strong for Papá," I told myself harshly each time I began to break down and weep.

Then I awakened Mamá. She refused to speak of departure. She sobbed, protesting that she must remain in Seville near Papá. She meant to try and have him released. In rising hysteria, she went on and on about how his friends in the court would vouch for him, how she would make them let her visit Papá in the dungeons of Triana.

"Mamá," I begged her, "it is hopeless. They will not let you see him; they will only imprison you too. Oh Mamá, the Holy Office will never let him go. No one would dare vouch for him. Everyone in Seville is afraid of the Holy Office. Soon they will take our house, all our servants, everything. We will be penniless and on the streets. Please Mamá, we must go now!" I grasped her arm in desperation. "Papá told me that the only thing that could help him endure what was coming was the knowledge that Manuel and you and I would escape with the Jewish ones."

The house fell eerily silent as Mamá lay quietly thinking. At last she sat up and took my hand. "You are right, my angel, so strong and determined like your father." Her eyes smiling through tears, she stroked my hand and said despairingly, "I cannot imagine life without my Paulos. For myself I care nothing. But for you and Manuel . . . we will go." Her lips were quivering. I nodded with relief and helped her into her traveling suit.

I ran downstairs and found Juanito, one of our scullery boys, about to stuff food in his mouth from the untended larders. Bribing him with food and the promise of more later, I sent him to the livery to fetch us a coach not far away. I was nearly wild with impatience waiting for him to return. He came back an hour later with a battered, old covered wagon and horse with an equally weather-beaten driver. They came clopping slowly down the street and I ran outside to direct the driver to the back of the house where we would be less noticed by prying eyes.

Mamá handed me the two large food hampers and asked me if I could fill them. I nodded, knowing she wanted as little to do with her beloved house as possible now. In the larders, I filled the baskets of food with fruits, hard sausages, skins of water and wine, a handful of nuts, a round of cheese, two mutton pies, two long loaves of bread, pouches of tea, a small crock of fruit preserve, anything I could stuff into the baskets. At the last moment, I paused, remembering that Jews do not eat pork. I picked up the sausages and turned them over and over. Such an everyday part of a Christian pantry. But now they would certainly look suspicious to the Jewish ones. Reluctantly I took all but one out of the basket. They would have been long-lasting assurance against starvation, lasting longer than any of the other food. But now, I reminded myself, we must begin to act, to think, like Jews. I would keep just one, in case anyone questioned our destination. I could wave the sausage about and speak about a picnic in the country, then toss the sausage away, before we reached the Jews in Cadíz. I searched through the baskets. There were other restrictions on food that Jews abided by, but I simply did not know them. Papá had mentioned several things in passing. But I didn't see how I could risk leaving any more food behind. On top and around the food I stuffed as much of Manuel's swaddling, sleeping gowns and linens as I could. Then I hauled the baskets out the scullery door and hoisted them into the wagon.

Mamá had gotten herself and Manuel into the wagon. She had walked down the stairs and out the back door and never looked back at the house.

The wizened old driver balked at the distance I proposed, even with two pieces of silver. It was only after I promised a third piece, at destination's end, that he agreed to make the trip.

As the wagon clattered down the street, I thought of a dozen things I should have brought—tinder box, pillows, Papá's dagger! But I dared not take the time to go back to fetch them. I looked warily around for soldiers, wondering if we would truly be allowed to leave. If Tomás or the Holy Office had a change of heart, a woman, a baby, and a girl in a rustic wagon from Seville would not be hard to find.

Hours later—long past the time that we were to have met Estaban de Gomez—our wagon jolted over the hard dirt roads. Mamá and I slid back and forth on the unpadded wooden seat, bumping into the hard sides, the baskets, each other. Holding my baby brother, I tried to brace myself with my feet, but Mamá did not seem to care how she was tumbled about. Once, jolted hard, her head hit the hard frame that held the dirty woolen wagon covering over us, but she barely noticed, just winced, staring vacantly into space.

"Mamá!" I reached to touch her, but she barely acknowledged me.

She was a broken woman now that Papá was gone. All her strength and courage for our escape these past weeks had come from a fervent belief that no matter how hard our life as Jews in a strange new land might be, we would all be together, with Papá to guide us.

But in the last hours she had sunk into a well of grief so deep that I feared for her. She held the baby so listlessly that I finally took him from her.

Parting the filthy woolen covering, I stared out into the empty fields before us. The sun hung hotly over the late afternoon horizon. It was Saturday, our planned day of escape. If all had gone according to plan, I thought bitterly, the four of us would have left at dawn and driven to the country where Papá would have collected his final taxes. Then, we would have enjoyed a leisurely lunch inside a fine carriage while we were driven to the road to Cadiz where Estaban de Gomez would have met us in the early afternoon.

By now I was sure Don Estaban had given up and gone away. No nobleman would hang about conspicuously for very long. Too many soldiers and spies were rumored to be about, and we were still leagues and leagues from the road to Cadiz. Our battered old covered wagon with its tired nag moved across the fields at a maddeningly slow pace. In the beginning of the journey, the driver had followed the banks of the Guadilquivir River, which snaked through the countryside from Seville to the gulfcoast of Cadiz. It was the surest way, but also the longest and slowest. When I complained, the driver mentioned a shortcut across the countryside. He said it was a more direct path to Cadiz, which would save us the long meandering river path. That manuever cost me another silver coin, which the driver pocketed immediately.

Even so, I had little hope of meeting Don Estaban now. With only two days left, my worst fear was not making it to the boats in time and I grew more worried about Mamá who seemed to sink deeper into silent despair now that we were far from home. From the pain in her eyes, I could see that she was back in Seville, searching for my father in dark and cold castle dungeons.

Manuel, who had slept most of the time in my arms, awoke and began to fuss, his tiny fist in his mouth, wanting the breast. Mamá didn't seem to hear him, so lost in herself was she. "Mamá, please!" I finally said, not wanting to hear him cry again. Gently I put the baby into her arms. Listlessly she came back to herself, lifted her jacket, and nursed him.

I parted the covering again and stared out at the landscape. We drove past farms, olive fields, citrus groves, and lovely villas drenched in golden light. It was my favorite time of day when light lasts its longest. Such beauty and tranquility seemed strange against the violence that had entered our lives. Faces and scenes flashed through my mind—beloved Papá, dearest Teresa, the good servants, my many relatives, dear Tía Mathílde, carefree girlfriends in new silk frocks, even Mamá, as she used to be, tasting from the cooking pots, always preparing for a fiesta, or family gathering. I looked at her now. Every line in her face seemed etched in grief and misery.

"Mamá!" I said despondently, and put my head on her shoulder.

"Angel," she said, and patted my face.

But I felt her remoteness, as if she slid slowly away from me and Manuel. No, no! I could not let myself think such thoughts. I must think forward to the future, to a new life among the Jewish ones. Mamá would get better among them. I began to practice the Shema, again and again. This is how I kept myself from going mad like my mother and sinking into listlessness and despair. Although I managed to get Mamá to take a bit of cider, I could urge little food past her lips. I feared that if Mamá did not eat or drink, her milk would dry up and she would not be able to nurse Manuel.

At dusk—it must have neared nine o'clock in the evening—the carriage came to an abrupt halt. I leaned forward, pushing aside the filthy curtains, and saw the driver wiping his brow on his sleeve.

"Señor," I called out, "why have you stopped?"

He turned and looked at me with little expression. "This is as far as we go," he said simply.

A huge stretch of field lay before us. Far in the distance was the dusky outline of a vast forest. We were entirely in the open! I could not see a road, let alone a place where a carriage might wait.

"But this is not the road to Cadiz!"

The driver pointed a long, gnarled finger in the direction of the forest. In front of us was a dirt path, barely outlined, beaten out by many feet. It disappeared down the empty field, a narrow country path made by farmers and country folk.

In dismay, I said again, "This is not the road to Cadiz where we must be taken!"

Again, the man pointed to the path in front of us, then to the forest beyond. "This path before you goes to the forest. The road to Cadiz is in that forest. No more than four, maybe five leagues from here."

"Four or five leagues? That is a full day's journey by coach! To walk will take much longer! Oh please, Señor, you promised to drive us to the road to Cadiz. It is nearly dark. Our f-friend is waiting there. Remember, I promised you an extra coin," I said with all the authority I could muster.

"Cannot do," said the old man, without emotion.

"Why not?" I demanded.

"Two reasons," he said, showing me two gnarled fingers. "First, my horse can go no farther. He is an old man like me." The man leaned over and patted the side of his nag. "Second, I do not go near the road with Jews. Many cutthroats and thieves go there."

"But, Señor, my father said the queen's soldiers guard the roads now." It was true. The Jews had paid mighty sums to have the soldiers of the Santa Hermandad guard the roads so that they could travel to the ships unaccosted.

"I want no part of that Jew business!" His voice was sharp and insistent. And that was that. If only Papá had been there. The man wouldn't have dared to break his obligation. But then Papá would never have hired so sorry a wagon and driver. I pulled back inside.

"No?" Mamá said shaking her head and gathering Manuel closely to her.

"No," I said sighing, "the driver says we must get out. He will take us no farther. We must walk the rest of the way to the Cadiz road. He says it's in the great forest ahead of us."

She sighed wearily, then, ever-so-softly, said, "Sí," and climbed out of the wagon.

I handed Manuel to her, collected our baskets, and climbed out. Stupidly, I had already paid the driver the other coins, leaving us no way to persuade him. We stood glumly as he turned his old horse and wagon around. Without so much as a last gaze upon the little family he so casually abandoned, he slowly drove away.

We trudged for perhaps a half-league, thoroughly discouraged, sagging under the weight of our baskets of food and Manuel. I longed to strip off my heavy traveling clothes. Mamá looked wretched and miserable, too. We had little chance of reaching the forest before nightfall, even less of meeting up with Don Estaban. I counted in my head: there were five days left on the expulsion order. There *might* be time to reach the port by foot. But without Don Estaban's help or his promised change of clothes, I was no longer sure we could carry out our daring transformation from New Christians to Jews.

My heart sank even further when I remembered Papá telling me that Don Estaban had intended to introduce us to some Jewish ones traveling along the road. With our change of clothes, he would have been able to tell them we were fellow Jews who had lost our way and were in need of simple guidance to the boats. Who would believe we were Jews now with our velvet finery, hidalgo traveling suits and rosaries about us?

Nightfall was slowly overtaking us. The forest, shrouded in eerie gloom, looked more than an hour's walk away. "Oh Mamá, we will be traveling in darkness," I said worriedly.

But in a voice of defeat, Mamá replied, "No, my Angel, I can't go on. I am so tired, I feel ill. We will have to stop here for the night."

fifteen

We Are Discovered upon the Road

We stood bewildered, searching the darkening country-side for shelter. On a small rise ahead of us I spotted the silhouette of a wild olive tree. Struggling up the hill, we dropped the heavy baskets and sank down. Manuel, hungry, began to bawl, making a terrible, mournful sound in the desolate night. Mamá, struggled to settle herself in all her finery, then fumbled with her jacket to nurse him.

I regretted that I had not brought a tinder box to make a small fire. Barely able to see, I pulled food from our baskets, and we ate hurriedly, jumping in fear at every sound. I was cheered though, that Mamá showed some appetite after our long day on the road.

A crescent moon began to shine, giving us a small bit of light to settle ourselves in. I remembered a story Papá had told me of how, during the season of harvest, Jews since ancient times have eaten and slept in small wooden booths under the moon and stars. In Hebrew the booth is called a *sukkah*. It is meant to remind the Jews that God is their shelter whether they are at home in safety or homeless and wandering. Papá would have been proud of me for remembering. I looked up at the spindly branches. "Gracias, Adonai," I said quietly. Tonight, a gnarled old olive tree would be our shelter, our sukkah.

While Mamá changed Manuel's swaddling, I hung the baskets of food from a low-lying branch and hoped that this measure would keep crawling insects away. Then I spread one of Manuel's clean swaddling cloths beneath the twisted trunk of the tree.

"See, it is not so bad here?" I said, cheered by food and a bit of rest. I thought Mamá must also be cheered, but suddenly she shuddered, gasped, and began weeping.

"Oh, Mamá, don't cry! I cannot bear it." Almost as quickly as I spoke, her crying ceased. Her silence then alarmed me even more. "Put your head here, Mamá. Rest yourself on this piece of swaddling."

"Gracias, Angel," she said in a quivering voice, patting the ground, "you lie next to me."

I kissed her on the cheek and she took my hand and kissed it back. But she had no more strength for tears or words.

"I hope you feel better in the morning." I stroked her forehead as Papá had done for me only last night. Like an obedient child, she curled up, pulling the bundle of Manuel in his blanket close to her. Within minutes she and my baby brother had fallen into deep exhausted sleep.

I lay down next to Mamá, pressing closely against her curled form. In spite of my exhaustion, I lay strangely awake, overtaken with fears. I tossed and turned on the uncomfortable ground. When I thought I could endure no more, the memory of Papá's voice and the words he had taught me broke through my fear: Shema Yisra'el, Adonai Elohanu, Adonai Echad. Lying in the darkness, I had a startling realization: I could no longer say the Avé Marias. Now the Shema had entered my mind and heart, shutting away my old Catholic life. That was the final thought I had that night. At last I plummetted to sleep.

I awoke to the dusk of early morning light. For a moment, I felt the soft velvety feeling that follows refreshing sleep. Then I sat up with a gasp. All came crashing back to me: the terrible scene of Papá being taken from us, Mamá's grief and listlessness, the strangeness of fleeing from home, the long, rough wagon ride, the abandonment by the Jew-hating driver. Gently I stroked the back of my sleeping mother, then leaned over and touched the bundle with Manuel. I stared at the wild olive tree above us and at the great forest ahead of us. None of it seemed quite real, nothing except Mamá's rosary beads wrapped around her hand.

As the sky brightened, I arose stiffly from the hard earth and looked around the vast empty land. Satisfied that we were alone, I went down the hill on the other side of the olive tree and relieved myself. Then I came around, reached into the hanging basket, took a small orange, and tore off a piece of crusty bread to eat. I gazed at the great forest looming ahead, shuddering to think of traveling through the dark forest alone, unprotected. I hoped the driver was right, that the road to Cadiz was no more than two or three leagues away and that we would not have to go too deeply into the forest to find it. For I had grown up on stories—real and make-believe—of murderous bandits and evil enchanters who lurked in the forests.

I sighed. It was no longer Saturday, but Sunday—too late to meet Estaban de Gomez at the crossroads, even if we managed to find it. Without Estaban de Gomez, there would be no special Jewish folk to guide us. We would have no way of changing our clothes. We looked exactly like what we were—illegally escaping hidalgos in our dirtied finery—not humble, expelled Jews. I fingered the rosary in my pocket, mulling over our problems. The rosary! We must remember to hide or cast our rosaries and crosses away, lest they be seen by Jewish folk. Yet we dare not cast them away too quickly, lest we be recognized as Christian hidalgos, who never traveled without them. My head spun with all of the complicated decisions to be made. Yet with all this against us, I knew that survival lay in the forest ahead and on the road to Cadiz. Only days remained until the last boats for Jews, sailed. There was no time to spare!

I bent down to arouse Mamá. Her eyes fluttered open, and she looked frantically down for the baby. When she saw him, she moaned, sat up and began to weep, her face in her hands.

"Oh, Mamá, I shall weep, too," I said, tears filling my eyes.

Mamá took several deep breaths and said, "No, no, I am better." She wiped her eyes on the swaddling that had served as her pillow. She looked up at the lightening sky, then down at Manuel, who had awakened and was happily examining a blade of grass in his tiny fist. "Isabel, we must try to reach shelter today, if only for the baby. I fear for him in this heat."

"Sí, Mamá, shelter, of course, but more importantly, the ships. We have only two or three days to reach the ships!"

"Ships," she said hollowly, as if the word had no meaning.

Reluctantly she rose, ate, and drank a bit. I breathed a sigh of relief.

At last we were packed up and on our way again. As I carried my brother, shifting his weight from arm to arm, I wished we had a long shawl to fashion into a carrier such as I had seen peasant women and servants use to carry their infants.

The sun shown bright in the sky. I turned to point out a colorful field of wild flowers to cheer my mother. But I stopped when I saw that her eyes had turned into darkened caves. The old driver had underestimated or lied about the distance to the forest and the road to Cadiz. By midmorning with the sun high in the sky, the forest still seemed leagues away. The meadow before us looked parched. The low yellowed grasses waved in the dry breeze. Our thirst was constant, though we dared not drink too much and empty our precious supply. We had been forced to stop already and drink several times. Mamá spilled a little water into Manuel's mouth from the leather jug and pulled the cap down over his head to keep the sun's burning rays from his face. His eyes stayed shut against the sun's glare.

How I longed for the comforts of home. I dreamed of the little bathing tin which Pascua had filled daily with cool water and I pictured the way she sometimes tossed the rose petals laughingly over my head into the water. I could almost feel the sea sponge she used to rub my back.

We sweltered in the intense heat in our heavy traveling clothes, weighed down with our secret pockets. The sun played tricks as it distorted the look of things in the distance. Once I thought I saw a dark pool of water just beyond us, only to see it disappear as a shadow on the land. Later, I saw another black spot on the ground and thought it was an animal lumbering in our direction. Then I realized it was little more than a scrub bush tumbling along the countryside.

Giant winged insects swooped alarmingly near our heads and large bees hovered near the food baskets, causing me to drop them and jump away several times. How ill-equipped for the outside world we were.

Late in the morning we reached hot, low meadow. The forest was quite near, just one more stretch of land! But Mamá, taking turns carrying Manuel with me, was trudging slower and slower. The sun was so bright we had to squint at the forest ahead. It had lost its sinister look of last night and now appeared cool and inviting. We began walking across the last stretch of sun-baked plain between us and the forest when another black spot, another mirage of water, suddenly appeared in the distance. I tried to ignore it but noticed that it did not go away.

No, it even seemed to grow in size and as I kept my eyes pinned on the growing dot I swore it was moving!

"Mamá, do you see the black spot? Isn't it moving?"

"Moving?" she said, raising a hand to shield her eyes. "Sí," she said frowning. "What can it be?"

"A wild bull or cow perhaps?" Papá had said many such animals roamed harmlessly in the forest. "If it is a cow, perhaps we may fill one of the empty skins with milk! I have seen this done many times on the farms Papá took me to," I added hopefully.

"What if it is a beast of some other sort?" Mamá said worriedly. We were completely in the open.

We walked on, hesitantly. Then she stopped.

"Look!" she said.

As our line of vision along the narrow trail changed, so did the shape of the dark form in the distance. Now it was a box, a moving box!

"It's a wagon," Mamá said with astonishment.

"With horses," I added, staring. "Could it be the old driver coming back for us?"

"It couldn't be, Isabel. He went back towards Seville. This is coming from the forest."

The sight of the wagon gave us a new worry. Stories of innocent travelers accosted and murdered along the roads were told endlessly in Seville. Only the major roads were considered safe, because the queen had installed her army of Santa Hermandad soldiers to protect travelers. But on this narrow trail we were at the mercy of any criminal or cutthroat. With no place to hide, we could do little but continue. We walked a bit farther. The vehicle drew close. Our eyes were riveted on the horse-drawn vehicle approaching us. Mamá turned to me.

"A coach," she said, "not a wagon."

"Could they be looking for us already, Mamá?" I said in rising panic. She knew that "they" meant the Holy Office.

"No, I do not *think* so. . . ." she said hesitantly.

"Perhaps someone is taking a ride in the country, Mamá. What is so bad about that?"

"Nothing, only . . ."

"Only?"

"What should we say we're doing here? Two hidalgo females and a tiny baby?"

"Could we not be country folk walking to the nearest town, to Cadiz?" I ventured.

"In these?" she said, pulling on her long skirt of fine broadcloth, much like my own, with rich piping all around it. Even the mantillas around our heads gave away our status as rich and privileged ones.

The coach was advancing. Mamá looked frantically for a place to hide, but we were completely in the open. The coach was now so close that we could hear the thumping of the horse hooves and see the outlines of the gold heraldic design upon its side. The coach of a nobleman, perhaps even a magistrate! I wasn't sure if the driver and passengers could see us, but whether they were gentlemen, criminals or officials, we would soon be face to face.

"Perhaps if we turn and go the other way. . . ." Mamá said, Manuel in one arm, grabbing me with her other arm and pulling me off the trail. "Let's go back across the field."

We ran stumbling in the opposite direction, the sound of wheels on the trail filling our ears. Then it was upon us, the feel of dust kicking up all around us, the sound of horse hooves thumping like thunder. And then . . . amazingly . . . nothing happened. It had passed us by!

We turned and ventured a look. At that very moment, the coach slowed. The driver pulled the horses to a standstill, then turned to stare back at us.

We froze in our place. I grabbed Mamá's arm. I could not be strong for us any longer. I clung fearfully to her like a little girl, and she stiffened with Manuel in her arms but did not say a word, watching the coach turn back towards us.

"Run, Mamá!" I tried to pull her, even as I knew it was hopeless to outrun a carriage with two horses.

With sickening speed the carriage drew up and the driver, with a large purple nose and a mouth missing many teeth, leered down at us. I prepared myself for the worst. And then, most amazingly, an absurdly cheerful face popped through the curtains of the carriage window. It was a gentleman's face with large astonished eyes set over a carefully curled moustache. We each stared at one another until finally the man spoke in a high, emotional voice.

"Buenos días, Señora, Señorita, little bebé!" His eyes flitted back and forth between the two of us and rested on the baby's capped head. He peered all around us. Then, before we could reply, the head went back inside and the door with the heraldic design swung open, and out jumped a short, dapper man, meticulously groomed from his polished black boots to his pomaded hair which was combed back into neat little waves against his neck. He twisted the ends of his moustache nervously as he looked us up and down. I felt self-conscious, knowing how dirty and unkempt we looked.

He glanced around the countryside. "You are all alone?" he spoke in a nervous voice.

"We are," Mamá answered. I kept my eyes downward.

"You are not accompanied by a man?"

"No," Mamá said shakily.

"You are sure?"

She nodded.

"You-you are not hidalgos?" he asked uncertainly. Mamá looked at me fearfully. I answered, "Sí, we are hidalgos." Of course, this was apparent by our clothes, but I offered no more, not knowing what he wanted. Perhaps he was some special sort of cheerful spy the Holy Office planted to catch Marranos attempting to leave the country.

"Then, what are you doing here?" the little man stomped his foot and shrilly demanded.

"Taking a walk!" I blurted out.

Mamá looked at me in surprise but it was the only thing I could think to say.

"Out taking a *walk*?" he asked incredulously, looking at Mamá.

She nodded.

He threw up his hands and looked up at his driver and began to mutter, "Out taking a walk."

The driver smirked and echoed, "Out taking a walk—in the middle of nowhere."

The short man threw up his hands. He shook his head in disbelief, and was about to step back into his coach when suddenly, he whirled around.

"Come, come now ladies," he said in a shrill, impatient voice. "I've no time for coyness. Where is he?"

"Who?" Mamá's voice quivered.

"Are you or are you not de Carvallos from Seville? The wife and daughter and baby son of Paulos de Carvallo, chief tax collector for our majesty's royal court in Seville?"

I gasped and caught my breath. "Estaban de Gomez!" I said in astonishment.

At the mention of his name, Mamá burst out crying.

"Aha! I knew it," he said triumphantly. "What hidalgos in their right minds would wander around like lost sheep? So? What have you done with him? Come, come, tell all. Do you know what inconvenience and expense you have caused me? All yesterday, I wait at the crossroads of the Guadilquivir trail and the road to Cadiz. I wait hours beyond my common sense. Then, I put myself and my driver and horse up at an expensive inn, for how can I, a nobleman, park myself and my fine rig at a cheap place? We had to search for a good inn far off the route. Those expenses will be charged to you including the oats for the horse!" he chattered loudly and shook his finger at us. "And when I had finally started for home, here you come promenading the countryside like the queen and her entourage, as if I, Estaban de Gomez, have all the time in the world!"

Mamá wept quietly. I stood speechless. He folded his arms and tapped his feet impatiently. "There, there now, my lady, what has happened? Where is your Paulos? Out collecting the rest of his relatives, I suppose? Emptying the dungeons of Triana perhaps? Gathering the rest of Seville? Doesn't he realize that a man of business like me has a schedule to keep?"

Then it was I who wept and revealed our terrible ordeals—Papá's arrest by the Holy Office, my brother Tomás's betrayal, our own desperate escape, and, finally, the desertion of the wagon driver who, without Papá, refused to take us to the road of the traveling Jews. All the while the jaunty little man tapped his foot nervously and listened with ever widening eyes. When I had finished my tale, he clucked and shook his head.

"Tch, tch. Why am I not surprised? The upper classes all betray each other. They sell each other and their cousins, too, for a few marivedos from the Holy Office! And you gullible ones," he shook his finger at us, "you should never have trusted a Dominican! Especially your own brother and son! He bargains to get your papá as the big prize for the Holy Office and lets his mother and siblings go, eh? Typical, typical. They are all crazy, obsessed fanatics mistaking people for firewood!"

He spoke as if we had foolishly allowed ourselves to have been duped of a few gold pieces by a dishonest shopkeeper instead of having lost our beloved papá to the Inquisition. But I knew from watching his large eyes grow sad that he took pity on us, that the scolding was his peculiar way of consoling us. I found myself starting to like this long-winded man with his gold rings and large cross hanging from his velvet collar. Mamá wiped her eyes with her kerchief, and we all stared at one another with an awkward silence.

"Well, what are you waiting for?" Don Estaban cleared his throat. "The outdoors is not good for the baby. He'll melt like wax in this sun." He mopped his face with a kerchief and held the carriage door open. When we hesitated, he said, "Come, come, ladies, I haven't got all day. I'm a business man, you know, with many pressing matters awaiting my attention. By the way, you didn't forget to bring your gold, did you?" he said suspiciously, as if to imply that having failed to bring Papá, we might easily have failed to bring our money as well.

I looked at Mamá, not knowing what I should reveal, but she swiftly shook her head to say no, we hadn't forgotten. He kissed his fingers three times.

"Muy bien!" he said. "Such good thinking on your part, my lady! Impoverished hidalgos will not get very far these days, trust me."

Only then did he step back and usher us into his well-appointed coach.

Sixteen

Don Estaban Reveals Papá's Secret

Exhausted, Mamá and I settled ourselves gratefully into Don Estaban's coach. After the clattering wagon that had violently bumped and jostled us across the fields, Don Estaban's coach swayed gently through the forest, a welcome relief. With the many soft cushions and pillows lining the long seats, we were able to lay Manuel down safely between us.

Don Estaban chattered endlessly. He insisted, among other things, that without him we would never have found our way—that the forest grew dense, that the road to Cadiz lay more than a full day's journey south; that traveling through the forest to reach the road to Cadiz was much slower than the coastal road he had planned with my father. Should soldiers appear along the path, he cautioned, we must appear at leisure, like a little hidalgo family out for a Sunday ride. He finished by telling us that we wouldn't reach the road to Cadiz until sometime the next day. We would have to stay the night together, he said a trifle apologetically.

Mamá and I looked at one another. Strangely, I was glad that we had to stay with Don Estaban. I had taken a liking to the gallant little man who spoke with his hands.

"Don Estaban," I said politely, "if you don't mind my asking, are you a-a Catholic or a secret Jew?"

"I?" he asked, polishing his rings on his kerchief, "I make the usual profession to the Catholic faith. Who dares not these days? Let us just say that I am one of the few men who appreciates—to use the biblical expression—a coat of many colors. I consider myself an educated, well-traveled man who understands the virtues of many colors, many peoples. Spain, you see, was once rich with many peoples, a leader among all the Christian nations in welcoming the genius of Islam, the gifts of Judaism, the fruits of economic prosperity!" He looked straight into my eyes. "Until that silly gullible queen and her fickle husband Ferdinand began to listen to that lunatic monk, Torquemada and his Holy Office henchmen. And now? To please Torquemada, our charming Catholic monarchs have kicked out the Moors and the Jews and glory in burning half the New Christian population too! They leave the Old Christian Spaniards to sit around and stare at each other like dumb oxen, wondering where everybody went! No tradesmen, no craftsmen, no merchants, no beautiful foreign women, no lively streets of commerce. No more coat of many colors." He shook his head mournfully. "Just a nation of dumb oxen all the same color, mooing at one another!"

Even Mamá couldn't help smiling at such lively descriptions. I could see that his talkative charm had won her over. She turned to him suddenly, and said, pleadingly, "Pray, Don Estaban, is there no hope for my Paulos?"

Don Estaban was slightly taken aback by the swift change of subject. He grimly looked down at his hands. Finally, he looked up at her. "I cannot lie to you, my lady. Once the Holy Office has arrested someone . . ." His voice trailed away, leaving the worst unsaid, and the tears that Mamá had held back began to spill down her face.

"How can you be sure?" she said, her voice cracking.

"Doña de Carvallo, even those who repent of their Jewish blood are put to death," Don Estaban said in as gentle a voice as he could. "The Inquisitor rewards the repentant by garroting them to death, so that they do not feel the flames of the stake. Not much advantage, alas. Besides," he added softly, "we both know that Don Paulos would never repent of his Jewish blood."

"But my husband is the chief royal tax collector over all Seville!" Mamá leaned forward, her hands held out as if Estaban de Gomez had the power to release my father.

"Mamá," I said sadly, putting a hand on her back.

"All the more reason the Holy Office will not let him go," said Don Estaban. "He is too lucrative a catch. First they will confiscate all his property. Then they will make him an example for others. Their specialty is to bring down sinners in high places. Even New Christian priests are not exempt."

"What if I went back and pleaded our case," cried Mamá, "what if I explained what a huge contribution he made for fifteen years to the royal coffers, how people loved and trusted him far and wide? I simply cannot believe—."

"Go back?!" Don Estaban interrupted. "Don't even think such a thing, my lady. The Holy Office is like one of those dangerous ocean currents. If you try to get close, you will find yourself and all your loved ones completely sucked in!"

Mamá sat back, dabbing her eye and stared bleakly out the window.

"Take heart, my lady, your husband will die a saintly martyr's death. Many will miss him in Seville. He was a most unusual man. A man who helps humanity is a scarce commodity in Spain these days."

"I would rather have a living husband than a dead saint!" she sobbed.

"Sí, sí. Of course, my lady," Don Estaban said, looking distressed.

"What do you mean a man who helps humanity?" I asked. "Do you mean how he helped get people out of debtor's jail and helped them pay their debts?"

"Sí, those were good things surely, but I was actually referring to his other work," Don Estaban said. "You know he always called it . . ." he hesitated, thinking, "a matzah. No, no." He waved his hands rapidly in front of him. "Matzah is that crispy bread of the Jews, your Papá told me. No, he called it not matzah but . . ." Don Estaban held a finger to his head as if boring into his own brain for the memory. "Mitzvah! That is it!" The finger pointed upwards, victoriously. He seemed quite satisfied with himself.

Don Estaban looked at me. "'Esty,' your papá would whisper to me, 'we are about to fulfill another mitzvah,' and I knew that we were about to meet and help some desperate Marranos leave this God-forsaken kingdom. It was a little secret code between us."

Mamá and I looked at one another in bewilderment. We knew nothing of this work of Papá's.

"You know this word of the Jews, mitzvah?" he asked.

I shook my head feeling ignorant.

"It means simply, 'a good deed.'" Don Estaban leaned forward and tapped me on the shoulder. "Good deeds, your papá always said, are the true pathway to heaven, not merely professing belief to this god or that, but giving to others. Ah, do not feel badly about your ignorance.

He had so little time to teach you about the Jews. So little time to help others, as well."

"What exactly did my husband do?" Mamá asked.

"You do not know? My dears, he helped many Marranos escape from Spain. He and I together. For several years we knew Seville was becoming more and more infiltrated with Holy Office spies. When he learned of Marranos desperate to leave the country, he would contact me. I know every port and escape route in Southern Spain. We worked like brothers together and it was such a lucrative profession for me. The Marranos were astonishingly wealthy and quite agreeable when it came to paying their way. When they couldn't your papá willingly paid for my services." Mamá and I looked at one another. Don Estaban sighed and shrugged. "It is the end of a wonderful, if all too brief, busy season."

"Busy season?" I said.

"Don't you see? The Expulsion Order of the Jews gave us an unusual number of people seeking escape these past four months. Many New Christians like you, became eager to leave the country. Of course, my work was ending anyway with the planned departure of your papá."

"But Don Estaban," I said encouragingly, "you may still help others as you are helping us."

"Ah, no. I am merely an errand boy," he said examining his immaculate nails. "I am most definitely not suited to the life of mitzvahs and heroics. A safe life behind courtyard walls surrounded by flowers, good food, amusing friends, fine wine—that is the life for me."

"But you are helping us," I protested. "You came looking for us even when we did not appear. That was very brave and good of you."

"Ah, but you are the family of my friend, Don Paulos. For him I would have searched the ends of the earth," he said, sighing deeply. "Yesterday I prayed that he had merely lost a wagon wheel somewhere along the road. Now I pray that it all goes quickly for him."

He looked imploringly towards heaven. Mamá turned away and I shuddered, for we all knew that he meant the terrible tortures of the Holy Office.

"Then you will not continue with the . . . the mitzvahs?" I asked.

"Señorita," he said, "I am one small man in a large and ruthless

Spain. Without your papá, I would not last three days doing such work. Besides, without your papá's contacts, things will not be so profitable anymore. I am, after all, a working man. No, Pedro, my driver, and I will go to Toledo after this. I think it will be wise to stay away from Seville since they intend to put on many more of those vulgar circuses they call the auto-de-fé." He shuddered again, and I imagined he was thinking of his personal safety.

The words auto-de-fé came back to pierce me like a sword and I began to weep softly.

"Isabel . . ." Mamá stroked my arm and looked at me with stricken eyes, as if imploring me not to cry.

"There, now, better to cry it all out now, before you are among the Jews," said Don Estaban patting my hand nervously. "Remember, they must not be told of your travails as a Marrano!"

We both nodded bleakly as Don Estaban looked heavenward and said fervently, "Mios Dios! Save us all!" In one swift movement, he crossed himself, lifted the giant cross to his lips, and kissed it for good luck.

Mamá had grown quite pale. She peered out the window. I wiped my eyes and blew my nose on the kerchief Don Estaban handed me. He began to chatter at length about politics and the pathetic state of affairs over all of Spain. I began to grow sleepy, all the while trying to keep that word in my head, mitzvah, a good deed. My dear Papá had done many good deeds.

Finally, Don Estaban ran out of things to say and leaned his head against a pillow and napped, giving Mamá, Manuel, and I a welcome respite of silence.

We stopped and ate from our food baskets and changed the baby's swaddlings once more before dusk. The driver disappeared into the woods. Don Estaban insisted that Mamá and I take a walk and stretch, saying it would help us sleep later. He sat on the ground leaning against a tree and held out his arms for the baby. I looked at Mamá. Her face betrayed her anxious distrust. I knew what she was thinking: how could she trust this man or anyone ever again when even her own son had betrayed her?

"Come, the two of you must rest," Don Estaban said matter-of-factly. "Tomorrow you will have no carriage, no Estaban de Gomez to give you respite from either bebé or your heavy baskets." He held his arms out insistently and I realized he was in his courtly manner issuing Mamá a command.

Reluctantly, Mamá handed Manuel down to him. We walked hesitantly down the wide, beaten-down path. Mamá kept her head turned, unable to take her eyes off Don Estaban holding Manuel. As soon as we reached a respectable distance, Mamá made a swift about-face and walked hurriedly back again.

We passed Don Estaban and the baby but he hardly noticed us. He was so engrossed in cooing and making faces at Manuel. Mamá and I walked a short distance in the opposite direction, until she made another swift about-face and hurried back toward Don Estaban. It went on this way for fifteen or twenty minutes, Mamá and I walking back and forth, keeping our eyes fixed on Don Estaban and Manuel.

"This is the last time," Mamá said quietly. We took one more walk down the road. When we turned to come back, the driver had reappeared and was squatting next to Don Estaban and the baby. Mamá looked at me nervously. We hurried back to find both men making faces and singing to my brother:

> "Little Caballero, Little Caballero,
> whither shall you go?
> and whom shall you smite?
> You will grow up soon to be a brave knight!"

๑

Mamá and I both bent down to peer into the baby's face. To our amazement, Manuel was smiling, his eyes shifting rapidly back and forth at the two men, who were twisting their faces into boyish, silly expressions. For the first time I regarded with interest Don Estaban's driver, Pedro. Though he had bad teeth and the rough ways of the lower classes, his face was full of kindness. I had a sudden wishful longing to stay with these two men instead of facing the world alone again. They had become like kindly uncles to us.

"You see my lady?" said Don Estaban handing Manuel back to Mamá, "already he shows the intelligence and good nature of a true caballero—a great knight."

"Just like the papá," said Pedro, in a husky voice and a strangely sweet smile that revealed his many missing teeth.

"Gracias. Oh, gracias, both of you," Mamá said, clutching Manuel as she hurried, weeping, into the carriage.

๑

Don Estaban instructed Pedro to proceed as far as possible before nightfall. I had forgotten to pack the fans and the heat inside the coach, with all our traveling clothes and cushions, made it unbearably warm. Finally I fell into a deep, exhausted sleep as the carriage swayed over the forest trail. When I awoke, eerie blackness surrounded me, and I heard the sound of snoring. The carriage was not moving. I realized the driver must have stopped for the night. I felt for Mamá. She was slumped against the cushions, the baby next to her in one of the baskets we had emptied for him. Don Estaban was snoring across from us, and the driver no doubt slept outside on the ground near by.

I was desperate to relieve myself, but frightened of going out into the dark forest alone. Finally, unable to wait any longer, I stepped over the feet of Don Estaban and felt for the door, hoping the squeaking carriage hinges did not waken everyone. Outside, Pedro's snores were loud and erratic. Cringing at every crunch of leaves, I went a short distance from the coach, amazed at the dark and frightening shapes of trees in the dead of night. How on earth would I manage a sea journey to a foreign kingdom if I was afraid of my own native forest?

I tiptoed back inside the carriage. The creaking hinges this time woke Don Estaban.

"Ah?" he said.

I stopped until his snoring resumed then in the darkness, I groped my way back to the seat, feeling inside the basket for Manuel. His little chest rose and fell evenly. Then, after turning and readjusting the cushions, I fell back to sleep.

It felt as if only minutes had passed when I was shaken awake by the sharp rocking of the carriage. Sitting up, I rubbed my eyes, surprised to see bright light, the trees moving past. Mamá was nursing Manuel modestly under her mantilla. Don Estaban was tapping his foot with impatience as he gazed out the window. Hours, not minutes, had gone by while I slept. It was midway through the next morning!

I blinked rapidly at Mamá who smiled and said in a thin, shaky voice, "Isabel, dearest, we're almost there."

My heart sank. How I hated the thought of leaving the coach, which had become like a tiny home.

But there was no way to avoid it. Don Estaban was already knocking hard against the wall above his head, signalling Pedro.

"¡Alto!" Pedro shouted to the horses.

A moment later, the coach came to a grinding halt. Mamá and I looked at one another in apprehension.

"Señora, Señorita," Don Estaban turned to us. "I am sorry to say . . ." he held his hands out in a gesture of regret, "this is as far as I go."

Seventeen

I Am Orphaned

We had pulled to the side of the road beneath the tall trees. Pedro was sent off with bread and cheese and a wine bottle to stretch himself in the woods. Don Estaban peered out the window in all directions before drawing back inside.

Nervously, he jumped up, turned around, and lifted the very cushions upon which he had been sitting. He pulled out a pile of folded cloths. "Here you are, my ladies," he said unfolding long, rough-hewn shifts made of stiff black material and laying them with a flourish upon the seat cushions. "Your new clothes," he said with a certain pride, "the garments of Jewish peasantry. Very nice, eh?"

I looked down at the plain clothes with long hanging tubes for arms and could not see the slightest nice thing about them. They were hideous and I told Don Estaban so.

"Hideous sí, but also authentic, Señorita. Many wear black in mourning for the homeland from which they are evicted. You will look like a little family of Jewish ones from the poor Judería scurrying to the boats."

I sighed, looking skeptically at the garments and the colorless little head scarves that went with them. Never in my life had I been forced to wear such poor and shabby garments.

"They are quite clean, my ladies," he said pushing them towards us. "The Jews are a fanatically clean lot, always washing, scrubbing, and cleaning things for their Sabbath. They change their clothes every week, without fail," he said reassuringly. "Now I shall step out for a stretch and you, my ladies, must quickly change your clothes. We cannot sit here all day. At any time the road may be flooded with Jews and soldiers. Once you are in these clothes, we must part quickly."

He bowed and climbed out of the coach. We both sat there, unmoving.

"Quickly now," said Don Estaban peering in, "time is flowing like a fast river stream. People might appear upon the road at any time. If soldiers come and want to peèr inside the windows, I cannot stop them," he warned and shut the door.

Our cheeks flushed in embarrassment, Mamá and I struggled out of our petticoats and traveling suits into the strange new garments, putting them over our precious undershifts lined with secret pockets, wrestling with the clothing in the cramped and overheated quarters. Even Manuel was not spared. We had to replace his richly colored woven blankets with several lengths of old and faded wool. Then Don Estaban was knocking on the door.

"Un momento," said Mamá, still tying the scarf to her head.

I sat clasping my arms about me in the long plain shift and scarf tied peasant-style around my hair. I felt immodest and undressed in the long shapeless shift, as if sitting in my petticoats and undergarments. To think that common folk went about in such insubstantial shifts as these!

"Well?" said Don Estaban impatiently.

"Sí, Don Estaban, you may open the door now."

He flung open the door and gasped a little. "So different," he said staring up at us in amazement. "Gone are my two hidalgo ladies. You two look quite the picture of Jewish peasants now, just the way you must look." He nodded in approval.

I looked away, feeling shorn and exposed. Mamá looked terribly haggard and pale now that she was in a thin, shapeless dress.

He stepped up into the coach and picked up the heavy brocaded traveling suits at our feet. "As for these," he said picking up our hidalgo clothes, "only a few Jews have acquired enough wealth in the Juderías to dress in luxury, maybe a physician's wife or a merchant's would own such finery." He quickly rolled up the clothes, and stuffed them into the cushions beneath his seat. He would sell them at a good profit, he explained. Beautiful clothing was a valuable commodity in the world.

Then Don Estaban turned and eyed the items we held and the jewelry we had been wearing—our crosses, our rosaries with the porcelain beads, our Book of Hours, which Mamá still held possessively in her lap.

"My dear lady—" said Don Estaban, gently but quite firmly, his hands open in front of her, "such things will only bring disaster for you now. You must relinquish yourself to your new life."

With trembling lips, Mamá handed over the last vestiges of our Sevillano life. It felt just as Papá had said, as if the warm cloak of Christianity was slipping from our shoulders. The objects clinked into Don Estaban's hands one by one. Mamá looked at her empty hands and refused to watch him stuff our belongings into the pockets of his jacket. I so wanted to tell Mamá that the golden mezuzzah was still tucked safely into my camisole. That, I knew, would help us with the Jewish ones. That, Don Estaban did not need to know.

"Have we come to the crossroads, Don Estaban?" I asked.

"We have passed the crossroads, Señorita. At some peril to myself, I have brought you onto the road to Cadiz, the road used widely by the Jews." He glanced outside to assure himself that the road was still empty. "You are very close to the Port of Cadiz, a league, maybe two. It is an easy walk. So close, you can almost smell the ocean." He sniffed deeply, pleased with himself. "Of course," he sighed, looking doubtfully at my pale mother, "now you will be truly on your own to find some Jewish ones to take you under their wing. I had approached a young Jewish couple who were to meet you on Saturday, for they were camping to avoid traveling on the Jewish Sabbath. Alas, I could not persuade them to wait any longer, when you did not come. They left with the others at dawn Sunday morning."

"How unfortunate!" Mamá said. "It would have been so helpful to have had Jewish ones to lead us and not to take to the road alone."

Don Estaban shrugged his shoulders. "My Lady, I tried to entice them to an inn for Saturday night, but the Señora was with child and after nightfall they refused even the marivedos I had offered them, planning to hurry to the ships at dawn, afraid they would not find room on the overcrowded ships. All are frightened lest they do not find a place aboard ship. It is, after all, the thirtieth of July. Only three days remain on the expulsion order. After that, *"Wheeeeek,"* he said, drawing his finger across his neck like an executioner's sword. "Remaining Jews will be sentenced to death."

"I-I am not sure we can go through with this," Mamá said mournfully, looking down at the baby in her lap.

"And I tell you that you and your children better secure passage today or tomorrow. The ships are already groaning under the weight of all the final travelers."

"I suppose, if we absolutely must . . ." she said in great reluctance.

"And now . . . there is one final matter," he said quickly, his eyes cast downward, holding his hands together at his mouth, as if in prayer. We stared at him.

"It is the trifling matter of money," he said and cleared his throat.

Mamá looked at me and nodded. We both turned away for modesty's sake and reached for coins hidden in our shifts. As we did, he said, "You understand, I am under heavy expense—my trusted driver, the horses, the inn, the food. . . ." He chattered almost apologetically. "And, of course, I work only infrequently, only when your papá asked me. Marranos do not escape everyday, and now that your papá is gone . . ."

Mamá gasped loudly.

He knew immediately that he had said too much. I took the coins out of Mamá's hands and gave him four gold marivedos, a handsome sum, indeed. I swallowed hard, staring at the coins in his hands. We had given him all the small coins we possessed. All that remained were large pieces, with no way to make smaller change. I feared paying huge coins for small bits of food, on the ship and in the new land.

Don Estaban seemed to read my thoughts. After rubbing the four coins together for several moments, he handed back one of them with only the slightest look of regret. "For the road," he said. "You will need it."

"Are you sure? Don Estaban?" I asked "You have performed for us a valuable service, which no one else could have done. You have earned it."

He coughed a little and waved me away. "Please," he said. "If your papá had been here, I would have demanded ten times that sum, trust me. Though he was walking away from most of his property and wealth, he was a most resourceful man. He would have prospered well in the kingdom of Turkey."

I knew the return of a gold piece was not an easy thing for Don Estaban. It was a true mitzvah, I realized, for I could tell that money brought him great pleasure and an even greater sense of security. I nodded and put away the coin quickly before he changed his mind.

Manuel grew fussy and while Don Estaban watched nervously outside, Mamá nursed him one last time before we had to leave the protection of the coach. When Pedro came back, Don Estaban ordered him to scout around the nearby trees to make sure there were no unexpected people about.

Then, as a parting gesture, he brought out food, a box holding dainty decorated cakes, and a flagon of wine. "Please, my ladies. You will not see such refined food for a long time." So we all partook, even Mamá, a little shyly. Don Estaban licked each of his fingers with relish after eating each cake, then wiped them carefully on a kerchief. Finally, after we had eaten and looked around the small compartment for things forgotten, there was nothing left to do but leave the safety of the carriage.

I looked at Don Estaban sitting on the edge of the seat. He was smiling and tickling the baby under his chin. We had been together only since yesterday, but I realized how much I had grown to like the little man with his nervous chatter and fastidious ways. I loathed to leave the safety and comfort of his cushioned carriage, especially knowing he worked alongside my father.

Don Estaban opened the door and stepped out with energy and grace, his mission complete. Pedro was standing guard at the edge of the forest. Don Estaban motioned for him to return, and the coach creaked and groaned above us as the man climbed back into his seat. Then Don Estaban glanced once more up and down the road. It was still deserted. He stood looking at us in the open door.

"Alas, there are no travelers about. What a pity. Saturday, at the crossroads, where I awaited you as originally planned, there was an endless stream of Jews resting along the roadways. But, I am sure there will be more last-minute stragglers, later if not sooner," he said philosophically.

My heart was in my throat as I stood in the door of the carriage. I looked forlornly at him.

"There, now, Señorita de Carvallo, do not worry," he said holding his arms out gaily, putting on a display of cheer for us, "you are very close now. It is not yet even noon. You will reach the port before sundown tonight."

He helped me step down from the carriage, and bowed to me as a gentleman would to a lady, ignoring my transformation into a peasant. Mamá stood distractedly at the door, holding the baby. I stared at her, seeing a look of desperation cross her face that I did not understand.

"Mamá?" I called.

She would not answer nor meet my eyes as she handed down the baby to Don Estaban who then handed the baby to me. Then she passed him the baskets, laden with our remaining food, and the baby's cotton swaddlings.

"My lady?" Don Estaban held his hand out to help Mamá out of the carriage, but she seemed to hesitate, as if she heard something in the distance. A second later, we all cocked our heads. Sí, it was the unmistakable sounds of music—a lute . . . the hollow pounding of drums . . . tambourines . . . the hearty sound of human voices. . . . People were singing! Don Estaban turned for a moment and listened, then smiled said, "Ah, music along the road to Cadiz most certainly means approaching Jews. They cheer themselves along with hired music from troubadours."

I looked at him with astonishment, remembering the pathetic vision of fleeing Jews I had seen with Papá. "They do?"

"Sí, it is true, Señorita. In the early days, after the queen's decree in March, they would travel moaning and wailing outside the city walls, crying of hunger and thirst and arousing many city people to pity and distress," Don Estaban explained. "Of course our great, compassionate queen would never allow such a thing as pity of Jews, you know. So the queen's soldiers were told to order the Jews to hire troubadours to drown out the distressing noise of their sufferings. What a clever queen we have, sí, Señorita?" he said mockingly. "Anyway, now the sound of troubadours are a good luck omen for the three of you!" He pressed his hands together in enthusiasm. "Jewish ones will soon be along, and you will find a way to fall in step with them. They will never be able to tell you apart from one of their own." He turned back to the coach, to help my mother. "Hurry, my lady, for they fast approach!"

Again, he held out his hand to Mamá, who stood looking down the road with dread from the carriage door. I watched her with Manuel in my arms and the two baskets at my feet.

Suddenly, Mamá shook her head violently. "No, no, Blessed Mary no!" she cried and shrank back inside the coach.

"My lady, what ails you?" exclaimed Don Estaban in alarm, flailing his arms. "What? What?" he flailed his arms.

Pedro jumped down beside Don Estaban, and we all looked aghast at my mother, who had fallen to her knees inside the carriage, weeping and wailing. "We must return to Seville!" she cried, her hands clenched pleadingly, "we must return to Seville!"

"Oh Mamá!" I begged, "baby Manuel, needs you! Mamá, please!"

I stepped forward and held out the baby. Pedro and Don Estaban turned their heads back and forth between me and my distraught mother.

"I cannot leave my Paulos!" she screamed. "Come back inside, Isabel. Bring the baby to me!" I started back into the carriage with the baby, but Don Estaban shook his head.

"Wait!" he commanded. "I will get her out."

The two men began urgently whispering. It occurred to me that Don Estaban and Pedro could easily overpower my mother and drag her out on the ground. For a moment I hoped they would. I stood behind them holding Manuel, hearing the sounds of approaching people, and I held my breath in terrible suspense, fearing for my mother, who wept hysterically.

Suddenly, Don Estaban shook his head, leaped inside the coach, and spoke urgently. "My lady, get hold of yourself! To return to Seville will mean certain arrest by the Holy Office, I assure you. You do not want that for your daughter or your son. They burn and torture even children!"

His voice was full of harsh warning. I stood paralyzed by the scene, helpless to change it, confused, panic enveloping me.

"Here," she sobbed desperately, pulling out her last gold and silver coins and holding them out in her hands. "Take it all. It's everything I have left. I give it to you to take us back to my Paulos!"

She wept and wept and neither Don Estaban nor Pedro made a move to take the money, but just stood looking with dismay at her and each other.

"Mamá, come to us," I screamed, frightened and shaken.

She seemed so strange and inconsolable. "Paulos! Paulos!" she cried on and on, "you will not know where we are!" And as she cried, she began to beat her head upon the wall of the coach.

The baby began to fuss and I jiggled him nervously in my arms to calm him. Don Estaban and Pedro peered down the curving road behind the coach, alarm on their faces. Music and the hubbub of voices were drawing louder every minute.

"Don Estaban perhaps I can convince Mamá . . ." I said, a growing uneasiness seizing me.

But he ignored me. "My lady, *please!*" he shouted at my mother, "won't you listen to reason?"

Behind the coach was a long bend in the road. In a moment or two a multitude of people would round that bend and find us. Don Estaban looked at Pedro and shook his head. The two men looked desperately at each other, then back to me and the baby.

"If the Jews think we are accosting their people, we will be reported to the queen's soldiers!" Don Estaban said, his voice rising. "We must get away from here now!"

Pedro, looking terrified, leaped back up to his seat and grabbed the reigns of the horses. Don Estaban turned back inside the coach once more. "You must go to your children now, my lady!" he commanded. "This is your last chance!"

"No, no," she sobbed. "I must return to Seville, to my Paulos. He is waiting for us! I must take the children home to their father!"

I shivered. I now knew Mamá was crazed with grief. She refused to believe that she could not save Papá! I stepped up to re-enter the coach, but to my dismay, Don Estaban, standing in the doorway, barred the way before I could get aboard with Manuel.

"No, Señorita!" he shouted in his own voice of hysteria. "Your mother has become unwell. Her ravings will betray you to the Jewish ones! You are only children—your life spreads out before you. Go forth as your papá wanted. Trust me! Paulos would never forgive me if I let his children. . . ." He was almost babbling as he reached outside for the handle and flung shut the carriage door!

"Oh no! Isabel! My baby! Please!" And I heard the sound of my mother's wild beating upon the wall.

"My lady! It is better this way! I will take you back to your Paulos. Calm yourself! I implore you!" I heard from behind the door. Then I heard my mother scream broken-hearted in a voice I knew I would never forget as long as I lived.

"My children, my children, I love you my children!"

At that moment Pedro, wild-eyed, unmindful of the shouts and cries within, jerked his two horses around with a savage energy and whipped them into a galloping retreat down the very road from which we had just come.

○

A cacophony of voices and music swelled in my ears as a large band of people appeared over the small rise and flowed onto the roadway towards me. The carriage clamored violently away, the dust rising in clouds high enough to reach my face. The crowd slowed, coughing and complaining, waving their hands at the carriage's ill-mannered retreat.

Shaking and trembling from head to foot, I had no choice but to step forward—a frightened, orphaned Ruth—clutching my wide-eyed baby brother.

Eighteen

I Encounter the Jewish People

My mother's last anguished cry rang in my ears. I could not take my eyes off the road and the tiny speck of carriage receding in the distance! "Mamá!" I said weakly. Shock robbed me of the strength to cry out or run after the coach. Dozens of people rounded the bend and jostled me as I stood clutching my baby brother, insensible, in the middle of the road.

"Move on, Señora!"

"You'll get hurt standing in the center of the road!"

"Move for the sake of your baby!"

Glaring looks, clucking mouths. Staring eyes. People swarming past. Dazed and confused, I picked up my two baskets in one hand and clutched Manuel with the other. My legs shook with fear and shock. No! I musn't faint and drop the baby! Hardly knowing what I was doing, I stumbled off the road into the woods and sank to the foot of a tree, sick and trembling with the weight of my burdens.

Black spots appeared before my eyes and I felt myself helplessly swirling down into darkness. Slipping sideways to the ground, I curled up and pulled the tightly wrapped bundle of Manuel close to me for comfort. How many minutes I lay in a swoon, I do not know. When I came back to myself, the singing and gay music sounded absurd to my ears. Manuel, mercifully asleep in the warmth of my arms, was unaware of the cruel fate that had abruptly turned him into an orphan and his sister into his sole protector.

Wearily, I sat up, leaned my head against the tree, and closed my eyes against fatigue, confusion, and pain. I had little idea how long I sat there, but all that time the noisy sounds of voices, music, and stomping feet never ceased. Were there hundreds or thousands of people? I did not know. It seemed as if all the Jews of Spain were surging endlessly down the road to Cadiz.

Gradually, the weakness in my arms and legs began to disappear. I opened my eyes and reached into my basket and drew deep gulps from my skin of spiced juice. But with the return of my strength, also came sorrow. How my heart ached for Mamá. Dear God, what would become of her, so heart-broken and lost from us all? I tried to tell myself that Don Estaban would take care of her, but I knew that if she could, she would somehow return to Seville, that she would try to free Papá, that the Holy Office would probably arrest her and—No! I put my hands up to my ears to stop the horrifying thoughts swirling in my head. I must not think of such things now, I told myself fiercely. I must think only of getting Manuel and me to safety. That is what my parents wanted. I forced myself to think of joining the Jews. But how could I bring myself to ask these people to take me in? How could I convince them I was truly one of them? To see them up close was to see an endless sea of strangers. No . . . I decided, I must wait until they all passed, then follow behind them unseen and sneak aboard a ship in a last minute rush.

Then Manuel awakened, interrupting my thoughts. With a wrench of my heart, I watched the tiny fist reaching to the open mouth in hunger! I gasped, realizing my baby brother's survival—and my own—depended upon my ability to convince these harassed, fleeing Jews, that I, too, was one of them. It was up to me now. I could hear my father's voice saying, "*Live.* Live the life you were destined for as Ruth. . . . It is the only thing that can help me endure what is coming!"

"Sí, dear Papá!" I whispered and struggled to my feet.

Clutching Manuel, I stared through the trees, thinking back to those first fleeing Jews I had seen that day so many months ago with Papá: the faces of the crying and haggard women, the bowed and bent men, the cheerless and sickly children, the old man who had dropped weeping to his knees, seeing his small belongings trampled in the wake of many feet, the fear and despair in all those people. It was all still sharp in my mind.

But as I stood there, hidden and watching, I began to realize I was witnessing a quite different kind of exodus here. These fleeing Jews, unlike those others I had seen, were dusty and weary-looking, sí, but far from downcast. Did my eyes deceive me? I walked forward a few feet closer. The longer I watched them, the more I realized that they were traveling almost *cheerfully* . . . accompanied—just as Don Estaban had said—by song and lively instruments. But there was something more than music that made these Jewish ones lively. I could see it in their faces—strength of spirit, determination, and even joy!

I could not fathom the meaning of such joy. These were people poor in dress like me but rich in spirit, their arms and backs laden with belongings tied upon them; their numerous children in tow, carrying many ragged bundles with babies like my own. Peasant girls my age with their long hair held back in scarves like the one Don Estaban had given me, skipped happily by. Even the women chattered together in lively whispers, like my own aunts and mother.

Young boys with soft caps and curious long sidelocks hanging curled below their ears walked arm in arm. The menfolk, their backs bent with fatigue and the weight of their many household parcels, managed to walk vigorously with faces full of hope. Most striking of all, were the many old ones, walking slowly, yet in quiet dignity. They held their heads so high, I could almost imagine them saying: "We go with pride and dignity. You cast us out to sea, but we shall merely float!"

In spite of my gloom, I felt cheered by the spirit of these folk and the music which swelled everywhere. I spotted at least four groups of troubadours moving among them, playing their instruments and singing lively tunes.

As one large group of people passed, yet another marched around the long bend of road. This time four young men linked arm in arm, their sidelocks bouncing gaily beneath their colorful caps, ignored the music up ahead and sang a stirring song of their own, as if shouting it to the heavens. I did not understand its words, but, of course, it had to be Hebrew! I tried to hear the words as they spilled out in repetition, but could only catch the first few: "*A-don O-lom A-sher Molah, b'te-rem kol y'tseer niv'ro* . . ."

Behind them, three heavily bearded men, faces glowing with sweat, backs laden with parcels, the hair below their caps shining silver in the blaze of sunlight, sang as vigorously as the younger men in front of them. One of them had kindly eyes, which reminded me of Papá's! When he chanced to cast his gaze in my direction, my heart felt like it broke open, sending waves of sorrow and grief through me. My eyes followed those dear-looking gentlemen down the road, but they did not glance at me again. My dress was so like the other girls and women, they must have thought I was another young mother resting by the side of the road.

"I am a Jewess, just like your own daughters!" I wanted to shout at their backs. But fear and timidness held me in agony silently to my spot.

"Mamá, Papá!" I sobbed. But only Manuel heard me. He looked up at me and made a cheerful noise in return. I slumped back down in exhaustion on the ground and clutched him to me. "My poor bebé, my poor, poor bebé!" I wept.

Suddenly, two short legs stood before me. I looked up and gasped. A small boy with long sidecurls and a soft cap stood before me staring down as I wept all over Manuel. And through the crowd, a young woman came pushing frantically past the trees.

"No, no, Yacov," she said and grabbed his hand. "*Lo siento*—I beg your pardon."

She pulled the curious child to her. I nodded and looked down quickly, feeling foolish and self-conscious at my teary face, my reddened, puffy eyes. I looked up as she hesitated for just a second, staring at me and Manuel. When our eyes met, she smiled quickly, shyly, nodding several times, then disappeared with her child into the jumble of people. I was blowing my nose on a clean swaddling cloth when yet another woman hastened towards me. This time I stumbled with Manuel to my feet, my heart beating frantically.

She was tall, attired in black, looking more well-dressed and dignified than the others, a woman of advanced years, gray wisps of hair about her face, a lacy mantilla tied softly around her head.

"Señora," she said firmly. I saw sharp probing eyes of swift intelligence, eyes that could quickly separate lies from truth! Those eyes now met mine, and I trembled. "You have gotten separated from your husband, your loved ones, up ahead?" She looked me over carefully. Surely, she suspected something.

Be careful! I told myself. Do not lie outright. But this question of a husband . . . I had not expected. "The b-baby is my b-brother," I stammered.

Her eyes flitted to my ragged bundle and the baskets a few trees away. Then—I could not stop her—she stepped forward and pulled my arms down to see inside the bundle. My heart felt as if it would leap from my chest. She stared at Manuel. Then, those eyes that missed nothing were back upon me.

She glanced around the forest and behind us, but saw no one. "You are not one of our people from Toledo, I do not think. Are you?"

I hesitated, not knowing what to say.

"The truth," she said in a quiet but demanding tone.

Swallowing hard, I shook my head no.

"I thought not. I recognize most of our people. But you are . . . one of us, no? You are a Jewess?"

I nodded slowly. "Sí, a Jewess," I said as convincingly as possible.

"What is the watchword of the Jewish faith?" she asked, her eyes boring into me.

I took a deep breath and said, "The Shema?"

"Say it."

"Shema Yisra'el, Adonai . . ."

"That's enough," she said, but still looked unconvinced. "Even false Jews can memorize a blessing."

"Wait, I have something . . ." I turned away from her and reached into my bodice and through the undershift, poking desperately through the stitches, until I brought forth my great grandmother's golden mezuzzah.

I could hear the slight gasp escape her lips.

"Put it back into hiding, quickly. The Edict says that gold and silver objects are not to be taken out of Spain, Señorita."

I slipped it back into my shift.

"Where are you going?"

"To the boats, Señora. To, to Turkey . . ." I dared not say more.

"You and the bebé are traveling to the boats alone?" she said incredulously. "Proper Jews travel in groups, with their own Judería . . ."

"Oh, Señora," the words began to tumble out, "my father was arrested . . . my mother taken . . . my brother and I left alone. . . ."

"No! Stop!" she interrupted sharply. "I do not want to know. What I do not know I cannot be forced to tell. All I need to know is that you and your bebé are Jews in need of help. Some other time, when we are well away from Spain, you may tell me your story."

I nodded nervously, wondering if she suspected we were Marranos.

She turned and looked through the trees up the road. I followed her glance and was shocked to see a man standing not too far away by the side of the road. He was watching us.

"My husband," she said in explanation. "My children are far ahead. We were summoned to see you."

"Summoned?" I said surprised.

"Sí. Sarah with her son Yacov came to tell me that she came upon you, a young Señora alone in the forest with an infant. You seemed upset, crying, as if lost and in trouble. . . ."

"Oh," I said. "The little boy and his mother." I looked up at the woman's face. She seemed to be thinking hard as she searched my eyes for something. I held my breath. She was, I suddenly realized, in the midst of a decision.

Finally, she took a deep breath. The piercing eyes softened slightly. She said, "You will join us."

"Gracias, Señora." I almost wept.

"Come along then. You must walk with my husband and I, and avoid Señor Levi for now."

"Who is Señor Levi?" I asked timidly.

"He is the president of our Toledo congregation. Someone you do not want to be questioned by." She took one of the baskets from my arm. As we walked towards her husband, she sighed wearily. For the first time I saw lines of weariness on her face.

"Praise God," she said. "We are nearly to the ships. A few hours at most, my husband says. It has been a long, dangerous journey of many weeks for our people. Soon, Señorita, by today or tonight, I hope, we will have sanctuary aboard a ship, a crowded ship, no doubt, but still a place of shelter, a small corner, or a bit of sitting space. In the worst of times Adonai has always provided the Jews with enough. Like the great exodus from Egypt, Adonai has guided our little exodus. In ten weeks, God has brought our entire congregation from Toledo with only seventeen deaths, mostly the sick, old ones near death anyway, and poor, frail Susanna, who died in childbirth. Well," she sighed deeply, "we mustn't complain. We must praise God even in the midst of hardship. We must say *Dayenu!* Had the Blessed One done much less for us, it still would have been enough."

I was thrilled by her words and longed to speak of Bisabuela Ruth and to share some Jewish stories and lessons Papá had taught me, but of course, I dared not. I followed silently behind her, as she strode ahead to catch up with her awaiting husband.

"Wait!" she turned and commanded, "I must speak to my husband." She approached him and began to speak rapidly in a foreign tongue—Hebrew, no doubt. But even in a foreign tongue, I could tell they were arguing, her husband uttering a long stream of dire-sounding words.

Finally, the señor said a few more words, then rolled his eyes and gave a shrug, as if he had given up. She turned and nodded quickly to me. I gathered up my things and found myself walking behind them in strained silence, sensing that my fate was hanging in the balance. At last, the señor spoke to his wife and turned and nodded to me. When she looked back and saw the baskets digging into my arm, she quickly took them away, giving one to her husband and one to herself. And then we were walking out of the woods onto the road with all the people. I looked at many of the dusty, weary-looking faces and marveled that such a large group of people had made it so far from Toledo, a town hundreds of leagues from Seville!

A number of worried-looking people were walking towards us and seemed greatly relieved to see the señor and señora. Were they people of importance, I wondered? They were both better dressed than many in the crowd, wearing dignified clothes of black. The señor turned to one of the men who had come looking for him: "Would you tell my children that we will join them soon?"

The señora turned to me and said, "Soon you will meet them."

I was about to ask her about them when suddenly, rounding the bend in the road, we were set upon by a group of nuns! They leaped out at us from behind trees, shouting and waving their arms. "Dios!" I said aloud, thankful that I hadn't let a "Blessed Mary" slip out in my surprise. As I grasped my sleeping brother, one of the nuns approached us with wild-looking eyes. "Repent, Jews! Now is your last time to accept Our Lord and Savior! Or be damned forever to hellfire and eternal damnation!"

To my horror, the wild-eyed nun turned to me and thrust the cross in my face!

Desperately, I turned and went around her.

"Save yourself and your child, Señora," she called as she followed me. I shivered. Why did she pick me? I wondered in panic. Could she sense my Christian background? Anxiously, I moved next to the señora who was busy waving them away.

She saw my distress and briefly put her arm around my shoulder. "Pay them no mind, my dear. They are Gentile proselytizers who are all along the roads. We simply ignore them."

"They frighten me," I said a little sheepishly.

She shook her head wryly. "The Christians try to the bitter end to convert us. Out of thousands of faithful, they have succeeded with only a handful of Jews, too fearful to face the uncertainties of foreign travel or to put their trust in Adonai.

"They will stay and become Marranos I suppose," she said with scorn, looking at me out of the corner of her eye. I said nothing, keeping my head down as if I were checking on Manuel. "Most Jews would rather be put to the sword than commit the ultimate sin of giving up Torah and the belief in One God. I am sure you feel the same way."

"But I wouldn't be here if some of my ancestors hadn't . . ." I blurted out.

"Say no more!" she held up her hand, glancing towards her husband who was engrossed in conversation with another man.

How grateful I was to the good señora for taking me under her wing. Yet she could never make me believe that my Bisabuela Ruth had sinned for choosing to live as a Marrano instead of dying by the sword. And what of Papá and Mamá? Can one judge what another does to escape pain or death?

"What I mean is," I persisted, remembering the words Papá had taught me, "the Bible says 'Therefore choose *life*.' Adonai, the giver of life, wants human beings to choose life above all things." There, I thought, meeting her eyes with a twinge of defiance, I had said what I had to say.

The señora stared at me, looking a bit surprised.

"My papá taught me that," I said glancing down at sleeping Manuel, my voice beginning to quiver, tears threatening to spill from my eyes.

"Your papá must have been a wise man, learned in Torah," the señora answered very gently.

Farther down the road a band of gypsies assailed us. "The end of the world draws near!" they screamed. "Buy these amulets from us before taking to the dangerous seas. They will bring you luck and protection!" They held colorful ornaments, crosses and rosaries of cut glass, which they thrust forcefully in our faces. I made the mistake of glancing at the bright baubles and they followed me, nagging me to buy. But I was not so fearful this time. It was the señora's husband who finally motioned for some troubadours to come over and drown the gypsies out with song until they gave up following us.

When it seemed as if we were safe again, the señora excused herself, telling me to keep her husband in view and that she would return soon. She hurried away into the crowd. The señor was avidly engaged in conversation with several men around him. I marveled at the way they wove Spanish and Hebrew through their talk like two colors of thread sewn together.

It wasn't the señora who returned a few moments later, but her daughter, a girl almost my own age. She came skipping toward us and stopped by the side of the señor.

"Shalom, Papá," she said and he kissed her affectionately on her head.

Smiling, she approached me and introduced herself as, "Zipporah." Her mother had asked her to take turns holding my baby brother, which she did, taking him happily into her arms.

"A little later I'll take you to meet my brothers and sisters, but not quite yet. They love babies, too, and will quickly snatch him away from me," she said, hugging Manuel.

"How many brothers and sisters do you have?" I asked.

"Six!" she said cheerfully.

Astounded, I looked at her.

"You are one of seven children?"

"Sí," she nodded, amused at my surprise. "It is not so many. The Lopez family has eight and the de Silva's have ten. And the Nunes, let's see . . ." She looked at me and shrugged. "I have lost count!"

I smiled as the girl chattered on. Seven children to argue over Manuel! It all seemed more good luck than I had dared hoped for. At last, I thought, the worst was over.

Little did I know that I was not to rest easy after all. I was about to discover my gravest foes. They were not the gypsies or Gentile proselytizers along the road, nor the Inquisitors or officials of the dreaded Holy Office, but the very Jews with whom I thought I had found refuge.

Nineteen

~~~

We Are Expelled

"You'd better take him," said Zipporah before we had gotten very far down the road. Manuel had grown wet and soggy in her arms and I pulled swaddling from my basket and changed him quickly, throwing the used swaddling in a small ditch that Zipporah amiably dug with a stick.

"Gracias for helping me, Zipporah. I'll carry my brother for a while now," I said shyly as we hurried to catch up with her father. I hoped she wasn't resentful at being sent to help me.

"Oh, I am happy to help. I love babies but you must call me Zippi! Everyone does. It is so much easier than Zipporah, which is such a mouthful to say. I wished I'd had a prettier name like Sara or Rachel or Judith. The Bible has so many good ones."

"Oh, but I like Zipporah," I said, trying to be assuring. "It is pretty and flows like a little sea wave. See? Zip-por-ah." I moved my hand up and down like a wave.

"Sí, perhaps," she said skeptically. "Anyway, Zipporah was the wife of Moses in the desert, but of course, you must know that." I nodded rapidly, as if I had known this too. "At least Mamá and Papá did not choose to name me after the *mother* of Moses." She gave me a mirthful look.

"I forgot . . . what is the name of the mother of Moses?"

"Yochebed!" she laughed. And I couldn't help laughing too.

"I see what you mean," I said.

"What is *your* name?" she asked. "You haven't said . . ."

"Isa . . . ." I said, but caught myself in horror. I cleared my throat noisily, hoping she did not notice.

"*Isa*, did you say?" She looked confused.

"Pardon me, my throat is so dry. Ruth is my name." I cleared my throat again. "Ruth de Cojano."

"Oh, Ruth! Now that's a pretty name. I wish my parents had . . ." she began but stopped abruptly, staring down the road ahead of us.

"What is it?" I followed her gaze. Someone was pushing roughly through the crowd.

"Something is wrong!" Zippi said.

"How do you know?" I asked.

"Señor Levi is coming! He must be looking for Papá. He never leaves the front of the line unless something is wrong. And look, my mother is following behind him, as well!" An angry-looking young man stomped toward us, with the señora hurrying behind him. When he reached Zippi's papá, he nodded with a great show of respect to the señor, falling in step with him, followed by the señora. Then to my dismay, Señor Levi turned around and gave me a cold stare but managed to avoid my own gaze. I could see that he regarded me with distrust and I shuddered, feeling panic rise within me. There was something in the way he looked at me that reminded me, ever so-slightly of Tomás, my older brother. Zippi and I looked at one another but her face showed only surprise and confusion.

Zipporah's father and Señor Levi now put their heads together and spoke, their voices rising in that strange language combining Spanish and Hebrew. The señora joined in and the young man stamped his foot impatiently and flung out his arms without looking the señora in the face. Again, he turned his cold eyes on me and spoke in perfect Spanish.

"*Como se llama?* Your name, señorita?" he demanded. I shrank back and caught my breath.

"Ruth," I said in a small, thin voice.

"Your whole name," he demanded, and his loud, sharp voice startled Manuel from his sleepy doze and he began to squall.

"There, there," said the señora who hurried to my side. She tried to scoop him into her arms, but, frightened, I held him tightly, which made him squall all the more.

"You will answer," the man said harshly without the slightest note of sympathy for the crying baby, "or I will speak to the soldiers who hover less than a half-league behind us. They are the queen's soldiers sent to protect the Jews."

I looked around me fearfully. Did he think I was a threat to the

Jews? As I stood there a growing crowd of Jewish onlookers came to see the commotion. Alarmed, I looked to the kinder señor.

"Sí, señorita," he said, nodding solemnly in agreement, "we need to know who you are. You must tell us your given family name."

I looked at the circle of faces staring at me. I was sure they suspected me of being exactly what I was—an illegal Marrano whose discovery by officials might jeopardize the entire Toledo community of Jews. Suddenly, I remembered Papá's prophecy: the hardest part of our escape would be convincing the Jewish ones that we were one of them.

My arms ached terribly. I wished I might lay my brother down for a rest but I did not trust any of these strangers with him, not even Zippi who stared at me with surprise. I felt weak and confused. Tears welled in my eyes and I feared I would weep and confess.

At that moment, the vision of my father flashed before me telling me to be strong. Like lightning it sent a jolt of courage through me. My mind cleared, my tears dried, and I thought: I am *Ruth*, who came to cast her lot with the Jewish people. No matter what these folk think of Marrano sinners, I, Ruth de Cojano, have a Jewish soul. Papá had told me that all the Jewish souls ever to exist had been present at Mt. Sinai when Moses received the Ten Commandments. The souls of those who ever had lived and all those who ever would live. And that included Marranos born thousands of years later and forced to live in secrecy. It struck me that I had as much right to be expelled with the Jewish people as did Señor Levi. I straightened myself and, though my voice still shook, I looked the disbelieving Señor Levi in the eye.

"I am called . . ." I began and all leaned near, hushed, to hear my words. "Ruth, Ruth de Cojano."

"She calls herself Cojano!" someone in the crowd shouted. "The child of a priestly family!"

"And this," I said raising the bundle in my arms, "this, is my baby brother . . . Mica." I took a deep breath and felt a stab of relief when Señor and Señora nodded encouragingly. Señor Levi, however, was not so easily appeased.

"Where are your people?" he demanded with irritation.

I took another deep breath. "You are my people," I said with as much conviction as I could muster.

"No, no, no!" Señor Levi chimed in, stamping his foot. "Where are your parents? Where is your own *familia*? Your own congregation? You do not belong with us. We are from the Toledo Judería. I know everyone and you are not one of us. Where are you from?"

I froze, unable to think of a reply. Barely in time, I remembered not to say Seville. No Jews had been allowed to live in Seville, I remembered Papá telling me, since 1391, since the forced conversions of Jews to Christianity. Since then, Jews had been allowed to live only in certain Spanish towns and then only in the crumbling walled Juderías. But which towns? Had Papá ever said? The name Cordoba flew into my mind. Teresa had just returned from Cordoba, speaking of all the Jews along the way. I had been there once. It lay only three days journey from Seville. But I had no idea if there actually were Juderías there or not.

"Cordoba," I lied. "I have come from Cordoba." I held my breath.

Señor Levi seemed to accept this. "Cordoba, I dare say, is much closer to Cadiz than Toledo. It is strange that the Cordoban Jews haven't long since sailed from Spain," he said, staring at me. I thought desperately for a reply, but could think of none. My mind stayed stubbornly shut.

"And your family, your neighbors in the Judería?" he demanded. "Where are they?"

"We were separated," I croaked out. "A terrible misfortune took place. . . . We, my baby brother and I, are orphaned." I looked desperately to the señora who stared back at me with pained eyes. "Mamá and Papá are both d-dead," I stumbled on. I simply couldn't tell them the truth of my parents; their fate was the fate of discovered Marranos, not the fate of Jews!

"How and where did they die?" persisted Señor Levi. "Was it plague?" The crowd of Jewish onlookers groaned in awesome dread at the word and stepped back away from me.

"Oh no!" I shook my head vehemently, "not plague. Bad men. They were . . . taken along the road . . . and killed!" I blurted out, tears welling up in my eyes. The crowd ah-ed sympathetically. Killed by a Jew-hating friar, I longed to tell them the truth, who happened to be their very own son!

"There, there, you have interrogated her quite enough, Señor Levi. Surely there is no need to go through it all now in front of everyone," said the señora insistently, stepping up to put her arm around me. "She must come with us. You can see she is only a girl with a tiny baby. What trouble could her presence cause?" I could see from the people's faces that her words carried force, not merely with the disbelieving Señor Levi but with the entire gathering.

Apparently the interrogation was not over yet. Señor Levi also held great sway over the community.

"Beloved Rabbi, Honorable *Rubisa*," the young interrogator said, "may I, the insignificant president of Toledo Judería's congregation, be so bold as to point out that we still do not know who she is. She could be in league with the Holy Office, bringing a Christian child to plant among us. Then, as so often happens, we Jews will be accused of kidnapping. She could even be a common wench and her babe looking for free food and refuge!" he said harshly.

I sucked in my breath at such cruel and vulgar suggestions and turned to the stunned crowd. Everyone seemed to be glaring at me. No one offered a word in my defense.

"In all due respect, she is not one of us. She is not included among our papers. I know everyone whose papers I carry," he said emphatically patting a bulging leather pouch strapped across his shoulder. "For all we know she might even be a Marrano." He fairly spat the word out with contempt. "May I remind all of you that it is highly illegal for a Marrano to leave the kingdom of Spain? Helping a Marrano escape is punishable by death! We have come too far on our own exodus to jeopardize our safety. I'm warning you, the soldiers and guards will check each and every document of identification with each and every person before we board ship."

A buzz of chatter ran through the crowd. I swallowed hard. Tears of rejection welled up in me. And then it struck me: he had called them Rabbi and Rubisa and showed them much respect. I looked at Zippi who hadn't taken her eyes off me. The names hadn't sunk in at first, but now I realized that these two, the señor and señora in their fine clothes, the parents of Zippi and her six siblings, who had befriended me, were none other than . . . the Toledo rabbi and his wife whom they called Rubisa. I looked at them all in amazement. It was my first encounter with a rabbi's family.

"Now, now," said the rubisa, waving away all of the man's accusations with her calm, even manner. "Surely you can see that she is a desperate young girl alone with her baby. She neither looks nor speaks like a wench but with gentility and she calls herself a Jewess, by a Hebrew name, like us." She turned to her husband, the rabbi. "Yosef, there are so many stray ones about. They get separated from their group or from their families. And she has said that her parents have been tragically taken . . . killed. In these terrible times, we must not forget chesed—'mercy,' for the stranger," she said imploringly.

But Señor Levi was shaking his head with angry impatience. "I beg your pardon, but compassion in the wrong place and time could spell disaster for our entire people, worthy Rubisa!"

"And I beg your pardon, Señor Levi, but we have already met with the worst disaster, in the Edict of Expulsion," the rubisa said sharply. "We have already lost most of what we had gained from a lifetime of work and raising families. Forced to travel the dangerous high seas, we must leave our ancestral homes and burial grounds, our Spanish homeland since the time of King David! We can do no worse, worthy President. I know you are angry. All of us are angry. But it would be a great mitzvah to let the girl join us."

At the word mitzvah, Señor Levi looked stunned. The idea had clearly never crossed his mind.

"We will find papers among the ones who have died since we left Toledo," the rubisa said. "The papers of Eliezer's wife, poor Susanna, may she rest in peace, a pregnant woman soon to give birth would help bring this girl and her baby aboard."

The rubisa appealed not only to Señor Levi, but also to the gathering crowd. "My friends, the Torah implores us to have compassion even in our own time of need. If we forget that, we shall be no different than our cruel Christian oppressors!" She turned to her husband. "But of course, the final decision is up to my worthy husband, our wise and learned Rabbi."

Murmuring ran through the crowd. I felt trapped as the curious people pressed in close but the rubisa looked encouragingly at me. Señor Levi for once was at a loss for words. And then the rabbi cleared his throat. I held my breath as all turned their attention to him.

"Señor Levi, our worthy president, I know you have our security at heart. For this we are in your debt. But I am satisfied that this young woman, a girl really, poses no real threat . . ."

Señor Levi's face flushed and he threw his arms up in frustration.

"Still," the soft-spoken rabbi held his hand up, "there is one practical matter to resolve before we proceed, dear one," he said to the rubisa.

My heart sank as Señor Levi looked up with renewed interest.

"This matter is beyond our control, Señorita," the rabbi looked at me almost apologetically. "It is the ultimate proof we must have for you to join us."

"Proof?" I said, thinking I might simply bring out the golden mezuzzah once again, as I had for the rubisa.

"The bebé," the rabbi continued, "he is your brother, Mica? You are sure he is male, not female?"

As the rabbi spoke, the harsh, forbidding President Levi leaned forward, eyes blazing. I shrank from his gaze.

"A-a boy baby. Of course I know he is a boy; he is my b-brother," I stammered out.

A murmur of excited whispers rippled through the crowd.

"Aha! See? Did I not warn you?" Señor Levi pounced upon my words. "She is a Gentile wench who brings this baby boy to plant among us. If we take her, she will report us to the soldiers, who will then have every excuse to arrest us or—or worse! Then the soldiers accuse us of kidnapping a high-ranking child of the nobility. It is just as the blood libels have always been carried out. Can you not recognize a gentile wench and her bastard child—or worse—a stowaway Marrano?"

Excited murmuring surged through the crowd. I realized the music had stopped, and dozens of strangers now stared openly at me. I looked to the rubisa, the rabbi, and Zippi for help. Although they had expressions of sympathy, they did not speak up in my behalf.

"Turn her over to the soldiers!" shouted a lone voice in the crowd.

I clutched my brother tightly. Was I not to fulfill Papá's dream of reaching safety after all? My mind raced with visions of horror and pain and doom.

"Mamá! Papá!" I began to weep uncontrollably, my tears spilling onto the baby's blanket.

"Can't you see she has been through a terrible ordeal?" said the rubisa, coming at last to my defense. "Where is our compassion for the stranger?" she chided the murmuring crowd. "Does not the Torah call us to help the widow, the orphan, the stranger?"

It was the rabbi who finally brought the crowd under control. "My people!" he said, putting his hand up. "My wife is quite right. To deny two children refuge at such a time would be a grave sin. Above all, we must show chesed to this young girl and her child. As the Talmud says: all Jews are protection for one another."

"That is if we are indeed all of us Jews!" called out Señor Levi.

Ignoring the remark, the rabbi turned to me. Clearly he, not Señor Levi, was in charge of things now. "Forgive me, child, but I must proceed with one last question: has your boy bebé . . . has he had the *brit malah*, the covenant with God?" The entire assemblage seemed to hold its breath at the question, but I did not comprehend.

In growing panic, I looked from one face to another. The rubisa stepped over to me and put her hand on my arm. "We are frightening you needlessly child. . . . My husband, the Chief Rabbi of Toledo asks if your baby . . . Mica . . . has had the blessed ceremony of circumcision performed upon the male genital? As you undoubtedly know," she said gently, "only a true son of Israel would dare have such a sacred ritual performed. A gentile or Marrano would never risk having a circumcised child among them. I am afraid without the brit malah, we could have no such child or his next of kin with us." She squeezed my elbow, a look of worry on her face. "Don't you see child, this would be a dangerous discovery not only for us but for you and the baby as well."

It was so unnaturally quiet, even the leaves could be heard rustling lightly in the breeze. How wrong you all are, I wanted to shout. Papá *had* brought the Marrano rabbi to my baby brother, a week after his birth. Papá had risked his life to give his newborn son the ancient rite of circumcision.

"Sí. He has had the circumcision," I said, almost joyfully.

A surprised "A-A-Ah!" surged through the crowd, while my stern inquisitor, the angry Señor Levi, persisted disbelievingly. "Sí? Sí, you say so easily? Then you must prove it and show us the child!" he screamed.

"Sí, show us! Show us!" many began to cry out.

Before I could protest, Señor Levi fairly snatched the baby from my arms, and the elbowing crowd pushed me aside. I could no longer see my baby brother. The people surrounding Señor Levi grew hushed as he fumbled with the blankets. Manuel, looking into that harsh, forbidding face, began to whimper.

Then the rubisa pushed to the center of the crowd. "Please, if you must, then allow me," she said, taking Manuel protectively in the cradle of her arm and deftly unwrapping his swaddling.

I held my breath. Please God, *please* God. I prayed the Marrano rabbi had done his job well. For if they did not see exactly what they wanted to see, my fate and my brother's would be sealed outside the Jewish people forever.

Murmurs rose from the crowd. My heart beat wildly as Señor Levi proclaimed, "Now Rubisa, we shall know the truth!" I stood on tiptoe and saw the last piece of cotton swaddling flung away. A hushed, unnatural silence filled the air. Then, before I knew what was happening, the crowd erupted in chant: *"Kosher! Kosher!"* In the background I heard my baby brother screaming frantically!

Desperately I tried to reach him, pushing through the crowd, not knowing what they might do to him, not knowing what this term kosher could mean.

"*Por favor!* Por favor—'please'!" I begged frantically.

Some people took pity on me, moved aside, and let me plunge through. At last I reached the center where the rabbi was holding my screaming brother and the rubisa was retying his swaddling. I looked at them in anguish, ready to snatch him away when the rabbi smiled and the rubisa said, "He is kosher, all according to Jewish law, my dear."

I nearly fainted in relief. All around me I heard the sound of cheers, excited talk, and laughter. People approached now smiling and welcoming me. Over and over I heard the word *Shalom*. And then it struck me: I had been accepted by these people. Like some great mother bird, the Jewish community of Toledo had swooped down and taken us under their protective wings. Dear Papá and Mamá, I fervently thought, if only you were here to share in this moment. I wanted to weep with joy and sorrow, all at once.

I turned to gather up my brother but there before me was the unsmiling face of Señor Levi! In all the excitement, I had nearly forgotten him. Before I could speak, he grudgingly nodded to me and finally, mercifully, turned and walked away into the crowd. I had robbed him of his vengeance upon a hateful Gentile world. I was no longer an alien force to be reckoned with, only a mere snippet of Jewish girl with a baby. Another *Sephardic* mouth to feed.

It was the rabbi who finally raised his hands and in a voice of authority, said what everyone already knew: "Dear friends and neighbors, the child is a true son of Israel, and this young girl has brought them both through hardship and tragedy, to be among their own Sephardic people. She is a true daughter of Israel! Welcome and Shalom to the Toledo Jewish Community, Señorita Ruth de Cojano!"

The sounds of clapping hands and cheering rose from the crowd. Zippi came to plant a small kiss on my cheek. I blushed shyly at all the attention. Then the rubisa herself handed me back my crying brother with a smile of triumph—and relief. The ordeal was over. Almost.

Suddenly, heavy thumping noises startled the crowd. In the excitement and shouting, no one had heard the steady approach of hoofbeats! Four of the queen's soldiers, members of the fierce Santa Hermandad, charged with keeping order in the Jews' long march to the seaports, must have heard the noise and come to see the disturbance. High atop their restless horses, the soldiers looked down disdainfully at us. One of them shouted: "What goes on here, Jews? A fiesta? In the middle of the road? Save it for the crammed, overcrowded boats that await you! Your time in Spain is nearly run out. Get along with you, all of you, money-grubbing, plague-bringers, stinking of garlic!"

With that, the crowd quickly dispersed. Many ran fearfully to catch up with the rest of their families who were far ahead. The four horsemen spread themselves menacingly across the road behind us, watchful that we moved on. The troubadours were quickly summoned to take up song and flute again.

And I? I found myself surrounded by the rabbi and rubisa's seven children. They had run back from the front of the lines to see what all the commotion was. Four boys and three girls all babbled in their foreign tongue to me and to themselves, not realizing I spoke no Hebrew, only Spanish.

By this time, Manuel was crying in hunger. A kindly young woman with a baby of her own was summoned. She took Manuel—that is

Mica—and nursed him generously under her modestly placed shawl as she walked.

As we marched the last league to Cadiz, I learned the rabbi was Yosef de Diaz and his wife, the rubisa, Leah de Diaz. Except for Zippi, it would take me a long while to remember the names of the other six children—Hannah, Hepzibah, Yoshua, Noach, Dovid, and Gershom.

I learned that our ship, the *Santa Angelo*, would be taking us as Papá had hoped to the great city of Istanbul where Jews had actually been invited by the Sultan. Zippi kept saying how she had heard Istanbul to be an awesome place of Turkish splendor. Of course I could not tell her how much I already knew about the "Turkish splendor" of the Moslem people—that they had once been our neighbors in Granada, just across the Guadilquivir River from my own city, Seville. For what would a proper Jewish girl be doing in Seville, where no Jews had been allowed to live for a hundred years?

Along the road, Zippi's handsome, slightly mischievous brothers chided me, for they had already begun to discover with astonishment how much I did not know of being a Jewess, not even that mixed-up Spanish-Hebrew language that I learned was called *Ladino*. "I know the Jewish blessings," I retorted and began to recite the Shema. The rubisa merely clucked and said that it was always a shame how many families went to lengths to educate their sons yet kept their girls ignorant of much Jewish learning.

My faced flushed deeply. I had to bite my tongue to keep from shouting the truth. I was not ignorant. My papá would have taught me everything, everything, I thought fiercely in silence. Yet when the rubisa looked at my stricken face, she said to all her children, "Ruth is a girl of great intelligence and love of Judaism. She will learn fast. Her papá was a righteous man who knew Torah."

"Did you know her papá?" said Zippi.

"Alas, no, my dearest," said the rubisa. "I can only see what he has beautifully molded." She smiled at me knowingly.

As the afternoon sun began to sink below the horizon, the salty smell of the ocean filled the forest air around us. I tried to sear into my mind the memory of this beautiful forest, of the land, my homeland. Very soon, now, I would take my last step upon this ancient land of my ancestors.

Then I would face nothing but ocean waters for weeks on end. I shivered to think of it. Already Zippi's brothers and sisters regaled me with horror stories of the terrible sea sickness that afflicted so many, of the pirates and ship's crew that sometimes preyed upon helpless, ocean-bound Jews. Señor Levi had already appointed a group of hardy men who had pledged to keep watchful guard over the community. We could only pray that measure would be enough. For the rest, we would have to take our chances on the good graces of the Gentile crew of the *Santa Angelo.*

The dozens of young children had grown very hungry, so before we reached the busy port, the Toledo community stopped one last time in the forest to rest and eat from their dwindling supplies of dried foods and bread. Zippi's gentle, soft-spoken father, the rabbi, blessed our meal of bread, olives, and nuts. Then he told me how the community had used precious traveling days each week on the road ritually slaughtering and roasting lambs on a spit, even baking bread and pots of fragrant rice in makeshift fires. Always fearful of not reaching Cadiz in time, the Toledo community nevertheless had to prepare a feast for the weekly rest day, Shabbat. "All these months," Rabbi Yosef said wistfully, "we have felt quite like the ancient Jews fleeing from Pharoah's Egypt."

The kindly young mother once more nursed Mica. I drew out my food baskets, magnanimously to share with the others, but the rubisa caught sight of the one plump sausage I had forgotten about. "Oh my, you've no doubt bought this basket from the gentiles, and they've put unkosher meat in here, my dear." Then she took the basket and pitched the entire contents into the woods—dried fruits, herbs, and everything!

I looked down with shame, but she merely shrugged and said, "Don't feel bad, Ruth. What you ate when you were all alone and struggling to survive is behind you. Now you will return to the purity of kosher food with your people."

I suddenly realized that everyone and everything of my former life had disappeared, except for my baby brother, Mica, and the golden mezuzzah of Great Grandmother Ruth—the single surviving heirloom of our family's once golden days as Jews in Spain. It was still in my shift, pressed close to my heart.

"Rubisa," I asked shyly as I helped pack up the family's belongings, "how is it that your people, I mean, your congregation from the Toledo

Judería, departs Spain with such joy and hope? I have seen other Jews flee Spain in a downcast state of chaos and hopeless weeping."

She smiled and said, "Indeed, we ourselves were weeping Jews many months ago when we began our chaotic flight from Toledo. Yet, as we went forward, we grew in strength and resolve to meet our fate with our heads held high. We decided we would not let the Gentiles see us go utterly defeated. My husband, the rabbi, endlessly encouraged us to keep together and find some measure of joy in our new destiny."

"Joy?" I shook my head in disbelief. "How can the Jews ever feel joyous at being hated and expelled by the Gentiles?"

"We make our own joy, my dear," said the Rubisa. "The Torah encourages us to find joy, even in the worst of times. 'Desire Fulfilled is a Tree of Life,' says the Torah proverb. Not to find joy in this life is to insult the *Ribbono Shel Olam*, 'the Master of the Universe.' That is why God has commanded us to celebrate the Shabbat each and every week, whether in the midst of great sorrows or not. Shabbat allows us to cease our daily labors and remember the joys of being alive."

"But it feels like God is punishing the Jews," I said.

"Oh no, Ruth, only troubled and cruel men, mere mortals, are punishing us, not God. I believe that Adonai will help us use this terrible expulsion from our homeland for good in the world somehow. Adonai sends us out into the far reaches of the world to spread ourselves and our Torah." The rubisa picked up her food pack wearily.

"Because the Torah has so many wonderful stories?" I asked, thinking of the ones Papá had only just begun to teach me.

"Not just stories, my dear. The Torah endlessly teaches the human race that love and chesed have the power to transform human beings from savage enemies to friendly neighbors. Sí, love and chesed can tame the cruel, barbarian places of this world."

I looked at the dusty, weary lady in gratitude and a shiver of excitement ran through me. I hoped I would be able to learn much more about the transforming power of Torah from the rubisa and her husband.

We started down the road again but a disturbing thought made me stop.

"Oh Rubisa," I turned to her, "perhaps God is punishing my family, taking my dear papá and mamá away. Perhaps we have been wicked . . .

somehow," I said, suddenly close to tears. I could never tell her that I feared that our family had sinned in the eyes of Adonai by living as New Christians.

"Oh, no!" The rubisa set her heavy pack down, took me by the shoulders, and looked kindly into my eyes. "Your parents sacrificed their lives so that you and Mica might live. And they, in turn, will live forever in you and your brother and in the generations that come from you both. You are a courageous girl, like that first Ruth, who chose her place among the Jews. Yet you are also like Miriam, who rescued her baby brother, Moses, the future leader of the Jews, from death. Who knows what you and your brother will accomplish in your lives?"

"Gracias, Rubisa Diaz, gracias," I said tearfully, wiping my eyes. I regarded the kind, wise rubisa in wonderment thinking she must surely have guessed the truth about our secret Jewish lives by now. Yet I knew it no longer mattered.

"Come," she said as she picked up her heavy pack again. "Let me recite for you in Spanish a passage from the Twenty-seventh Psalm. It is a prayer to bring you comfort." And, as we trudged down the road with our burdens, she chanted in a sure, lilting voice:

"Though my father and mother abandon me
The Lord will take me in
Show me Your way, O Lord
And lead me on a level path."

And then the Toledo Judería, my newly adopted people, was back on the road, approaching the end of one long journey, preparing to begin yet another on the high seas.

As we rounded a bend in the road, we were accosted once more by a group of well-meaning nuns and friars who called us "the poor pathetic Jews of Spain," and offered us one last chance to convert to Christianity and remain on Spanish soil.

As we started to pass them, the two eldest sons of the rabbi—Yoshua and Noach—shook their heads and scoffed.

"In the name of Our Lord, young men, let me baptize you," called out a friar as Noach and Yoshua passed him, "and we will let you stay in Spain!"

Yoshua turned and defiantly called over his shoulder, "The only way you'll ever baptize us, Brother John, is to sink the ship you're expelling us on!"

Unruffled, the friar moved smoothly down the line to accost yet another.

"The Christians never give up on us, do they?" said Noach, irritably, shifting the heavy pack on his back.

Then things moved swiftly, for an eager scout had run ahead and come back to tell us that the Port de Cadiz was but a few dozen paces beyond the next bend in the road.

"We'll be in good company! They say the boats of the great map maker Cristobal Colón are docked just beyond the boats of the Jews," the excited scout reported.

A few minutes later, the entire Jewish community came to a sudden and complete stop in the middle of the road. The music ceased. The crowd grew hushed and serious. Only the rabbi could be heard chanting with closed eyes what I realized were Hebrew blessings. Though standing in the back of the crowd, Zippi leaned and whispered into my ear—*"It's the Shehekiyanu*—the prayer of thanksgiving—that Adonai has allowed us to reach this moment alive, together."

My heart soared with a brief flitting joy. Sometime soon, I thought, I must remember to show Zippi the beautiful golden mezuzzah hidden closely to my heart. Then on a sudden impulse, I said aloud a familiar prayer of thanksgiving of my own:

"Adonai, my God in my thoughts, Adonai, my God on my Lips, Adonai, my God in my heart." But this time, I made no sign of the cross. Zippi, looking sideways at me and jiggling fussy Mica, said, "What prayer is that? I don't know that one."

"It's just a special one I made up when I was a little girl."

"Here, take your brother," she said suddenly, thrusting him into my arms. "There is something I want to say also." As I settled Mica in my arms, she turned towards the road behind us and with upraised arms shouted, "I spit on the name Isabel!" In a most unlady-like way, she bent and spat upon the ground.

Shocked, I stared at her. My heart leaped with panic in my chest. How had she learned my Sevillano name?

She looked at me, her eyes shining with mischief and continued. "And I spit on the name Ferdinand!" And spitting again, she added, "Wicked monarchs of Spain who expel the Jews! May their names sit with the devil himself!" She looked at me with my open mouth and said, "Well, don't you?"

My heart still beating wildly, I handed my brother back to her. She watched approvingly as I raised my hands to the sky. "I, Ruth de Cojano," I shouted, "spit on the name Isabel and I spit on the name Ferdinand! And I spit on the name Tomás!" I blurted out my brother's name before I knew what I had said. Shocked, I threw my hands to my mouth.

"Who is Tomás?" Zippi said in surprise.

How could I tell her about my wicked Dominican brother who had betrayed his own father? My mind raced feverishly for a reply. Suddenly, from some forgotten spot in my brain, a name leaped up at me. "Tomás de Torquemada, of course, the hateful monk who convinced the queen to expel us!" I yelled.

"Of course! How could I have forgotten? You're so clever," said Zippi. "Let's spit on the name of Tomás!"

We spat on the ground and looked at each other with impish satisfaction.

Then Zippi, holding my brother, Mica, and I, hurried ahead and joined the others. All around us were the sounds of praying, quiet murmuring, and soft weeping. We looked at one another. Even on our toes, we couldn't see around the huge throng of people. At last the crowd inched forward and I caught sight of what the others were gawking at and shuddered to my very bones.

For there, within shouting distance, were the frighteningly immense and powerful ships that were soon to turn us into human driftwood, fulfilling the king and queen's Edict of Jewish Expulsion, and exiling us from our ancient Golden Spain *forever.*

Glossary

abuela, abuelo (Spanish): Grandmother, grandfather.

Adonai (Hebrew): One of the Sacred Hebrew names of God, familiar to all Jews in prayer and translated as My Lord.

"A-don O-lom A-sher Molah b'te-rem kol Y'tseer niv'ro..." (Hebrew): "The Lord of all, who reigned supreme . . ." the stirring song that Isabel heard the Jewish men sing as the Toledo Jewish community marched to the boats of expulsion. Adon Olom was written by the great Jewish poet Solomon Ben Juda Gabirol who lived in eleventh-century Spain and whose songs and prayers are still sung in our synagogues today. This wondrous song would have been familiar to Spanish Jews in 1492.

¡Alto! (Spanish): Stop or halt.

Amidah (Hebrew): The central prayer of every Jewish worship service, recited each morning, afternoon, and evening, on the Sabbath, and every Jewish Festival.

auto-de-fé (Spanish): "Act-of-faith." The public ceremony in which people found disloyal to Catholicism were burned alive at the stake, before jeering and wildly cheering crowds. For over four hundred years, many thousands of discovered Marranos—secret Jews—were put to death in autos-de-fé in Spain, Portugal, Italy, and other European nations.

Avé María: Also called Hail Mary. The traditional Catholic prayer of greeting to Mary, Mother of Jesus.

baptism: The ceremony of initiation or conversion to Christianity.

barrio (Spanish): Neighborhood.

bebé (Spanish): baby.

bisabuela, bisabuelo (Spanish): Great grandmother and great grandfather.

Book of Hours: Small Catholic prayer books carried by worshippers to indicate time of day for prayers and the prayers to be said.

Brit Milah (Hebrew): "The sign of the covenant." The ceremony in which the foreskin of the male infant's penis is removed.

bueno, buena (Spanish): Good, fine, well.

buenos días (Spanish): Good day.

caballero (Spanish): Pronounced "ca-ba-yero." The traditional term for a knight or nobleman or horseman.

caliph (Moslem): The title for the spiritual leader of the Moslem people.

catechism: Instructions given in question and answer format about the Catholic faith.

Chamotzi (Hebrew): Blesssing for the bread.

chesed (Hebrew): Mercy, compassion, giving.

Cristobal Colón: The Spanish pronunciation of the name Christopher Columbus.

circumcision (Hebrew): The ceremony in which the foreskin of the male infant's penis is removed. See above, **Brit Milah**.

Cojano (Spanish): Pronounced "Co-ha-no." The name of Cohen among Spanish Jews. Just as in English, the name Cohen indicates that a family is descended from Cohanes, the High Priests of ancient Jewish times.

converso (Spanish): A religious convert to Christianity. In Spain the New Christians who were known to have once been Jews were often called conversos. Isabel and her family are referred to as both conversos and New Christians.

Dayenu (Hebrew): A song of the Exodus of the ancient Jews fleeing Egypt. The word means "much less would have been enough for us—God gives us more than we need." At Passover and other times, Jews say Dayenu! to remind themselves that even in hardship, God is there, bestowing gifts of hope and survival.

Dios or Mios Dios (Spanish): God or My God.

Don, Doña (Spanish): Lord, Lady. The Medieval terms to address a man and woman of high birth or wealth.

The Edict of Expulsion: The infamous proclamation of King Ferdinand and Queen Isabel ordering the expulsion of every Jewish man, woman, and child from Spain. As the last ship of Jewish emigres set sail from the Port of Cadiz on August 2, 1492 the Niña, the Pinta and the Santa Maria—the fleet of Christopher Columbus—could be seen, about to set sail on its sea voyage the very next day.

El Rápido (Spanish): "The swift one." The name of Teresa's horse.

fiesta (Spanish): A party, festival, or holiday.

gracias (Spanish): Thank you. [**Muchas gracias**: many thanks.]

hidalgo (Spanish): Pronounced "ee-dal-go." Nobleman, Noblewoman. A member of royal lineage or any person of wealth, title, or prestige.

¡hola! (Spanish): Pronounced "o-la." Hello.

Holy Office of the Inquisition (Spanish): The organization of terror founded by Queen Isabel and the Catholic Church to eradicate all non-Catholic peoples from Spain, Portugal, and Europe, which operated for more than three centuries.

juderías (Spanish): The ghettos of Spain, walled neighborhoods in which Jews were separated by law from the rest of the Spanish population.

Kiddush (Hebrew): Blessing for the wine.

kosher (Hebrew): Food that is ritually clean according to the dietary laws of the Jewish people. However, the word is often used to describe anything that is ritually proper or acceptable in Jewish life. That is why the Jews chant "Kosher! Kosher!" after examining Isabel's brother Manuel and seeing that he has been properly circumcised according to Jewish law.

Ladino: The language of Spanish Jewry, mixing both Spanish and Hebrew together in much the same way that the Yiddish language of Eastern Europe mixes Hebrew and German together.

league: Spanish mapmakers used this term instead of miles, the unit of measure for travelers in fifteenth-century Spain. In Spanish the word is legua. A league equalled 2 and one-half of our miles. However people often guessed—and badly—at the number of leagues from one point to another.

limpieza de sangre (Spanish): The infamous certificate of "purity of blood." It supposedly proved that a Spaniard did not have the offensive "taint" of Jewish blood in their family ancestry.

mantilla (Spanish): Pronounced "man-tee-ah." Woman's shawl, worn about the head and shoulders and often made of ornate fabric and lace.

marques, marquesa (Spanish): Pronounced "mar-kays, mar-kay-sa." Male and female titles of European nobility, ranking below duke and duchess and above count and contessa, distantly related to royalty.

Marrano, Marranos (Spanish): The word means swine or something filthy and unclean, and was the Spaniard's derisive term for all secret Jews.

mezuzzah (Hebrew): Doorpost. The tiny prayer scroll-inside-the-container that has been the signpost of the Jewish home since ancient times. The prayer scroll contains two passages from Deuteronomy.

mi amiga (Spanish): My friend.

mitzvah (Hebrew): Good deed, an unselfish act. It also refers to the performance of one of the Jewish laws or commandments.

muy bien (Spanish): Very good.

New Christians: Former Jews, who had been forceably converted to Christianity in 1391.

quemadero (Spanish): Pronounced "kay-ma-der-o." The burning place where the condemned Judaizers and heretics were lashed to the stakes and burned alive on the public square before crowds of peasants and nobles.

patio (Spanish): The inner courtyard and gardens of affluent Spanish homes, often built behind tall, enclosing walls.

plaza (Spanish): A large public square in a city.

rabbi (Hebrew and Ladino): Spiritual leader of the Jewish people. In Spanish countries the rabbi might also be called "Chochma," meaning wise man, just as the Yiddish-speaking Jews of Europe often call their rabbis "Zaddik," meaning riteous or saintly man.

rubisa (Ladino): The wife of the rabbi. Similarly, the Yiddish-speaking Jews of Europe call the wife of the rabbi, rebetzen.

sanbenitos (Spanish): The humiliating "garments of shame" (ugly yellow or white shifts for both men and women with big red crosses painted on the front) worn by condemned prisoners of the Holy Office of the Inquisition.

Santa Hermandad (Spanish): The horseback soldiers throughout Spain known as the "Holy Brotherhood," started by Queen Isabel, in her quest to end lawlessness and criminal activity which was rampant in Spain when she took office. In 1492, they served to make sure the Jews left Spain as instructed by the monarchs.

Santa Maria del Popolo (Italian): Saint Mary's of the People. The name of the great cathedral church in Seville, named for a church in Rome.

Shaddai (Hebrew): The Almighty. One of the sacred names of God in the Torah and the name depicted on the mezuzzah, the signpost of the Jewish home.

Shema (Hebrew): The foremost prayer of Jewish faith proclaiming the belief in One God. Throughout history, martyred Jews have gone to their deaths uttering the Shema.

Señor, Señora, Señorita (Spanish): Common terms for Mr., Mrs., and young lady.

Sephardic (Hebrew): The term that refers to Spanish Jews. The Sephardim today are descendents of Spanish Jews.

Sevillano (Spanish): Pronounced "Se-vi-ya-no." A resident of Seville.

Shehecheyanu (Hebrew): Pronounced "She-he-chee-ya-nu." The prayer of thanksgiving in which Jews thank God for survival, for reaching each moment in time.

sí (Spanish): Yes.

sultan: The political leader of Turkey or other Moslem kingdoms.

tía, tío (Spanish): Aunt, uncle.

Torah (Hebrew): The Five Books of Moses and the most sacred document of the Jewish people, written on parchment and rolled into scroll form.

un momento (Spanish): One moment.

vaya con Díos (Spanish): God be with you. Teresa's final goodbye to Isabel.

Acknowledgments

It has been a pleasure to work with Dan Sharon, and the other friendly librarians of the Asher Library of the Spertus College of Judaica in Chicago, who found numerous sources and answered many questions over the years. Special thanks must go to Shari Lowin, who researched the poetry and prayers of the Sephardic poet, Solomon Ben Juda Gabriol, who gave us the hymn Adon Olom in the eleventh century.

I am also grateful for the thoughtful and expansive collections of Judaica found at the Illinois libraries of Arlington Heights, Wheeling (Indian Trails), and Prospect Heights.

My heartfelt appreciation must go to editorial assistant Nomi Eve Buch for her meticulous and challenging analysis of the narrative and characters. And to Christine Sweeney, Tara McFadden, and Lisa Weinberger for their skillful copyediting of a complex, three-language manuscript.

Finally, I must express deepest gratitude to my editor, Bruce Black, who has made my first experience as a novelist a rich and *hamish* one. His insightful, caring criticism created a wonderful dialogue between us about the fate of Isabel and her family.